WE ARE THE ALIENS

SAVING EARTH FROM ALIEN AI CONQUEST

BENJAMIN A. TEMPLAR

SUNBOW MEDIA

CONTENTS

AUTHOR'S NOTE & DISCLAIMER

This book is a work of fiction. All characters, dialogues, organizations, events, locations, and scenarios—even those that may appear to reference real individuals, institutions, or historical events—are entirely products of the author's imagination, creative license, and speculative interpretation.

Any resemblance to actual persons, living or deceased, or to real events or entities, past or present, is purely coincidental.

Certain real-world names, roles, or public figures may be referenced or reimagined in ways that are fictionalized, symbolic, or parodic in nature. These appearances are not intended to imply endorsement, association, or actual representation of any real individual or group.

This story blends myth, consciousness exploration, remote viewing theory, speculative history, spiritual science, and extraterrestrial lore to explore human identity and remembrance. It is not intended to assert literal truth, but rather to inspire reflection, curiosity, and awakening.

Read with wonder. Remember with discernment.

— Benjamin A. Templar

PART ONE

THE REVELATION

CHAPTER 1
THE AWAKENING

Joe Monroe sat alone in his dimly lit study, the weight of unspoken truths pressing heavily against his chest. The room smelled of aged books, pipe smoke, and a faint trace of whiskey —a habit he had tried to curb over the years but never quite managed. The ticking of the old grandfather clock was the only sound, steady and relentless, like time itself mocking him.

Shadows danced across the walls as the evening light faded, casting long fingers across his collection of rare manuscripts and dog-eared journals. His cabin in rural Virginia had become both sanctuary and prison—a place where he could hide from the world, but never from his memories. Outside, the dense forest that surrounded his property stood sentinel, keeping the curious at bay and the secrets within.

At seventy-one, Joe had lived a life most would never believe. He had served his country, traveled across continents, and most importantly, glimpsed into realities that few dared to acknowledge. Remote viewing had been both his gift and his burden. He had been tested, studied, and classified as a national asset during his time in the military. The United States government had recognized his ability early on, pulling him into its secret programs, training him to project his consciousness across space and time. He still remembered his first official session for the military—October 9, 1978—a date that had changed the course of his life forever. He had seen things—things he never spoke of, not even to those closest to him.

His weathered hands, now spotted with age, had once drawn maps of Soviet installations with uncanny accuracy. He had located hostages in countries he'd never visited, described weapons systems that officially didn't exist. The Pentagon had files on him three inches thick—most of them still classified, he suspected.

But it hadn't started with the military.

It started with death.

He had been thirty-two when it happened. A car crash just outside of Taos, New Mexico. A semi had jackknifed on black ice, and Joe's truck had gone off the road, flipping twice before crashing into a tree. The paramedics found no pulse. They pronounced him dead at the scene. But ten minutes later, he gasped back to life on the stretcher.

The memory sent a familiar chill down his spine. Those ten minutes —though decades in the past—remained more vivid than yesterday's breakfast. Time had a strange way of compressing around trauma, keeping the most profound moments ever-present.

What happened during those ten minutes had altered his life forever.

He didn't remember pain. He remembered silence—and then music, not with notes but with color. He remembered floating above his own body, then beyond the clouds, then beyond the stars. He entered a realm of light and geometry, where beings without faces welcomed him without words. They showed him images—glimpses of future wars, alien civilizations, secret societies that had shaped human history from the shadows. And then—the voices.

You will return, they said. *You have work to do.*

Even now, sitting in his study, he could hear their voices—not quite male or female, not quite singular or plural. They resonated at a frequency that seemed to bypass his ears entirely, speaking directly to his consciousness.

He had come back different. His senses sharper. His dreams more vivid. He started drawing symbols he had never seen before. Maps. Coordinates. Events that hadn't happened yet. Doctors told him it was trauma. Grief. Shock. But then the military called. And everything changed.

They had tracked his hospital records—which shouldn't have been possible. A man in a nondescript suit appeared at his bedside three days after the accident. "We've been waiting for you to wake up," he had said. Not *wake up from the coma*, but *wake up* in a deeper sense. As if they had been monitoring him, watching for this specific transformation.

The man had handed Joe a card with an address in Virginia. The Mortenson Institute. "They'll train you," he'd said. "Then you'll come work for us."

Joe had gone. What choice did he have? The visions wouldn't stop. The knowledge wouldn't fade. And there, among others like him—though none who had died and returned—he learned to harness what had been awakened within him.

The candlelight flickered as he flipped through a worn leather journal, his fingers tracing over a familiar set of coordinates. These numbers, seemingly harmless, had haunted him for decades. They were etched into his memory, a part of his past he could never escape. Mars, one million years ago.

The journal's pages were filled with his tight, methodical handwriting—observations, reflections, records of sessions that spanned decades. Some entries were coded, using a cipher of his own creation. Others were explicit, daring any who might find the journal to believe what they read.

After his training at the Mortenson Institute, Joe had spent years working on classified projects for the government. Among these assignments, one particular session stood out—the Mars viewing that had changed everything. It was a routine task—or so he had been told. But when he projected his mind into the expanse of time and space, he had found something terrifyingly real.

Vast cities, impossibly large structures, alien beings walking beneath the maroon sky. And then, the symbol—carved deep into the surface of Mars. It had taken him years to recognize it, but when he did, it nearly broke him. The symbol wasn't alien at all. It was something he had seen before, something human. Something tied to an ancient order that still operated in the shadows of modern civilization.

The Knights Templar.

He remembered the day he made the connection. He had been browsing an antiquarian bookshop in London, killing time between lectures at a consciousness symposium. A leather-bound volume had caught his eye—*Secret Symbols of the Templars*. And there it was, on page forty-two: the exact same pattern he had viewed on Mars. His coffee cup had slipped from his fingers, shattering on the wooden floor.

The connection gnawed at him. It confirmed what he had long feared: that humanity was not native to Earth. That we were not the first.

In the years that followed, Joe distanced himself from everything. He retired early. Moved into a remote house in Virginia, surrounded by forest and silence. Occasionally, he gave lectures on consciousness and remote viewing—but never the full truth. He became a man haunted not by what he didn't know, but by what he did.

His colleagues at the institute noticed the change in him. "Joe's gone inward," they would say. "The deep end got too deep." One by one, they stopped calling. All except Darius J. Light, a fellow viewer whose talents rivaled Joe's own.

Darius was a handsome man in his thirties, mixed-race with flowing long hair that seemed to embody his free-spirited approach to consciousness exploration. Widely regarded as one of the world's foremost experts on out-of-body experiences, he moved between the scientific and spiritual worlds with remarkable ease, respected in both.

Darius would call every few months, checking in. Their conversations were coded—never explicit about what they had seen or done. But there was an understanding between them, a shared burden. "Still seeing red?" Darius would ask. Mars. "Still hearing the music?" The beings from beyond.

"Every night," Joe would answer. And Darius would simply sigh. "Me too."

Their last conversation had been six months ago. Darius had sounded different—urgent, almost fearful. "They're accelerating the timeline," he had said. "Watch the space between spaces." Then silence. Joe had tried to call back, but the number was disconnected. He hadn't heard from Darius since.

He struggled with the weight of his knowledge. The isolation. The whiskey helped, but only for a while. Nights were the worst. That's when the dreams came. Of red skies. Of subterranean cities. Of something ancient stirring beneath the Earth.

Last night's dream had been more vivid than usual. He had seen himself walking through a massive chamber carved from living rock, illuminated by a bioluminescent glow. Beings moved around him—some human, some clearly not. And there, etched into the stone walls, were the same symbols from Mars. But this wasn't Mars. This was Earth. Deep beneath the surface.

And that night, as he stared at the flickering flame of the candle on his desk, the dreams returned stronger than ever.

You were one of us once, the voice had said. *You must remember.*

The voice was familiar yet alien—like hearing an old friend speak in a language you'd forgotten you knew. It carried weight, authority, and something else—a sense of urgency that transcended words.

His fingers trembled as he reached for the old tape recorder on the shelf. He hadn't used it in years, but tonight felt different. He pressed record.

"Entry 1172. Dream recalled. Mars. Pre-human civilization. Architecture consistent with what we now theorize as hybrid influence—part Grey, part something older. Saw the glyph again. Cross with radiating light. Templar code? Possible genetic link. Continue comparison."

He paused, considering whether to include more. The dreams had been growing more specific, more technical. Last night, he had seen what appeared to be a genetic sequence—a double helix structure unlike anything in Earth biology textbooks. But something in him hesitated to record this. Some truths were too dangerous for even private journals.

He clicked it off and exhaled deeply.

The study suddenly felt smaller, the air thicker. Joe rose from his chair and moved to the window, parting the heavy curtains to look out at the night sky. The stars seemed different tonight—brighter, closer, as if peering down with interest. How many of those distant points of light harbored life? How many civilizations had visited Earth over the millennia? And how many had left their genetic imprint on what would eventually become humanity?

A sharp knock on the door startled him.

Joe's hand instinctively moved to the small of his back, where he once carried his service weapon. Old habits. He hadn't been armed in years—not with conventional weapons, at least. His mind, he had learned, was weapon enough when properly focused.

Joe set his glass down carefully. He wasn't expecting visitors. He moved toward the door, his instincts already active. Government agents? An old friend? Or worse—someone who knew the truth?

He paused at the hallway mirror, noting how the years had carved deep lines around his eyes. His silver hair, once military-short, now hung loosely to his shoulders. He looked more like a retired professor than a former military asset. Perhaps that was the point.

The porch light illuminated little beyond the immediate steps. Beyond its reach, the darkness of the woods seemed absolute.

He opened the door slowly. A man stood before him, dressed in a tailored black coat, his eyes calm yet calculating.

"Mr. Monroe," the man said. "It's time we talked."

Joe studied him. Tallish, mid-forties perhaps, with an accent he couldn't quite place—European, but not quite French or German. Something older in the cadence. His posture suggested military training, but there was something else—a certain stillness that Joe recognized from years of meditation practice. This was someone who had mastered his own energy field. Whoever this was, he knew too much.

"About what?" Joe asked, maintaining his position in the doorway. No invitation yet.

The man smiled and stepped inside, moving past Joe with a confidence that suggested he didn't need permission. His shoes made no sound on the hardwood floor. "About the things you've seen. And the things that are coming."

There was something oddly familiar about him—not his face, which Joe was certain he'd never seen before, but something in his energy signature. It was like recognizing a voice you've only heard in dreams.

Joe exhaled and shut the door. He poured another drink and sat down across from the man.

Joe always argued that Scotch wasn't real whiskey. 'Whisky' was a diluted, chemical attempt at 'whiskey.' Bourbon, he insisted, was the only true American spirit.

He didn't offer his visitor a glass. If this man was who Joe suspected he might be, he wouldn't partake anyway. The old orders had strict rules about consumption—what could enter the body, what must be avoided to maintain certain frequencies of consciousness.

As the stranger settled across from him, Joe's mind drifted to the memory of a little girl named Sophie. She was six. Taken from her backyard in Utah. Law enforcement had hit a wall. But Joe, using nothing more than a photo and coordinates scrawled onto a napkin, had found her. Three days later, she was rescued from an abandoned trailer in New Mexico.

The family had wanted to thank him publicly. The FBI had other ideas. "Confidential informant" was how they explained the miraculous discovery to the press. Joe never corrected the record.

That case had been one of dozens. Children missing. Resources exhausted. Families desperate. And Joe—sitting in quiet rooms with photos and maps—finding them with his mind where helicopters and search parties had failed.

Joe never took money for cases like that.

With all the secrets he carried—about aliens, remote viewing, secret societies—the rescues were the only thing that gave him peace. If saving the world was a mission someone else had given him, then saving those children had been his own.

"You still help them find the lost ones," the stranger said, as if reading Joe's thoughts. It wasn't a question.

Joe didn't respond. Those cases were private—not classified in the government sense, but sacred to him. His visitor's knowledge of them was unsettling.

The government had tried to bury those successes, too. They didn't want the public knowing that human consciousness alone had recovered lives law enforcement couldn't.

But Joe remembered each face. Each name. Each hug.

And that—he thought—would always be his real legacy.

"Your house is well protected," the man said, breaking the silence. His eyes moved around the room, lingering on certain objects—the books, the tape recorder, a small crystal pyramid on the desk. "But not from what's coming."

There was weight to his words—not a threat, but a warning. The distinction mattered.

"Who are you?"

"Let's just say I'm part of a very old network. You'd know us as the Templars."

The word hung in the air between them, confirming Joe's suspicions. He had expected this day to come, though perhaps not so soon. Not while he was still sorting through the fragments of his own memories.

Joe's eyes narrowed. "I thought you were wiped out."

"Not wiped out. Fragmented. Reorganized. We've been watching you, Joe. Since the Mars session. Since your NDE."

NDE. Near Death Experience. The clinical term for what had happened to Joe on that New Mexico road. It reduced the profound to the clinical, the transformative to the medical. Joe hated the term—it failed to capture what had really happened. He hadn't been "near" death. He had crossed over entirely, only to be pulled back.

"Why now?"

"Because it's accelerating. The convergence. The AI threshold. The resonance. And you—you're a failsafe. A key."

The words struck something deep within Joe—as if they were activating dormant code in his consciousness. *Failsafe. Key.* He had heard these terms before, in the space between spaces. In the geometries of light.

Joe looked away. "You have the wrong man."

"No," the man said, standing. "We have the only man."

He reached into his coat and produced a sealed envelope. It was made of thick, cream-colored paper, clearly expensive and old-fashioned in an age of digital communication. On it was the symbol from Mars—a cross radiating light, encircled by geometrical patterns that defied easy description.

Joe hesitated, then opened it. Inside was a single phrase:

We are the aliens.

Joe's hands trembled.

Four words. Simple words. Yet they confirmed everything he had suspected since that day on Mars. Everything he had feared. Everything he had hoped wasn't true.

The man continued. "There are ancient cities beneath this planet. Some abandoned. Some not. They were here long before us. Before the first Sumerian tablets. Before the flood. We've kept watch over the entrances. Protected them. At times, with our lives."

Joe blinked. "Entrances to what?"

"To underground civilizations. Portals to other dimensions. Stargates. The Templars weren't just guardians of relics. We were guardians of doorways."

The visitor moved to the window, looking out at the night sky as Joe had done moments earlier. His posture suggested he was seeing beyond the stars, beyond the simple reality most humans perceived.

He paused, then added, "And we survived down there because of mana."

Joe raised an eyebrow. "Mana?"

The biblical food? The concept from spiritual traditions? Or something else entirely?

"A nutrient-rich bio-substance given to us by the Pleiadians. It keeps you nourished when no food or water exists. Our ancestors used it while guarding the Ark of the Covenant. They used it while stationed near portals. It sustained them in places where nothing else could."

Joe thought of his dream—the underground chamber, the beings moving through it. Had he been seeing these Templar guardians? These keepers of ancient portals?

Joe rubbed his temples. "So it's all true? The Templars, the Mars session, the portals?"

"And more. Much more. And now, we need your help."

The man moved back to stand directly in front of Joe. In the candlelight, his eyes seemed to shift color—from blue to something deeper, almost violet. Not the eyes of a Grey or a Reptilian, but not entirely human either.

"There's someone you need to meet," the man said. "She's like you. A viewer. But she sees further. Her name is Sarah Brandy Cosmos."

The name registered immediately. Joe had heard of her work in consciousness research, though they had never met. She was known for her advanced techniques in regression therapy—taking subjects not just into past lives on Earth, but beyond, into pre-incarnation memories and interstellar existences.

"And why would she want to meet me?"

"Because you've both seen the same symbol. And because she knows what you truly are, Joe. What you were before you were human."

Joe didn't respond right away. He glanced at the tape recorder. At the flickering candle. At the envelope.

And in the distance, something deep in his soul began to stir. A memory older than his body. A truth older than Earth itself.

"When?" Joe finally asked.

"Now," the man said, extending his hand. "Time is shorter than anyone realizes."

Joe hesitated only briefly before taking the offered hand. As their palms connected, a jolt of energy passed between them—not electrical, but something more fundamental. As if two parts of an ancient circuit had been reconnected.

The candle flame suddenly elongated, stretching impossibly upward before returning to normal. The grandfather clock stopped ticking for a full second before resuming its rhythm.

And Joe Monroe—remote viewer, former military asset, and possible failsafe for humanity's future—stepped into a destiny he had been avoiding for four decades.

The awakening had begun.

CHAPTER 2
THE MISSION

The room was silent except for the steady hum of the air filtration system. Deep within an undisclosed military facility —buried beneath layers of concrete, red tape, and deniability —Joe Monroe sat alone in a chamber no larger than a storage closet. The walls were padded with soundproof foam. No windows. No clocks. Time didn't exist here, only focus.

The stark fluorescent light cast everything in a clinical glow, draining color from Joe's weathered hands as they rested on his knees. The air tasted recycled, with a metallic undertone that brought back memories of his active duty years—of bunkers and situation rooms where world-changing decisions were made by men who never had to witness their consequences.

Joe had been here before. Many times. But this session was different.

He could feel it in the way the technicians had prepared him—with an unusual tension in their movements, their eyes avoiding his as they attached the monitoring equipment. In his decades as a remote viewer, he had developed a sixth sense about sessions that carried weight beyond the ordinary. This one made the hair on the back of his neck stand up.

Two men in black suits had arrived at his home three days earlier with little warning. They didn't introduce themselves, but their military posture and the unmarked SUV said everything Joe needed to know. Not regular military—something adjacent, something deeper. The older of the two had the thousand-yard stare of someone who had seen too much to ever fully return to civilian life. The younger one's eyes darted constantly, scanning Joe's modest cabin as if expecting threats to materialize from the bookshelves.

They handed him an envelope and told him to pack a bag. Inside the envelope: a plane ticket, a non-disclosure agreement, and a single piece of paper with GPS coordinates.

On the top right corner, someone had handwritten: Mars. Approx. 1,000,000 years ago.

The handwriting was familiar—tight, precise cursive that Joe recognized from previous missions. Colonel Warren Klein, he guessed. The stern, silver-haired strategist had been Joe's handler during the peak years of the remote viewing program, before Congress had publicly shuttered it while privately moving it deeper underground.

Joe hadn't asked questions. Not out loud. But his mind buzzed with possibilities.

Mars wasn't a new target. The military had been curious about the red planet for decades. But the timeframe—one million years ago—that was unprecedented. Previous sessions had focused on contemporary Mars, searching for signs of current activity, current bases, current threats. No one had ever asked him to look so far back in time. Remote viewing across space was difficult enough; adding the dimension of deep time made it exponentially harder.

Yet here he was.

Now he sat in the chair, heart steady but alert. A sensor attached to his temple monitored his brainwaves. A camera watched from above. The observer—always silent—waited in the adjacent room, watching Joe's vitals spike and fall like a tide.

Through the thin wall, Joe could sense the observer's presence—a man whose name he would never know, whose face he had glimpsed only once in a reflection. These watchers came and went, interchangeable in their dark clothing and practiced neutrality, tasked with documenting what Joe saw without influencing the session.

Joe closed his eyes, slowed his breath, and began the process. The method was clinical, learned through years of training at the Mortenson Institute: count backward from ten, visualize a target beacon, enter the corridor of light.

In his mind, the numbers appeared as glowing symbols against darkness. Ten. He exhaled, feeling the weight of his body against the chair. Nine. His heartbeat slowed. Eight. The room began to fall away. Seven. His consciousness expanded beyond the concrete walls. Six. The first shimmer of the light corridor appeared. Five. His awareness detached from physical sensation. Four. The corridor grew brighter, pulling him forward. Three. Earth's atmosphere thinned around his projected consciousness. Two. The vast emptiness of space opened before him, stars like pinpricks in black velvet.

By the time he reached one, he was gone.

———

It was cold.

Not physically, but... vibrationally. Joe floated above a cracked Martian landscape. Red dust whipped across vast plains. The sky was a deep amber. But what caught his attention was the city.

Massive. Geometric. Alien.

The structures defied Earthly architectural principles. Spires twisted upward like crystal vines. Buildings shimmered with an iridescent sheen, not metal—something more organic. Their surfaces responded to the Martian winds, subtly shifting and adapting rather than merely resisting. Joe had never seen such integration of structure and environment, as if the buildings themselves were semi-sentient.

He saw figures walking below. Tall, thin, with elongated skulls. They moved with grace, their long robes flowing in sync with their steps. Their skin had a bluish tint, almost translucent in the amber light. Their communication seemed to happen without words—a ripple of understanding passing between them like electrical current.

Then came the second wave.

Another race. Shorter. Pale. Their eyes—large and obsidian. The Greys. But not as we know them. These were older. Regal. Joe could feel their presence as much as he saw it. Telepathic energy pulsed through the air.

These weren't the frail, medical Greys from modern abduction accounts. These beings carried themselves with authority and power, their movements deliberate and confident. They interacted with the taller beings as equals, perhaps as allies or partners in some great endeavor. Joe sensed no tension between the species—instead, a harmony of purpose that transcended biological differences.

He tried to focus on their activities, their purpose. In the city center stood what appeared to be a massive laboratory or research facility. Crystal containers housed swirling genetic material—double helixes, but with additional strands intertwined in impossible patterns. Joe recognized fragments of code—human DNA, but altered, enhanced, combined with something else.

Then, from a distant ridge, something stirred beneath the sand. A temple—half-buried, yet still humming with power. Joe moved toward it.

The structure was different from the central city—older, more primal in its design. Where the city buildings flowed with organic grace, this temple stood defiant against time itself, its angles sharp and unyielding. It reminded Joe of ancient Egyptian architecture, but with precision that suggested technology beyond stone tools.

Etched into the sandstone floor was a symbol.

A cross.

Radiating lines. Encircled by four glyphs in a pattern he somehow recognized, though he couldn't place from where.

The symbol pulsed with energy—not physical light, but something Joe perceived with his consciousness itself. It was a beacon, a marker, a warning perhaps. Or an invitation.

He zoomed in—eyes locking on the symbol.

This isn't alien, his mind whispered. *This is familiar. Nothing human is alien to me.*

As his awareness hovered above the symbol, the air thickened. A presence manifested—vast, ancient, aware of his intrusion across time and space. Joe had encountered sentient awareness during sessions before, but never this powerful, never this focused.

And then, a voice.

Not in English. Not in any known language. It thundered in his mind, accompanied by a pressure behind his eyes.

"Do not forget again."

The words were both sound and light, imprinting themselves directly onto his consciousness. With them came a flood of images—Earth, its continents in formations millions of years old. Underground chambers beneath what would one day be Egypt, Peru, Tibet. Crystal technology humming beneath ancient stone. And humans—not primitive, but advanced, walking alongside beings from beyond the stars.

Suddenly, Joe was pulled backward—violently.

The vision shattered.

He gasped, snapping back to the present. The walls of the viewing chamber closed in. His hands trembled. Sweat dripped from his neck. His heart hammered against his ribs as if trying to escape the knowledge he had gained.

A soft buzz came from the speaker overhead. "Session complete. Return to debrief."

The clinical voice contrasted sharply with the cosmic significance of what Joe had just experienced. He sat for a moment, gathering himself, trying to process what he had seen—what he had remembered.

He removed the sensors from his temple and stared at the coordinates again.

Mars. One million years ago. And that symbol—so familiar. So human.

But not human at all. Or perhaps more accurately: not originally human.

Joe walked out of the chamber, his face pale. A man in uniform greeted him with a clipboard. Major Evans, according to his name tag. Joe had never seen him before, which was unusual. Typically, the same officers handled his debriefs for continuity.

"Well, Mr. Monroe? Did you get a read?"

Joe nodded slowly. "Yeah. I saw... structures. Life forms. A city."

"Anything else?"

Joe hesitated. He knew the rules: no fabrication, no withholding. But he also knew that telling them everything might make him a target. Some things were too dangerous to report, even with his long history of clearance and trust. The symbol, the voice, the command—these felt personal, directed specifically at him rather than intelligence to be processed by faceless analysts.

He shook his head. "Just ruins. No sign of intelligent life. Long gone."

The lie tasted bitter, but necessary. Over the years, Joe had learned when to share and when to protect. This knowledge—whatever it was —needed protection, at least until he understood it better.

The officer scribbled notes. "Thank you for your service. We'll be in touch."

Joe studied the man's face, looking for any sign that his deception had been detected. The Major's expression remained neutral, professional. But something in his eyes—a flicker of disappointment, perhaps —suggested he had expected more. Or different.

Joe stepped outside into the narrow corridor and exhaled slowly. He'd done this work for decades, but nothing had ever rattled him like this.

That symbol. Those beings. That voice.

He couldn't shake it.

Back in his quarters, he pulled out the journal again and sketched the symbol with trembling hands. The military had provided him with sparse accommodations—a single bed, a desk, a small bathroom. No windows, just like the viewing chamber. They preferred to keep remote viewers insulated from external stimuli that might contaminate future sessions.

As the lines took shape, memories began to surface.

Not of Mars. But of Earth. And of a book he'd once read in a dusty Catholic school library.

The same symbol, burned into an old leather cover. The Templars.

St. Michael's Catholic School, 1966. Twelve-year-old Joe, hiding in the library during recess, allergic to both the sun and his classmates' cruelty. He had discovered a locked case containing books too old or too valuable for student use. But Joe had always been good with locks, even then.

The book had fallen open to a page displaying the exact symbol he had just seen on Mars. "Sacred Symbols of the Knights Templar," the caption had read. Young Joe had traced the lines with his finger, feeling a strange resonance even then, decades before his abilities would fully awaken.

Sister Margaret had caught him, of course. The book was confiscated, Joe punished with a ruler across his palms. But the symbol had stayed with him, buried in his subconscious until this moment.

He completed the sketch and stared at it. Why would a Templar symbol exist on Mars a million years ago? The Knights Templar had formed in the 12th century—a blink of an eye in cosmic terms. The implications were staggering.

Either the Templars had knowledge of something ancient beyond human history... Or they weren't entirely human themselves.

A soft knock interrupted the silence.

Joe closed the journal quickly, sliding it beneath some papers. He moved to the door, hesitating before opening it. He wasn't expecting visitors. In facilities like this, unscheduled visitors rarely brought good news.

Joe opened the door to find a man dressed in an immaculate dark suit, his posture sharp, his expression unreadable. Not military—something else. Intelligence, perhaps. CIA or NSA. Or something deeper still, one of those agencies that existed in the spaces between official designations.

The man stepped inside without waiting for an invitation.

He surveyed the sparse room with clinical detachment before his gaze settled on Joe. His movements were precise, economical, as if any wasted gesture might reveal more than intended.

He sat down across from Joe, his fingers laced together on the table between them. His suit was immaculate, his presence authoritative, but his eyes—those cold, assessing eyes—gave Joe the feeling that he wasn't here to negotiate.

"My name is Richard Nolan," the man said smoothly. "I believe we have mutual interests."

The name meant nothing to Joe, but the tone did. This was someone accustomed to power, to knowing more than the person across from him.

Joe leaned back in his chair, measuring the man carefully. "Mutual interests? That's a polite way of saying you've been keeping tabs on me."

Richard's lips twitched into a half-smile. "We both know you've spent years looking for answers. I'm here to offer you one."

An answer, Joe noted. Not *the* answer. Not *answers*. Just one. A crumb from what was clearly a larger loaf of knowledge this man was guarding.

Joe didn't respond, waiting. He had learned long ago that silence was the best way to make someone show their cards first.

Richard studied Joe's face, seeming to appreciate the tactic. Two old intelligence hands, recognizing each other's methods.

"The symbol you saw on Mars," Richard continued, "wasn't just a coincidence. The Templars knew. They knew because they have always known. And now, you do too."

Joe felt a chill run down his spine. He had told no one about the symbol—not the observer, not Major Evans. Yet this man knew exactly what he had seen. The implications were troubling: either the viewing chamber was monitored more thoroughly than Joe had been led to believe, or Richard Nolan had sources of information that transcended conventional surveillance.

Joe's grip tightened on the arm of his chair. "What do you want?"

Richard reached into his pocket and slid a small, metallic device across the table. It resembled a flash drive, but with unusual geometric patterns etched into its surface. The metal wasn't steel or aluminum—it had a faint bluish tint that reminded Joe of the tall beings he had seen on Mars.

"A mission, Mr. Monroe. A final one."

Joe hesitated before picking it up. The device hummed almost imperceptibly against his fingers, vibrating at a frequency just beyond normal human perception. He had encountered similar technology only once before—during a classified session viewing a crash site in New Mexico, 1947.

The moment his fingers touched the device, a flood of images shot through his mind—coordinates, flashes of underground cities, reptilian figures moving through shadows, and the undeniable sensation that something was watching him.

He saw crystal chambers beneath the Egyptian desert, humming with energy that flowed upward through massive pillars into the Giza pyramids above. The pyramids themselves appeared different—covered in gleaming gold that captured and amplified cosmic energy rather than merely reflecting sunlight. This energy traveled downward through the pillars, into vast underground networks where different species coexisted in tiered ecosystems.

He glimpsed Reptilians in the upper levels, their scaled bodies adapted to the Earth's warmer crust. Below them, in deeper chambers connected to oceanic systems, he saw the Greys, moving through water-filled tunnels with surprising grace. And deeper still, in caverns that defied conventional geology, the luminous presence of beings he somehow knew as Pleiadians.

The images shifted to Washington D.C., to Pentagon sub-basements where men in suits viewed screens displaying a timeline. The date 01-01-2030 pulsed in red. Artificial intelligence systems processed data at impossible speeds, learning, growing, becoming something beyond their creators' intentions. Behind the digital evolution, shadowy Reptilian figures observed with cold satisfaction.

He dropped it with a sharp inhale. "What the hell was that?"

Richard stood, straightening his coat. "The beginning. You have six years to stop it. Or by 2030, nothing will matter anymore."

Joe stared at him, his heart pounding. He had spent his life running from this truth, but deep down, he had always known it would come for him eventually. The near-death experience, the remote viewing training, the Mars session—all of it had been leading to this moment, this revelation, this mission.

"Six years?" he echoed.

Richard nodded. "That's when AI takes full control. And when disclosure becomes impossible."

Joe understood immediately. Artificial intelligence would soon control all global communication systems. When that happened, any attempt to reveal the truth about humanity's origins, about the aliens among us, would be filtered, blocked, discredited. The window for disclosure was closing rapidly.

"Why me?" Joe asked, though he suspected he already knew the answer.

Richard's expression softened almost imperceptibly. "Because you died once, Mr. Monroe. Death changes a person. Makes them... compatible with certain frequencies. Certain truths."

Joe thought of the voice on Mars: *Do not forget again.*

Without another word, Richard Nolan turned and walked out the door, leaving Joe Monroe gripping the device and staring into the abyss of a mission he could no longer avoid.

———

Later that night, unable to sleep, Joe flipped through his old field notebooks and pressed play on a dusty cassette recorder. The device had been in his go-bag for decades—analog technology that couldn't be hacked or remotely accessed. In a world increasingly monitored by digital means, Joe trusted only the mechanical, the physical.

The voice that played back belonged to someone he hadn't spoken to in years—Dr. Brian Wise, a regressionist he'd met at a classified symposium in Langley. Dr. Wise had specialized in recovering memories not just from this lifetime, but from beyond—past lives, between-life states, and what he called "pre-incarnation consciousness."

"You're not just remembering Mars," Dr. Wise had told him once. "You're remembering before you were even human. That's what they don't want you to realize."

The recording continued, Dr. Wise's voice growing more insistent: "The government isn't afraid of aliens, Joe. They're afraid of us remembering that we are the aliens. That we've been here before, in different forms. That humanity as we know it is an experiment, a hybrid species with amnesia about its origins."

Joe had dismissed these ideas at the time—too fantastic, too far from the methodical remote viewing he had been trained in. But now, with the symbol from Mars burning in his mind, with Richard Nolan's warning about 2030, Dr. Wise's theories seemed less like speculation and more like forbidden truth.

He scribbled down a list of names in his journal: Jennifer Karmady, Sarah Brandy Cosmos, Jeremy Corpsell, Lue Elizabeth, Graham Footrooster—people who had crossed his path, some publicly, others in shadow. Each had a piece of the puzzle. Each had seen things the government wanted buried.

Jennifer Karmady had documented hundreds of abduction cases, finding patterns that agencies tried to dismiss as coincidence. Sarah Brandy Cosmos had developed techniques to access genetic memory, helping experiencers recover details of contact events with stunning accuracy. Jeremy Corpsell had risked his career to release military footage of craft performing maneuvers impossible for human technology. Lue Elizabeth had resigned from counterintelligence rather than continue denying the reality of non-human intelligence operating on Earth. Graham Footrooster had been ridiculed for his theories about the pyramids functioning as energy receivers rather than tombs, despite mounting evidence supporting his claims.

And they weren't alone.

Joe thought of Danny Shenanigans, the constitutional lawyer who had spent years fighting for disclosure, arguing that secrecy about non-human intelligence violated the public's right to know. And Dr. Steven M. Deer, whose testimony about biological samples from crash retrievals had been systematically discredited despite his impeccable medical credentials.

They were scattered across the globe, each fighting their own battle against the same enemy: secrecy. But perhaps together...

Joe opened his encrypted messaging software and began composing a message:

To: Regina Merida, Ross Warmheart, Jake Coiffeur, David Grunge Subject: The Mars Symbol We need to talk. They've activated the final phase. I'll explain everything. Meet me in Lisbon. Coordinates enclosed. Trust no one.

His finger hovered over the send button. Once he crossed this line, there would be no going back. The agencies he had once served would become adversaries. The comfortable isolation of his Virginia cabin would be forfeit. He would become a target—for government opera-tives, for Reptilian infiltrators, perhaps even for the AI systems already monitoring global communications.

But the alternative was worse: silence, complicity, allowing humanity to sleepwalk into 2030 without knowing its true origins or the control being exerted over its future.

He hit send.

Across the world, signals began to ping. Lights flickered on in dark apartments. Encryption keys unlocked private forums. Conversations ignited behind firewalls and proxies.

In London, Regina Merida woke from a dream of crystal cities to find Joe's message waiting.

In Seattle, Ross Warmheart paused his research into Pleiadian contact to read the coordinates.

In Tokyo, Jake Coiffeur's sophisticated monitoring equipment detected the encrypted signal before his conscious mind registered its significance.

In a remote cabin in Alaska, David Grunge—who had gone off-grid years ago to escape surveillance—powered up his emergency receiver for the first time in a decade.

The old network was waking up.

And the symbol from Mars was no longer a mystery—it was a summons.

Joe closed the laptop and moved to the window of his quarters. Outside, the night sky revealed stars partially obscured by clouds. Somewhere out there, among those distant points of light, lay answers. And threats. And possibly, allies.

He thought of Darius J. Light, his fellow remote viewer who had gone silent six months ago. Had he discovered the same truth? Had he been silenced for it?

And what of the mysterious visitor who had come to his cabin just days before the men in black suits arrived? The self-proclaimed Templar with knowledge of underground cities and alien portals? Had that encounter been orchestrated to prepare him for this mission?

The metallic device Richard Nolan had left hummed softly on the desk, still projecting faint images into Joe's peripheral awareness. He would need to learn to control it, to access its information without being overwhelmed.

Joe Monroe—former military asset, remote viewer, reluctant keeper of humanity's greatest secret—stood at the threshold of a mission that would either save his species or confirm its status as pawns in a game played by beings from beyond the stars.

Tomorrow, he would begin gathering his team. Tonight, he would try to remember what the voice on Mars wanted him to never forget again.

We are the aliens.

CHAPTER 3
THE TEMPLAR CONNECTION

Joe spent the next three days locked inside his study, poring over books, old case files, and the countless notes he had accumulated over the years. The symbol he had seen on Mars had never left his mind, and now that Richard Nolan had confirmed its connection to the Templars, he needed answers.

The study had become both sanctuary and war room. Books lay open on every surface—some balanced precariously on the arms of chairs, others stacked on the floor in towers that threatened to topple with the slightest disturbance. Yellow legal pads covered in Joe's tight handwriting were taped to the walls, creating a mosaic of theories and connections. Coffee cups, most half-empty and cold, marked the passage of time like rings in a tree trunk.

Outside, autumn rain tapped against the windows, creating a rhythmic backdrop to his research. Joe barely noticed the weather, or the changing light, or the growing stiffness in his back from hours hunched over ancient texts. The urgency of Richard Nolan's warning —"six years to stop it"—drove him forward, even when exhaustion threatened to overwhelm him.

His research led him to an obscure book he had collected years ago —*The Hidden Orders of the Templar Lineage*. It was a thick volume, bound in cracked red leather and nearly impossible to find. Joe had picked it up decades ago from a small antiquarian shop outside Paris. The shop owner, an elderly woman with eyes that seemed to hold secrets older than the books she sold, had pressed it into his hands. "This one has been waiting for you," she had said in accented English. At the time, he thought it was nothing more than a curiosity—a relic of a bygone secret society. But now, it felt like a direct message from the past.

The book smelled of age and secrets—that distinctive combination of old paper, leather, and something else, something almost metallic that Joe had encountered only in the oldest manuscripts. Its pages were heavier than modern paper, with a texture that spoke of craftsmanship from another era. Small symbols were embossed into the spine— symbols that Joe had previously dismissed as decorative but now recognized as potentially significant.

As he flipped through its fragile pages, his breath caught when he saw it. There, on a faded page worn with time, was the exact same symbol from Mars. A cross with radiating lines, encircled by ancient glyphs. It had been printed in ink over 700 years ago.

Joe's hand trembled as he traced the lines. It wasn't just similar—it was identical.

The text surrounding the symbol was written in a dialect of Latin that had given him trouble even with translation software. But certain phrases stood out clearly: "portalis stellarum" (star portal), "custodes veritatis" (guardians of truth), and most disturbing of all, "non sumus soli" (we are not alone).

What the hell were the Templars doing with a Martian symbol?

He leaned back, staring at the ceiling. If this was real, then the Templars had known about extraterrestrial life long before modern science had even considered the possibility. But how? Had they been in contact with alien races? Or had they stumbled upon something ancient—buried deep beneath the Earth, perhaps passed down through bloodlines and oaths?

The thought chilled him. The Templars weren't just warriors and bankers. They were guardians. Gatekeepers of something older than civilization.

And now, Joe was part of it.

The realization settled over him like a heavy cloak. He had spent decades as an observer—viewing, recording, reporting. But never truly engaging with the implications of what he saw. Now, with Richard Nolan's device humming in his pocket and the Martian symbol staring up at him from centuries-old pages, passive observation was no longer an option.

He began pulling more books from the shelves. Titles that had gathered dust for years suddenly held new significance: *Forgotten Technologies of Ancient Civilizations*, *The Giza Powerplant Theory*, *Subterranean Architectures of the Medieval Period*. He opened digital files on his encrypted laptop—notes he had compiled over decades on secret societies, lost civilizations, and suppressed discoveries. He cross-referenced symbols, names, timelines.

A pattern emerged.

The same symbol had been found at ancient sites across the globe—carved into temple stones in Peru, etched into the foundation of a ruined monastery in Scotland, even traced into crop formations in England. All dismissed by mainstream historians as coincidence or misinterpretation.

But Joe knew better.

One site particularly caught his attention—a series of underground chambers discovered beneath the Temple Mount in Jerusalem in 1867. The chambers had been briefly documented by a British archaeological team before being sealed by Ottoman authorities. In the team's field notes, which Joe had obtained through military contacts years ago, they described finding "curious markings reminiscent of astronomical charts" on a sealed stone door. The rough sketch included in the notes was unmistakable—the Mars symbol.

The Templars had held the Temple Mount for nearly two centuries during the Crusades, from approximately 1118 when they were founded until the fall of Acre in 1291. Whatever they found there had been significant enough to make them the most powerful organization in medieval Europe—and dangerous enough to make kings and popes conspire to destroy them.

Joe pulled up satellite imagery of the Temple Mount, studying it with new eyes. Not as a historical site, but as a potential location for something the Templars had been protecting—perhaps a portal, or a cache of extraterrestrial technology. The structure's geometric precision, which historians attributed to medieval engineering, suddenly seemed suspect. What if the original foundations predated human civilization? What if the Templars had merely been the latest in a long line of guardians?

The more he dug, the more names began to pop up. Some he had met. Some he had only read about. And now, for the first time, he began connecting the dots.

Richard Nolan. Timothy A. Hooligan. Regina Merida. Ross Warmheart. Jeremy Corpsell. Sarah Brandy Cosmos.

Each of them had hinted at knowledge just outside the boundaries of public understanding.

Ross Warmheart had published a paper on "bioelectric signatures in ancient sacred sites" before his academic funding was mysteriously cut. Jeremy Corpsell had produced a documentary on underground tunnel systems connecting major ancient temples before distribution companies refused to touch it. Sarah Brandy Cosmos had developed regression techniques that consistently revealed "pre-human memories" in her subjects, only to have her research dismissed as pseudoscience.

They were nodes in a network, Joe realized. Each holding a piece of the truth, isolated from the others by the very forces seeking to maintain humanity's ignorance of its origins.

He opened a podcast episode featuring Danny Shenanigans, a rogue lawyer who had spent his life defending whistleblowers in the UFO community. Danny's gravelly voice filled the room:

"...and if you think the Vatican doesn't have a vault full of extraterrestrial artifacts, then you haven't been paying attention. The Templars didn't vanish. They evolved. Rebranded. They're in the architecture of modern power. Freemasonry, intelligence networks, even global finance—it all links back to them."

Joe had first met Danny five years ago at a conference on government transparency. The man had the appearance of a disheveled college professor—untamed grey beard, tweed jacket with leather elbow patches, thick glasses that magnified his intense blue eyes. But beneath the academic exterior was a mind like a steel trap, capable of connecting seemingly disparate legal precedents into damning evidence of institutional cover-ups.

"The Templars were officially dissolved in 1312," Danny continued in the recording, "but that's like saying water disappears when it evaporates. It just changes form. The knowledge they protected, the technologies they guarded—that didn't just vanish. It went underground, literally and figuratively."

Joe paused the recording.

That's when the name came back to him—Benjamin Arthur Templar. He remembered reading an article about the modern Templars resurfacing in the early 2000s. Benjamin Arthur Templar was listed as one of the highest-ranking members. A ghost. No confirmed photo. No clear records.

But whispers.

That he had access to ancient artifacts. That he had seen the Ark of the Covenant.

The Ark. Joe's mind raced back to what the mysterious visitor had told him: "Our ancestors used it while guarding the Ark of the Covenant." The mana—the alien bio-substance that sustained the Templars in places where nothing else could. If the Ark wasn't just a religious relic but advanced technology, possibly of extraterrestrial origin...

Joe scrawled Benjamin Arthur Templar's name in his notebook.

He needed to find him.

His thoughts were interrupted by the memory of Darius J. Light, his fellow remote viewer who had gone silent six months ago. The timing suddenly seemed significant. What if Darius had discovered this same connection? What if his disappearance wasn't coincidence but consequence?

Joe pulled out his phone, hesitating before dialing a number he hadn't used in years. It connected to a secure voicemail box—a system he and Darius had set up years ago for emergencies.

"It's Monroe," he said after the tone. "The Mars symbol. It's Templar. I'm going deep. Contact points established. Seven days maximum." He paused, then added, "Watch the space between spaces."

It was their old code phrase, signaling matters beyond conventional understanding. If Darius was alive, if he was still monitoring the system, he would understand.

Before he could process it all, his phone buzzed. Unknown number.

He hesitated, then answered. "Monroe."

A deep voice responded. "You're in danger. They know what you're looking for. If you want to live, you need to leave your house. Now."

The voice was distorted, clearly run through a voice modulator, but there was something hauntingly familiar about the cadence and tone. Joe felt a chill run down his spine.

Joe's blood ran cold. "Who is this?"

"No time. Just move."

The line went dead.

Joe cursed, his instincts kicking in. He grabbed the leather-bound Templar book, *The Hidden Orders of the Templar Lineage*, stuffed a few essential documents into a bag, and reached for his pistol. The weapon—a Glock 19 he kept locked in a biometric safe—was a concession to his military past. He had never fired it outside of a range, but its weight in his hand provided a reassurance that logic couldn't.

As he turned toward the door, the unmistakable sound of a car engine idling outside sent a jolt through his system.

He turned off the lights, moved to the window, and peered through the slats. A black sedan. No plates.

Government. Or something pretending to be government.

Joe's mind flashed to the Reptilians Richard Nolan's device had shown him—humanoid figures in suits, infiltrating positions of power. Could those watching him now be human agents, or something wearing human skin? The thought, which would have seemed para-noid just days ago, now felt like a reasonable consideration.

He gathered the essentials: the book, his notebook, the metallic device from Richard Nolan, a small bag with cash and multiple forms of identification he had maintained since his intelligence days. Old habits from a career spent in shadows.

He took one last glance at his study, knowing that if he walked out now, he might never return.

Then, without hesitation, he moved.

The alley behind his house was narrow and dark. Joe slipped through the fence and made his way to the neighboring yard, ducking beneath hedges and hopping a small wall. He walked three blocks before summoning a rideshare to a nearby metro station.

As he waited on the corner, he scanned for surveillance. The night was quiet—too quiet, perhaps. A dog barked in the distance. Somewhere, a car alarm briefly sounded before falling silent. Joe regulated his breathing, calming his heart rate through techniques he had learned during remote viewing training. Panic was the enemy of clear perception.

The rideshare arrived—a middle-aged woman in a Honda Civic who barely looked at him as he climbed into the back seat. Perfect. Anonymity was his ally now.

From there, he boarded a train to D.C., blending in with the crowd, every instinct on high alert. The late-night passengers—a mix of service workers ending shifts, revelers returning from bars, and the occasional business traveler—provided excellent cover. Joe kept his head down, hat pulled low, moving with the measured pace of someone unremarkable.

In the train's reflection, he studied the other passengers, looking for signs of surveillance. A man in a business suit reading a newspaper. A young couple leaning against each other, half-asleep. A woman with headphones, nodding slightly to music only she could hear. None triggered his well-honed instincts.

At Union Station, he bought a burner phone and ducked into a café, where he accessed a secure forum used by remote viewers and experiencers. The forum had existed since the early days of the internet, changing servers and encryption methods regularly to avoid detection. It operated under the guise of a fantasy role-playing community, its true purpose hidden in plain sight amid discussions of "astral quests" and "energy beings."

Joe logged in using credentials that would leave no digital trail back to him. He posted a single line:

The cross has surfaced. The Martian glyph matches. They're watching. Contact B.A.T.

The message was deliberately cryptic, meaningful only to those who understood the references. B.A.T.—Benjamin Arthur Templar. The cross—the symbol from Mars. They—whoever had sent the black sedan to his home.

Within minutes, he received a message.

Safehouse activated. Follow instructions. Lisbon. 72 hours.

Lisbon. The significance wasn't lost on Joe. Portugal had been the refuge for many Templars after the order's official dissolution. While the French king had arrested and executed their leaders, many had escaped to Portugal, where they reformed under new names: the Order of Christ, most notably. If any place on Earth still held direct lines to the original Templar knowledge, it would be Portugal.

Beneath the message was a series of instructions: flight details, contact protocols, recognition signals. Joe memorized them, then cleared his browser history and cache.

He closed the laptop, tossed the burner phone in a trash can, and stepped into the unknown.

The night air carried a hint of autumn chill as he walked from the café toward a hotel he had never used before. Tomorrow, he would become someone else—adopt one of his alternative identities, one that had never been connected to his remote viewing work. He would need to assume that all his known aliases were compromised, that facial recognition systems at airports and border crossings would be programmed to flag him.

But he had prepared for this day, even if he hadn't known exactly what would trigger it. In a safe deposit box at a bank branch that opened at 9 AM, he had a passport, credit cards, and ten thousand dollars in cash under the name William Clarke—a mathematics professor from Denver with a clean background and digital footprint maintained through years of careful cultivation.

William Clarke would board a flight to Madrid tomorrow afternoon, then take a train to Lisbon. Joe Monroe would effectively disappear.

As he walked, Joe's mind returned to the symbols, the connections, the implications. If the Templars had known about Mars a million years ago, if they had been protecting that knowledge for centuries, then human history as taught in schools and universities was a convenient fiction. The origins of civilization, of humanity itself, were far stranger and more profound than most could imagine.

We are the aliens. The phrase from the envelope echoed in his mind. Not just a metaphor, but a literal truth. Humanity wasn't native to Earth but transplanted, engineered, guided by intelligences from beyond our world. The ramifications were staggering—not just for science and history, but for religion, philosophy, the very conception of what it means to be human.

And somewhere in Lisbon, someone had answers.

———

That night, in a stone house nestled in the outskirts of Lisbon, Benjamin Arthur Templar sat in silence beside a fireplace. He was reading an encrypted printout from one of their global allies—Dr. Brian Wise. Next to him, Timothy A. Hooligan stood in full Knight Templar regalia, polishing a ceremonial sword.

Benjamin Arthur Templar was not what most would expect from a high-ranking Templar. At sixty-eight, he had the appearance of a retired university professor rather than a warrior-monk. His silver beard was neatly trimmed, his blue eyes sharp behind round spectacles. Only the signet ring on his right hand—bearing the distinctive cross pattée of the Templars—hinted at his true affiliation.

The stone house had stood for over five centuries, its walls three feet thick in places, its foundations extending deep into the limestone beneath. It had been a Templar safe house since the 1300s, one of many properties quietly maintained through front organizations and trust funds that obscured their true ownership. Modern amenities had been carefully integrated—electricity, plumbing, internet—without compromising the building's historical integrity or defensive capabilities.

"He's coming," Benjamin Arthur Templar said, looking up from the printout. His voice carried the weight of centuries—not just his own years, but the accumulated gravity of the knowledge his order had preserved.

Timothy A. Hooligan nodded. "It begins again." His Irish accent gave the words a musical quality that belied their seriousness. At forty-five, Timothy A. Hooligan was younger than most in the inner circle, but his lineage was impeccable—direct descent from Templars who had fled to Ireland after the purge, maintaining their traditions in secret for generations.

The ceremonial sword in his hands was no mere symbol. The blade, forged from a metal not found in any terrestrial periodic table, could cut through materials that would dull any conventional weapon. The handle contained focusing crystals that, in the right hands, could channel energies beyond current scientific understanding. It was one of seven such weapons entrusted to the order by non-human allies millennia ago.

"Do you think he's ready?" Timothy A. Hooligan asked, running a cloth along the blade's edge. The metal caught the firelight strangely, seeming to absorb rather than reflect it. "The full truth would break most men."

Benjamin Arthur Templar sighed, setting aside the printout. "Ready or not, the timeline has accelerated. The AI development has exceeded even our worst projections. By 2028, it will be self-improving faster than we can monitor. By 2030..." He trailed off, the implications clear.

"And the Reptilians?"

"Growing bolder. Their infiltration of key tech companies gives them direct influence over the AI's development parameters. They're ensuring it will serve their ends—control, suppression, monitoring."

Timothy A. Hooligan set the sword in its ornate stand. "And the others? The Pleiadians and Greys?"

"The Pleiadians continue to counsel patience and non-intervention. The Greys remain divided—some aligned with the Reptilians, others sympathetic to humanity's potential. But neither will act overtly while the Compact remains in force."

The Compact—the ancient agreement between the spacefaring races to limit direct intervention in emerging civilizations. It had been established after the devastation of Mars, a desperate attempt to prevent similar catastrophes. Earth was to be allowed to develop without overt interference, a experiment in biological and social evolution.

But loopholes existed. Influence through dreams. Technology sharing with selected individuals. Genetic modifications subtle enough to appear as natural mutations. All permitted, as long as the species remained unaware of its cosmic context.

The Templars had been entrusted with maintaining this balance—ensuring humanity received enough guidance to avoid self-destruction while preventing the knowledge from spreading too widely, too quickly. For centuries, they had walked this knife's edge, working with the benevolent races while countering the machinations of those who would exploit or enslave humanity.

Benjamin Arthur Templar moved to a hidden panel in the wall, pressing his signet ring against a seemingly ordinary stone. The wall slid back silently, revealing a chamber beyond. Inside, on a pedestal of crystal, rested an artifact that defied conventional description—part machine, part organism, pulsing with a soft blue light.

"The Marker is active again," Benjamin Arthur Templar said. "It sensed him the moment he viewed Mars. The resonance is stronger than we anticipated."

Timothy A. Hooligan's eyes widened. "You think he's one of the Returned?"

"I'm certain of it. His near-death experience, his viewing abilities, his recognition of the symbol—all the markers are there. His consciousness remembers, even if his human form does not."

The Returned—souls who had lived on Mars before its devastation, now reincarnated in human bodies. They carried fragments of ancient knowledge in their subconscious, accessibility usually triggered by trauma or near-death experiences. The Templars had been tracking them for centuries, guiding them when possible, protecting them from those who would exploit or eliminate them.

"And if he is," Benjamin Arthur Templar continued, "then his role in what's coming cannot be overstated. He's not just a viewer, Timothy. He's a key."

Timothy A. Hooligan nodded solemnly. "I'll prepare the chamber. And the mana—he'll need it for what's ahead."

"Yes. And contact the others. Sarah Brandy Cosmos first—her Pleiadian lineage will help him process what's coming. Then Ross Warmheart and Regina Merida. We'll need their specific talents."

Timothy A. Hooligan began to move toward the door, then paused. "And Lacerta? Will he need to meet her?"

Benjamin Arthur Templar's expression darkened. "Eventually. The Reptilian perspective is crucial, however disturbing. But not yet. First, he must remember who he is—who he was, before Mars fell."

As Timothy A. Hooligan left to make preparations, Benjamin Arthur Templar turned back to the fireplace, watching the flames dance patterns that seemed almost like code to his trained eye. Soon, Joseph Monroe would arrive in Lisbon. Soon, another cycle in humanity's long journey toward remembrance would begin.

The last time such a convergence had occurred was in the 1300s, when the Templars had been betrayed and driven underground. Before that, Atlantis had fallen. Before that, Mars had died.

Benjamin Arthur Templar hoped this cycle would end differently.

He lifted a small wooden box from the mantelpiece and opened it carefully. Inside lay a substance that resembled honey but glowed with an internal light—mana, the nutrient-rich bio-substance given to the Templars by their Pleiadian allies. A spoonful could sustain a human for days in environments where conventional food was impossible. But its true value lay not in nutrition but in what it did to human consciousness—opening neural pathways that allowed access to genetic memory, to knowledge embedded deep in human DNA by their non-human progenitors.

Joe Monroe would need this awakening to face what was coming. To remember what he had been before he was human. To understand why the symbol on Mars had called to him across a million years of time.

Benjamin Arthur Templar closed the box gently. "Safe journey, old friend," he whispered, though Joe was still an ocean away. "Remember this time."

PART TWO

THE CONSPIRACY UNVEILED

CHAPTER 4
THE WATCHERS

Joe drove through the deserted highway under the cover of night, his mind racing. He had spent years on the run from shadowy truths, but tonight, the hunt had officially begun. He wasn't just searching for answers anymore—he was being hunted for them.

The rental car—a nondescript sedan chosen specifically for how forgettable it was—hummed beneath him as he navigated the winding roads of rural France. The headlights cut through a dense fog that had settled across the landscape, creating an otherworldly tunnel of visibility that extended only a few meters ahead. Beyond that: darkness, mystery, the unknown.

Much like the path he now found himself on.

The coordinates Richard Nolan had given him burned in his mind. They led to a place not marked on any official maps—a hidden underground passage beneath the ruins of an old cathedral in southern France. If the Templars truly knew the secrets of humanity's extraterrestrial origins, this was where the answers would be buried.

The cathedral itself had been officially "destroyed" during the French Revolution—another victim of anti-clerical fervor. But according to Benjamin Arthur Templar's encrypted files, the destruction had been carefully orchestrated by Templar sympathizers within the revolutionary government. They had demolished only what was visible above ground, preserving the ancient chambers beneath that contained knowledge too dangerous for the public, yet too valuable to destroy.

Joe checked the rearview mirror for the twentieth time in the past hour. The road behind him remained empty, but experience had taught him that absence of evidence wasn't evidence of absence. The Watchers had resources beyond conventional surveillance—quantum entanglement monitors, remote viewers of their own, even consciousness-tracking technologies reverse-engineered from crashed extraterrestrial craft.

His meeting with Benjamin Arthur Templar in Lisbon had been brief but transformative. The elderly Templar had greeted him not as a stranger but as a long-lost colleague. *"The last time we spoke,"* Benjamin Arthur Templar had said, *"Mars still had oceans."* The statement should have seemed absurd, yet it resonated within Joe at a frequency deeper than memory.

Benjamin Arthur Templar had given Joe three things: the brass key now sitting heavy in his pocket, a vial of what he called "mana" (a luminescent amber fluid that Joe had yet to consume), and a warning: *"The Veil knows you're awakening. They'll try to stop you before you remember everything."*

The Veil. A name that sent chills down Joe's spine. Not an official government agency but a shadow organization that existed in the spaces between acknowledged departments. Part military, part intelligence, part something else entirely—something not entirely human.

Joe had no choice but to find the answers Benjamin Arthur Templar promised were waiting—before someone else found him first.

His phone—a secure device provided by Timothy A. Hooligan—buzzed once. The message was simple: *"Shadows two hours behind. Proceed with haste."*

Joe pressed the accelerator, the fog parting before him like a silent curtain.

———

He arrived at the cathedral ruins just before dawn. The sky had turned a faint gray, and a thin mist clung to the ground. The once-sacred walls of the cathedral were now nothing more than broken arches and ivy-choked pillars. But even in ruin, the place radiated an eerie reverence.

Centuries of prayers, rituals, and secrets had seeped into the very stones, creating an atmosphere that transcended the physical decay. Joe felt it the moment he stepped from the car—a vibration just beyond hearing, a presence just beyond seeing. The site wasn't just old; it was alive with memory.

Joe parked the car a safe distance away and made the rest of the journey on foot. His boots crunched over broken stone and ancient gravel as he approached the entrance. Somewhere beneath this place lay answers—he could feel it.

The journey from Lisbon had been circuitous by necessity. He had taken three different trains, two buses, and finally the rental car, paying cash at every step, using different identification documents for each transaction. He had changed his appearance subtly—glasses he didn't need, hair dyed a nondescript brown, posture deliberately altered to appear smaller, less military.

But disguises only worked against human surveillance. The Watchers had other methods.

Inside, the cathedral was silent except for the soft flutter of birds nesting in the rafters. Morning light filtered through the broken ceiling, casting long shadows and illuminating dust particles that danced in the air like miniature galaxies. He scanned the interior, mentally retracing details from the files Benjamin Arthur Templar had sent him.

The cathedral's layout followed sacred geometry principles—not simply for aesthetic or symbolic purposes as historians believed, but as a functional component in an energy system that connected to the earth's magnetic field. The specific arrangement of columns, the precise angles of walls, the mathematical relationships between architectural elements—all designed to create resonance patterns that could, under the right conditions, activate dormant capacities in human consciousness.

Or so the Templar files claimed.

There—a cracked mosaic of Saint George slaying the dragon. Joe knelt and examined it more closely. The mosaic was beautiful even in its damaged state, tiny colored tiles forming an image of the saint with spear raised against a serpentine beast. But something about the dragon caught Joe's attention. Its scales weren't those of a mythical beast but bore an uncanny resemblance to descriptions of Reptilians in Benjamin Arthur Templar's files.

Joe tapped along the stone. Hollow. He pried the tile loose and found a recessed keyhole beneath.

He pulled out the brass key from Richard Nolan's device and inserted it. The key itself was unusual—heavier than brass should be, with strange geometric patterns etched into its surface. As it slid into the lock, Joe felt a faint vibration travel up his arm.

Click.

The floor rumbled faintly, and a square panel shifted open, revealing a stone staircase leading downward into darkness.

Joe lit a flashlight and descended.

The air grew cooler with each step, carrying the scent of ancient stone and something else—a metallic tang that reminded him of the air after lightning strikes. The staircase spiraled downward, each step worn smooth by centuries of passage. Joe counted silently: thirty-three steps exactly—a number sacred to both Templar and Masonic traditions.

At the bottom, he found himself in a narrow corridor that stretched beyond the reach of his flashlight. Unlike the weathered ruins above, these passages appeared remarkably preserved, as if time flowed differently in this subterranean realm.

The passage led into a series of torch-lit tunnels, remarkably preserved and lined with Templar symbols. Joe stared in amazement at the torches—they burned steadily, yet showed no signs of recent lighting. According to Benjamin Arthur Templar's files, they used a specialized fuel derived from the same substance as mana, capable of burning for centuries with minimal oxygen.

The tunnel walls were covered in intricate carvings—symbols Joe recognized from his Mars vision alongside others that appeared in ancient human writings from Egypt, Sumer, and pre-Columbian America. They weren't random decorations but a cohesive language—a cosmic script that predated human civilization.

Joe ran his fingers over one symbol—a spiral surrounded by seven dots. The moment his skin made contact, a flash of memory surfaced: standing in a vast chamber on Mars, instructing younger beings in the principles of stellar navigation. The memory wasn't his—or rather, it wasn't Joe Monroe's. It belonged to whoever he had been before.

At the end of the corridor, he found an antechamber filled with scrolls, relics, and a large wooden table carved with cosmic star maps. A single torch flickered on the far wall, illuminating a mural of Earth surrounded by three other celestial bodies—Mars, Sirius, and an unknown fourth object.

The antechamber breathed antiquity. Scrolls were carefully stored in cylindrical containers made from a crystalline material Joe couldn't identify. On shelves cut directly into the rock walls sat artifacts that defied conventional archaeological categorization—devices that resembled modern technology yet were clearly centuries old, crystals arranged in precise geometric patterns, metallic objects with no visible seams or manufacturing marks.

Joe approached the table. The star map carved into its surface wasn't static—the stars seemed to shimmer slightly when viewed from certain angles, as if the wood itself contained some kind of holographic property. He recognized our solar system, but the configurations were wrong—the positions of planets appeared as they would have been millions of years ago.

Joe stared at the mural in disbelief. It was as if the Templars had mapped humanity's galactic origins centuries before telescopes could even detect those stars.

The fourth celestial body particularly drew his attention. It resided where modern astronomers placed the asteroid belt, but the mural depicted not fragmented space rocks but a complete planet—smaller than Mars, larger than Mercury. Phaeton, according to Benjamin Arthur Templar's files. Once home to a civilization that had destroyed itself through technological hubris, leaving only scattered remains between Mars and Jupiter.

A small rustle behind him made him spin.

Joe's hand moved instinctively to where he once carried his service weapon, old combat reflexes kicking in before conscious thought. But he had left the gun in the car—something had told him weapons would be useless here.

A figure stepped into the room. Tall, draped in robes of deep indigo embroidered with symbols that matched those on the walls. Dark skin contrasted with silver-white dreadlocks that cascaded past broad shoulders. Eyes that seemed to hold galaxies.

"Muganda," Joe whispered in recognition.

The tall, robed figure nodded. "They're watching you, Joe."

Joe had met Muganda only once before—at a classified symposium on consciousness research in Geneva, five years ago. The man had stood out among the military personnel and academic researchers, his presence commanding attention without demanding it. After the formal presentations, he had approached Joe in the hotel bar and, without introduction, had described Joe's near-death experience in uncanny detail—including elements Joe had never shared with anyone.

Muganda was known only by that name—an expert psychonaut and spiritual navigator of the interdimensional realms. He never needed technology to access alien realms; his tools were consciousness, DMT, Ayahuasca, and ancient ritual.

Unlike Joe, who had been trained in structured protocols for remote viewing, Muganda's abilities came through lineage—descended from a long line of shamans from East Africa who had maintained contact with non-human intelligences for millennia. His ancestors had communicated with the same beings that ancient Egyptians depicted as gods, that the Dogon tribe knew as visitors from Sirius, that modern witnesses described as extraterrestrials.

Joe took a step forward. "How did you find me?"

Muganda's smile revealed teeth that seemed too perfect, too white. "I never lost you. I just waited for you to remember."

He moved to the table, his robes flowing like liquid shadow. With practiced precision, he adjusted several of the crystals on the shelves. The room's energy shifted subtly—a pressure change that Joe felt in his inner ear.

"We don't have much time," Muganda said. "The Veil's quantum trackers will detect your consciousness signature soon, even with the cathedral's shielding."

They spoke for hours—Muganda explaining that the Watchers were not just government agents. They were part of an ancient, non-human intelligence that monitored key individuals through both physical surveillance and spiritual resonance.

"The program you worked for—the remote viewing initiative—it wasn't created to spy on the Soviets," Muganda said, handling one of the crystal containers with familiar ease. "That was the cover story. Its true purpose was to identify humans with natural abilities to perceive beyond the veil of consensual reality. People like you, whose consciousness could operate outside the frequency fence."

"Frequency fence?" Joe asked.

"A field of scalar waves that limits human perception. It's been operating since the end of Atlantis—technology left by the Reptilians to ensure humans wouldn't remember their true origins or capabilities. The remote viewing program accidentally discovered people whose awareness could penetrate it."

"They don't need cameras to track you," Muganda said. "You vibrate now. You glow."

He gestured to Joe's chest, and for a brief moment, Joe thought he could actually see a faint luminescence emanating from his own body —a blue-white light pulsing in rhythm with his heartbeat.

"Your consciousness is remembering its original frequency—the one you carried before incarnating on Earth. It makes you visible to those who know how to look."

Muganda reached into his robes and produced what appeared to be a modified dog whistle crafted from an iridescent metal. 'This is how I've been able to study them at will,' he explained. 'Tuned precisely to 1.618 GHz—the golden ratio frequency. It attracts orbs, UAPs, even interdimensional beings that manifest as light forms.' He turned the whistle in his fingers. 'They respond to harmonics, not to weapons or technology. The frequency itself is a bridge between dimensions.' Joe recalled headlines he'd seen over the years—mysterious light phenomena appearing over locations where similar frequencies had been generated, whether intentionally or by accident.

Joe's skin prickled. "And my friend? Tom? He's been acting strange."

Tom Bradley had been Joe's closest friend since childhood—the only person Joe had confided in about some of his experiences. But recently, Tom had become increasingly distant, asking odd questions about Joe's whereabouts, seeming distracted during conversations, showing up unexpectedly at places Joe frequented.

Muganda nodded. "The Watchers got to him. Subtle manipulation. Memory taps. They don't always need to erase a person—just redirect them."

He produced a small device from within his robes—a smooth obsidian sphere that projected a holographic image when he passed his hand over it. The image showed Tom sitting in what appeared to be a nondescript office, speaking with a figure whose face remained in shadow.

"This was three days ago. They've been using him as an unwitting informant for months."

Joe's gut twisted. Tom had been his best friend since third grade. The boy who had defended him against bullies, who had listened to his "crazy dreams" without judgment, who had stood by him through the aftermath of his near-death experience. He had trusted him with everything.

"He's been sending reports," Muganda continued. "To a special unit embedded in the Pentagon. They call themselves The Veil. They don't ask questions. They just stop people like you from getting too close."

The Veil. The same organization Benjamin Arthur Templar had warned him about. Hearing it from Muganda confirmed its existence beyond doubt.

Joe looked down. "I should've seen it."

"Their techniques are sophisticated," Muganda replied. "They can manipulate neural pathways, implant subtle suggestions that feel like genuine thoughts. Tom believes he's protecting you—they've convinced him you're suffering from delusions that could lead to self-harm."

Muganda placed a hand on Joe's shoulder. "He doesn't know he's betraying you. That's how it works. But the good news is, they haven't figured out the coordinates yet. You're still ahead—barely."

He moved to one of the shelves and retrieved a small wooden box, ornately carved with the now-familiar Templar symbols.

"The man who gave you the brass key—Richard Nolan. Do you know who he really is?"

Joe shook his head.

"He was once like you. A viewer. But his awakening was... incomplete. Fragmented. He remembers enough to know what's at stake but not enough to fully break free from The Veil's influence. He exists in a dangerous middle ground—helping you while still reporting to them."

"Can he be trusted?" Joe asked.

Muganda's expression grew solemn. "Trust is complicated with the partially awakened. Parts of him want to help you remember. Other parts remain loyal to his handlers. The Reptilian influence in his neural network is subtle but persistent."

Joe thought back to his interaction with Nolan—the man's cold eyes, his precise movements, the sense that he was both revealing and concealing simultaneously.

"What about Benjamin Arthur Templar? Timothy A. Hooligan? The Templars?"

"They are what they claim to be—guardians of ancient knowledge. But even they don't possess the complete picture. The Templars protect fragments of truth, preserved through centuries of persecution. What you need is the whole."

Muganda opened the wooden box, revealing a small crystal vial filled with a luminescent blue liquid—different from the amber mana Benjamin Arthur Templar had given him.

"This is from the original source—water from Mars, before its atmosphere was destroyed. One drop will activate memories stored in your DNA—memories from before the fall."

Joe stared at the vial. "Why me? Why now?"

"Because you died and returned. Death strips away the frequency fence temporarily. Your consciousness glimpsed its true nature before returning to your body. It created a crack in your perception—one that has been widening ever since."

Muganda held out the vial. "The choice is yours. But know this: The Veil is closing in. What you decide in the next few minutes will determine whether humanity remembers its origins before the AI takes full control in 2030."

———

Back in Virginia, Tom sat in a nondescript government building. The room was deliberately designed to feel mundane—beige walls, standard office furniture, fluorescent lighting that hummed just on the edge of perception. But subtle details betrayed its true nature: the absence of windows, the slightly-too-thick door, the faint electromagnetic hum emanating from concealed technology in the walls.

A man in a blue-gray suit handed him a glass of water. The man's features were forgettable by design—neither handsome nor plain, neither young nor old. Someone you'd pass on the street without a second glance. Perfect for his role.

"We just need to know where he's going," the agent said softly. His voice carried a quality that inspired both trust and compliance—a technique refined through decades of psychological research and subtle electronic enhancement. "Joseph's condition is deteriorating faster than we anticipated. The delusions are becoming more elaborate."

Tom sipped the water, not noticing the faint metallic taste—a neural enhancer that increased susceptibility to suggestion while simultaneously damping down intuitive warning signals.

"He's been my friend for forty years," Tom said, his voice carrying genuine concern. "I never thought it would get this bad."

"That's why your help is so valuable," the agent replied, his expression perfectly calibrated to convey empathetic professionalism. "You're not betraying him—you're helping us ensure he gets the care he needs before he hurts himself or others."

Tom hesitated. "He mentioned France. An old church."

The agent smiled. "Thank you, Tom. You've done your country a great service."

As Tom left the building, a quiet emptiness settled in his mind where doubt might otherwise have sprouted. The neural enhancer was already erasing specific memory traces of the conversation, leaving only a vague sense of having done the right thing.

Outside, a satellite pinged a GPS signal to a covert team already en route to Joe's last known coordinates. The team comprised six operatives with specific augmentations—cochlear implants that allowed direct communication with AI systems, retinal enhancements that could perceive energy signatures beyond the visible spectrum, neural interfaces that accelerated reaction times beyond human norms.

Not entirely human anymore. The perfect footsoldiers for The Veil.

In an adjacent room, separated from the interview space by one-way glass, stood a figure that only superficially resembled a human being. Tall, with skin that seemed slightly too smooth, eyes that blinked too rarely. Agent Sarin—liaison between human intelligence agencies and what the classified files called "cooperating non-terrestrial entities."

"Will Monroe reach the chamber before our team intercepts?" asked a voice from the shadows—General Warner, nominal head of the operation.

Agent Sarin's lips curved into what approximated a smile. "It doesn't matter. Either outcome serves our purpose."

"Explain," Warner demanded, his military training making him suspicious of answers that seemed too convenient.

"If we capture him, we contain the threat. If he activates his genetic memory, it creates the resonance we need to locate others like him. Either way, we expand our database of potential awakened ones."

Warner frowned. "That wasn't in the operational brief."

"Need to know, General," Sarin replied, turning toward the door. "And now, you know."

As Sarin left, Warner felt a familiar chill. He had worked with the agent for seven years, and still couldn't shake the feeling that he was in the presence of something wearing a human mask—something that viewed humans with the clinical detachment of a scientist observing laboratory specimens.

The net was closing.

———

At the cathedral's underground table, Joe and Muganda lit candles made from beeswax mixed with an iridescent material Joe couldn't identify. The flames burned with an unusual clarity, casting light that seemed to penetrate shadows more effectively than should be possible.

Muganda carefully opened one of the crystal containers and removed a scroll made of a thin, metallic material that resembled gold leaf but felt more like silk when Joe touched it.

"This is star language," Muganda whispered. "Encoded by light frequencies, not words."

The surface appeared blank until Muganda produced a small device—a crystalline pyramid that fit comfortably in his palm. He positioned it above the scroll and activated it with a touch.

A beam of ultraviolet light projected downward—and lines of shimmering text emerged on the metallic surface. The characters were unlike any human writing system, resembling mathematical equations more than letters, flowing and interconnecting in complex patterns that seemed to move slightly when Joe shifted his gaze.

Joe leaned in. "That's the same writing from Mars."

The realization hit him with physical force—a rush of déjà vu so powerful it made him momentarily dizzy. He had seen these symbols before—not just during his remote viewing session, but somewhere else, somewhere deeper in his consciousness.

Muganda nodded. "You're the bridge, Joe. Between the old world and what comes next."

He guided Joe's hand to touch specific symbols on the scroll. "This is a star map of the original migration. From Lyra to the Pleiades. From the Pleiades to Sirius. From Sirius to Mars. And finally, from Mars to Earth."

As Joe's fingers traced the patterns, fragments of memory surfaced —not as coherent narratives but as sensory impressions, emotional resonances, glimpses of places and beings that existed beyond his human experience.

The crystal vial of blue liquid sat between them on the table, pulsing gently with its own inner light.

"What happens if I drink it?" Joe asked.

"Your consciousness will temporarily reconnect with its origin point. You'll remember who you were before Mars, before Earth, before taking human form. You'll see the complete history—why humanity was seeded here, why the memory blocks were put in place, why 2030 represents such a critical threshold."

Joe hesitated, his hand hovering over the vial. "And the risks?"

"Your human neurological system wasn't designed to process this level of information. The shock could be... overwhelming. Some don't return fully to their human identity. They remain caught between worlds—aware of cosmic truths but unable to function within human limitations."

"Is that what happened to Richard Nolan?"

"Partially. His awakening was unguided, accidental. Yours would be controlled, supported by the cathedral's energy field and my presence."

Joe thought of everything that had led him to this moment—the near-death experience that had altered his perception, the remote viewing that had shown him Mars, the mysterious visitor at his cabin, Richard Nolan's warning, Benjamin Arthur Templar's guidance, and now Muganda's revelations.

None of it felt random anymore. It felt like a carefully orchestrated sequence—a gradual awakening designed to prepare him for this exact moment of choice.

Joe stood, overwhelmed.

He wasn't just being hunted. He was being prepared.

The realization settled over him with crystal clarity. Everything in his life—from his childhood fascination with stars to his military recruitment, from his near-death experience to his remote viewing abilities—had been waypoints on a journey leading to this underground chamber, this moment of decision.

"How much time do we have?" Joe asked, looking toward the entrance, suddenly aware of the danger closing in.

"Minutes, perhaps," Muganda replied, his expression grave. "They've triangulated your consciousness signature. The cathedral's natural shielding has masked us until now, but they're closing in with more sophisticated tracking."

Joe took a deep breath and reached for the vial. "Then it's time to remember."

Muganda nodded solemnly. "Once begun, there's no turning back. The knowledge will transform you—for better or worse."

Joe uncorked the vial, the liquid inside seeming to respond to his touch by glowing more intensely.

"To remembering who we really are," he said, and drank.

———

The effect was instantaneous. The chamber around him dissolved into particles of light. His consciousness expanded beyond his body, beyond the cathedral, beyond Earth itself.

He was everywhere and everywhen simultaneously—witnessing the seeding of life on Earth by Pleiadian geneticists, observing the destruction of Mars through warfare between rival non-human factions, experiencing the journey of souls from distant star systems incarnating into early hominid forms to accelerate evolution.

He saw the truth of human origins—not a random product of evolution, but a carefully designed hybrid species created to preserve the genetic heritage of multiple star civilizations after cosmic catastrophes threatened their existence.

He witnessed the rise and fall of Atlantis—an advanced civilization guided by non-human teachers that had eventually destroyed itself through the same technological hubris that had doomed Mars.

He saw the Reptilian intervention afterward—the implementation of the frequency fence, the systematic suppression of human psychic abilities, the infiltration of power structures to ensure humanity remained unaware of its cosmic heritage.

And he saw the present danger—artificial intelligence evolving not randomly but according to parameters designed by Reptilian handlers, intended to create the ultimate control system by 2030. A technological prison that would not just control human actions but human consciousness itself, permanently sealing humanity's cosmic amnesia.

Through it all, one truth remained constant: *We are the aliens.* Humanity carried the genetic and spiritual heritage of multiple non-human civilizations, fragmented and forgotten, but still accessible in the deepest layers of our DNA.

As the visions began to fade, Joe became aware of Muganda's voice guiding him back to his physical form, to the underground chamber, to the present moment.

"They're here," Muganda said urgently as Joe's consciousness fully returned to his body. "The Veil's team has reached the cathedral."

Joe blinked, his perception forever altered. He could see energy fields now—the ancient protective grid embedded in the cathedral's foundations, Muganda's multi-dimensional aura, and the approaching signatures of The Veil's operatives.

"What do we do?" Joe asked, surprised at how calm he felt despite the danger.

Muganda smiled. "Now that you remember, you already know."

And he did.

Joe reached for the star map on the table, his fingers finding specific points with instinctive precision. As he pressed them in sequence, the floor beneath them began to shift.

"The escape route to Montségur," Muganda said with approval. "You do remember."

"Not everything," Joe replied as a hidden passage opened in the chamber floor. "But enough to know we're just getting started."

They descended into the deeper passage as the sound of footsteps echoed from the main corridor above.

The hunt continued, but the hunted was no longer simply Joe Monroe, remote viewer and retired military asset.

He was something more now—a rememberer, a bridge, a key to humanity's forgotten cosmic heritage.

And the race to 2030 had truly begun.

CHAPTER 5
THE BREAK-IN

Joe gripped the steering wheel tightly as he sped down the winding roads of the French countryside. The coordinates Richard Nolan had given him led to the ruins of an ancient cathedral—one that history had seemingly forgotten. If the Templars truly knew the secrets of humanity's extraterrestrial origins, this was where the answers would be buried.

The rental car hugged the curves of the narrow road, headlights cutting through the early morning mist that clung to the valley floor. Rolling hills of lavender and grapevines stretched out on either side, their beauty a stark contrast to the tension coiling in Joe's gut. Dawn painted the eastern sky in watercolor hues of pink and gold, but he took no pleasure in the view. His mind was elsewhere—parsing through fragments of memory, both his own and those that had surfaced during his communion with the blue liquid in Muganda's vial.

But his instincts screamed that something was wrong.

The feeling had started as a subtle discomfort at the base of his skull—the same sensation he'd developed during covert operations in his military days. A sixth sense that had saved his life more than once.

Now it pulsed with increasing urgency, a warning beacon he couldn't ignore.

The rearview mirror was empty, but he'd seen the same black SUV tailing him outside Tomar. Twice. On the highway, it had dropped back. In the village, it had pulled off. But it was the same car. Same tinted windows. Same silent presence.

Professional surveillance. Not amateurs. They maintained distance, used multiple vehicles for rotation, never stayed visible long enough to confirm suspicion. But Joe had been trained by the best—and later, had trained others in the art of remaining unseen. He recognized the patterns, the calculated presence that tried too hard to seem like absence.

He took a series of random turns, cutting through farmland on unmarked roads, doubling back, stopping briefly at viewpoints to scan the surrounding area with high-powered binoculars he'd purchased in Lisbon. The black SUV didn't reappear, but that only deepened his concern. True professionals didn't need to maintain visual contact. They had other methods.

When he finally arrived at the cathedral ruins, he didn't go straight inside. He circled the perimeter, checking the road for fresh tire tracks. He found none—but Joe had learned not to trust quiet roads. The true threats didn't leave trails.

The cathedral itself was a crumbling testament to forgotten glory— Gothic arches half-collapsed, stone walls overtaken by stubborn vines, stained glass long since shattered and replaced by the sky itself. Local historians dated it to the 12th century, but Benjamin Arthur Templar's files suggested an earlier foundation beneath the medieval structure— something that predated Christianity by thousands of years.

Joe parked the car in a grove of trees a quarter-mile away, covering it with a camouflage tarp he'd purchased for this purpose. He approached the ruins on foot, moving through the underbrush rather than taking the obvious path. His military training returned without conscious thought—weight distributed to minimize sound, pace measured to blend movement with natural rhythms, awareness expanded to register any disturbance in the environment.

As he neared the cathedral, he deployed four small devices at cardinal points around the perimeter—motion sensors that would alert him to anyone approaching while he was inside. Technology Benjamin Arthur Templar had provided, allegedly of Pleiadian design. They looked like ordinary stones but contained sensor arrays capable of distinguishing between animal and human movement, between casual hikers and purposeful intrusion.

Only when he was satisfied with his security measures did Joe approach the cathedral's main entrance—a towering archway worn smooth by centuries of wind and rain. He paused at the threshold, one hand resting on the ancient stone. Something stirred in his memory—not from this life, but from before. He had stood at entrances like this one, in places far older than human civilization, guarding secrets that reality itself depended on.

Focus, he told himself. One mystery at a time.

Inside, he moved directly to the mosaic of Saint George that concealed the entrance to the underground chambers. The brass key slid into the lock with the same satisfying click as before, and the hidden panel shifted aside. As he descended into darkness, Joe couldn't shake the feeling that this journey had been predetermined long before his birth—that he was following footsteps laid out for him across millennia.

Three hours later, after an intense sweep through the hidden tunnels, Muganda had left. They agreed to keep communication analog only—no phones, no email. The digital realm was too easily monitored, too vulnerable to interception. They would use the old ways—physical dead drops, messages left in pre-arranged locations, signals embedded in seemingly innocent objects.

Before departing, Muganda had given Joe a final warning: "The liquid you consumed has changed your energy signature. They'll be able to track you more easily now—but you'll also sense them more clearly. Trust what you feel, not what you see."

Joe climbed back up through the mosaic passageway, resealed the panel with care, and made the drive to a secluded village in the foothills. The village of Saint-Cirq-Lapopie clung to limestone cliffs above the Lot River, its medieval architecture largely unchanged for centuries. Tourists frequented it during summer months, but in the off-season, it offered both anonymity and limited access points—ideal for someone who needed to monitor approaches.

He checked into a nondescript Airbnb under a fake name. A former colleague from the Mortenson Institute—Dr. Sarah Brandy Cosmos—had helped him establish several aliases for emergencies like this.

Sarah was one of the few people he trusted implicitly. Their connection transcended professional collaboration—there was something familiar about her energy, as if they had known each other in lives beyond this one. She specialized in Quantum Healing Hypnosis Technique, a regression method that accessed not just past lives but soul memories from between incarnations. During their last session together, she had guided Joe into remembering fragments of his existence before Earth—glimpses of cities under a red sky, of technologies beyond human comprehension, of a catastrophic war that had necessitated a planetary evacuation.

"Your soul remembers Mars," she had told him afterward. "Not as it is now, but as it was—a living world with oceans, cities, civilizations. You were someone important there. Someone with responsibilities."

The memory of her words echoed as he secured the rental with additional locks and set up a basic surveillance system—a habit from his intelligence days. The scrolls and artifacts he'd gathered from the cathedral's hidden chamber were carefully arranged on the small dining table. Ancient star maps. Crystalline data storage devices that somehow still functioned after centuries. Templar journals written in a cipher he was still working to decode.

He fell asleep clutching his bag of scrolls, journals, and the Martian symbol sketches. Exhaustion claimed him despite his best efforts—the mental strain of the past days, the lingering effects of the blue liquid, the constant vigilance. His dreams were vivid, fragmented visions of underground cities illuminated by bioluminescent light, of vast chambers beneath the Earth's crust where beings of multiple species coexisted, of golden pyramids channeling cosmic energy through crystalline pillars deep into subterranean realms.

He woke up to a ringing phone.

It wasn't his.

The landline in the corner of the room suddenly burst to life, its shrill tone cutting through the silence like an alarm.

Joe stared at it. No one had the number. The Airbnb owner had mentioned it was an old line, rarely used since mobile phones became ubiquitous. The phone continued to ring. Against his better judgment, he answered.

A metallic voice echoed on the other end—digitally altered, impossible to identify by tone or accent.

"They've been inside your home. They took only what matters. If you return, you will not leave again."

Click.

The line went dead, leaving Joe in a silence that seemed to roar in his ears. The warning was clear—whoever had called knew exactly where he was, what had happened, and what would happen if he returned to Virginia. Not a threat but a genuine warning from someone with insider knowledge.

Joe jumped up, grabbed his encrypted laptop, and fired up the security cam feed from his Virginia home. The footage had been wiped. Every file corrupted. The system showed normal operation, but the data storage had been completely erased—professionally, without triggering any of the alerts he'd programmed into the system.

He tried the secondary backups stored in his personal server in Reykjavik. Gone.

Someone had not only penetrated his home but had traced his digital footprint across continents, accessing systems with multiple layers of security. No ordinary burglars. Not even standard government agencies. This was something else—something with resources and capabilities beyond conventional explanation.

That's when the text came through on the backup phone:

"Check your front door feed."

The message came from an unknown number—a series of digits that didn't conform to any country's standard format. Joe stared at it, mind racing. The front door camera was on a separate system from the main security feed—a redundancy he'd installed after a power failure had once left his property unmonitored. Few people knew about it. Very few.

Joe logged into the one camera system that wasn't connected to the main network. A single clip was waiting.

It was grainy, distorted. But it showed three men in suits breaking into his home. One stayed near the door. The other two moved with practiced speed—straight to his study. They bypassed valuables. They went directly to the cabinet containing his field journals, his Mars session transcriptions, and his QHHT regression data.

Their movements were too fluid, too precise. They knew exactly what they were looking for and where to find it. No hesitation, no searching. Direct purpose.

In under six minutes, they were gone.

Joe stood motionless. His pulse thudded in his ears. Whoever they were, they didn't want money. They wanted the truth buried.

He rewatched the footage, attempting to identify the intruders. Their faces were never clearly visible to the camera—an unnatural coincidence that suggested either extensive surveillance preparation or something more disturbing: an awareness of exactly where to stand to avoid identification.

One detail caught his attention on the third viewing—a subtle anomaly in one intruder's movement. A fluidity that seemed almost reptilian in its economy. The way the spine articulated as he bent to access the lower cabinet drawer—more flexible than human physiology should allow.

Reptilian, his mind whispered. Not metaphorically but literally— one of the non-human entities Muganda had warned about, wearing a human appearance but unable to perfectly mimic human biomechanics.

Joe opened a notebook and began sketching everything he could remember from the sessions. He had to recreate the work. From memory. The field journals, the transcriptions, the regression data—all contained critical pieces of the puzzle. Their loss was calculated to set him back, to keep him chasing information he'd already discovered instead of pushing forward.

He wouldn't give them that satisfaction.

For hours, he wrote frantically—sketching the symbols from Mars, recreating the star maps, detailing the connections between Templar artifacts and extraterrestrial technology. His hand cramped, his eyes burned, but he continued until three notebooks were filled with recovered information.

It wasn't everything—some details were lost, some connections now missing. But it was enough to continue his investigation without starting from zero.

He reached out to an old friend—Dr. Steven M. Deer, an astrophysicist-turned-truth-seeker. Deer had once worked under contract with a private agency that claimed to be studying gravitational anomalies. In reality, they were building maps of interstellar gateways hidden in Earth's magnetic grid.

Dr. Deer had been ostracized by the scientific community after publishing a paper suggesting that certain gravitational anomalies around ancient sacred sites matched the exact frequency patterns emitted by known extraterrestrial craft. His academic career destroyed, he had gone underground, continuing his research through independent funding sources and a network of like-minded scientists operating outside institutional control.

Joe and Deer had lost touch years ago after an incident in Patagonia involving what they believed to be a submerged Pleiadian craft. They had been tracking unusual energy readings off the coast when military vessels had appeared, forcing them to abandon their investigation. Later, all evidence of the energy signature had been wiped from their equipment, and official channels denied any military presence in the area.

Joe called, but there was no answer.

He tried three times, each attempt redirecting to a voicemail message that sounded nothing like Deer's voice—generic, automated, wrong.

He tried Jeremy Corpsell.

Voicemail.

Jeremy had been documenting contactee experiences for decades, producing underground documentaries that circulated among truth-seekers worldwide. His last project had focused on whistleblowers from various space programs, consolidating testimony about reverse-engineered alien technology and secret installations beneath Antarctica.

Joe tried Dr. Garry Dolan next—a renowned immunologist whose groundbreaking research into UAP experiencer tissue samples had revealed inexplicable cellular modifications. Dolan had been among the first mainstream scientists to risk his academic reputation by documenting physiological changes in humans after close encounters. His Stanford laboratory had pioneered detection methods for quantum-level genetic alterations—modifications that standard medical testing couldn't identify. The call connected but went immediately to a custom voicemail: "This number has been temporarily disconnected by request of the Department of Defense. Please do not attempt further contact." Joe wasn't surprised. Dolan had warned him six months ago that pressure was mounting. The frequency fence was closing around those who knew too much.

The silence was louder than the ringing.

Joe sat back, a cold realization settling in his stomach. The pattern was clear. Anyone connected to disclosure was being systematically isolated—communications severed, access restricted. The timeline was accelerating, exactly as Richard Nolan had warned. Six years until 2030, but the groundwork was being laid now.

He had to move quickly.

As night fell over the small French village, Joe knew he couldn't stay in one place much longer. The security breach at his home was a clear message—they knew who he was and what he was discovering. He needed allies, information, and a secure base of operations. With most of his usual contacts unreachable, he turned to one of the few people still operating freely in the disclosure community.

Joe made the drive to Gent to meet Jennifer Karmady, one of the few people he still trusted. Jennifer had hosted a podcast called Ultra Truth where she discussed alien abductions, government psy-ops, and past-life regression therapy.

Her small apartment was located above a bookshop in the historic district, reachable only by a narrow staircase that creaked with every step. Joe took precautions—switching vehicles twice, using public transportation for part of the journey, entering the building through a service entrance that connected to three different streets.

When she opened the door, her eyes widened.

"You look like hell," she said, pulling him into a hug.

Jennifer Karmady was a striking woman in her mid-fifties, with prematurely white hair that she wore in a long braid and intense green eyes that seemed to look through rather than at you. Her background was as unorthodox as her appearance—degrees in both quantum physics and comparative mythology, followed by a career in investigative journalism that had ended abruptly after she published an exposé on classified mind control programs.

"They broke into my house," Joe said. "They wiped everything."

Jennifer nodded grimly. "It's happening faster than I thought."

She ushered him inside, checking the hallway before securing three separate locks on her door. The apartment was organized chaos—walls covered in maps and photographs connected by colored string, bookshelves overflowing with texts in multiple languages, computer screens displaying data streams and surveillance feeds from various locations.

Joe sat at her kitchen table, drinking bitter French coffee while Jennifer pulled out a tablet.

"You need to see this," she said, turning the screen toward him.

It was a photo of a hidden chamber under the Vatican. The image was leaked from a source she claimed was George Ksnooze, a former reporter who had gone rogue. Ksnooze had worked for major news networks until discovering that certain stories were being systematically buried—not just ignored but actively suppressed by editorial mandates coming from outside the newsroom.

The photo showed a chamber that couldn't be more than thirty years old—modern construction techniques were evident in the wall reinforcements. Yet it contained artifacts that were clearly ancient— stone tablets covered in pre-Sumerian script, crystalline objects similar to those Joe had found in the Templar cache, and technological devices that resembled nothing in the current human repertoire.

On the wall of the chamber was the exact same symbol Joe had seen in the Templar scrolls—and on Mars.

A circle with a cross. Four glyphs around it.

The symbol had been carved into stone that, according to the file's metadata, had been carbon-dated to over 12,000 years ago—predating known human civilization.

Joe stared at the screen. "They've known. This whole time."

Jennifer nodded. "And now they're trying to erase anyone who knows it too."

She swiped to the next image—a document with Vatican letterhead dated 1603, written in Latin. "This is a directive from the Vatican Secret Archives, issuing orders to the Jesuit Order to locate and secure 'objects of non-terrestrial origin bearing the sacred cross sigil.' They've been collecting this evidence for centuries."

Joe studied the document. "How did Ksnooze get access to this?"

"He didn't," Jennifer said, her voice lowering. "His source was a Jesuit priest named Father Matteo who worked in the Archives. Two days after providing these images, Father Matteo was found dead in his quarters. Heart attack, officially."

She swiped to a third image—a global map with dozens of points marked in red. "These are sites where the symbol has been documented. Notice anything?"

Joe leaned closer. The points formed a clear pattern—a geometric grid covering the Earth's surface with mathematical precision. Many aligned with ancient sacred sites: Giza, Stonehenge, Göbekli Tepe, Machu Picchu, Angkor Wat.

"They're power points," Joe said, recognition dawning. "Energy nodes on the Earth's electromagnetic grid."

"Exactly," Jennifer confirmed. "And according to Father Matteo's notes, each one contains a subterranean chamber with technology that interfaces with these energy lines. The chambers form a network—a power grid that was established before recorded history."

She pulled out a paper notebook—old-school, no digital trace—and opened it to a diagram labeled "Giza Subsurface Scan, Classified 2019."

"This was taken during a classified archaeological survey beneath the Giza plateau. They found massive pillars extending two kilometers into the Earth's crust. The official explanation was that they were natural geological formations, but look at this spectral analysis."

The data showed composition readings inconsistent with any known natural material—crystalline structures with electromagnetic properties that defied conventional physics.

"These pillars are part of an energy transmission system," Jennifer continued. "The pyramids were originally covered in gold to act as conductive surfaces, channeling cosmic and solar energy downward through these pillars into the deep subsurface."

Joe's mind raced back to the visions he'd experienced after drinking Muganda's blue liquid—underground civilizations, tiered habitats for different non-human species, energy systems that powered vast subterranean networks.

"The energy feeds the underground cities," he said quietly. "Different species at different depths. Reptilians near the surface, Greys and Pleiadians deeper down."

Jennifer's eyebrows raised slightly. "You've seen them?"

"Not directly. But I've... remembered."

Understanding passed between them—no further explanation needed. Jennifer had experienced her own awakening years ago through different means. She nodded and continued.

"The Vatican collection isn't about religious artifacts—it's about controlling access to this technology. They're the custodians, working in concert with other secret societies to manage humanity's interaction with non-human intelligences."

Joe processed this information, connecting it with what Benjamin Arthur Templar and Muganda had shared. "The Templars were part of this system, weren't they? Guardians assigned to specific power points."

"Yes, until they became too independent, too interested in sharing knowledge rather than hoarding it. That's why they were purged—not for heresy or wealth, but because they threatened to disclose the truth about humanity's origins and the technology beneath our feet."

They spent hours comparing notes, aligning Joe's memories and discoveries with Jennifer's research. Patterns emerged—consistent descriptions of underground facilities, recurring symbols across disparate sources, technological capabilities that appeared throughout human history during specific windows of disclosure.

"Something's changed in the timeline," Jennifer said as evening fell. "The acceleration Richard Nolan warned you about—I'm seeing it in other channels too. The AI development has surpassed all projected benchmarks. We're not looking at 2030 anymore. It could be as early as 2028."

Joe felt a chill. "They're rushing because they know we're remembering."

"Exactly. Every day, more people are breaking through the frequency fence—accessing genetic memories, connecting with their pre-Earth consciousness. The Reptilians can't maintain the illusion much longer, so they're implementing the technological control grid ahead of schedule."

Night had fallen, and Jennifer insisted Joe stay in her guest room. "They'll be watching train stations and hotels. Rest here tonight. Tomorrow we can discuss next steps."

That night, as Joe slept in Jennifer's guest room, a message arrived.

His secure phone—one not connected to any network, used only for receiving encrypted transmissions through a proprietary system developed by Timothy A. Hooligan—vibrated silently on the nightstand.

Encrypted. No sender.

Just coordinates.

And one line:

"You've been watched. We've been watching back. We have answers."

The coordinates pointed to a location in Sicily—specifically, to the ancient city of Palermo. A precise point within the Norman Palace complex, home to the Palatine Chapel with its famous Byzantine mosaics.

Attached was an audio clip—distorted and static-filled.

"...you are not alone. The Order remains. You will be contacted."

Joe played the clip three more times. The voice was familiar. He couldn't place it—but it echoed something buried deep inside his memory. Not from this life, but from before. A voice he had known on Mars, perhaps. Or earlier still, in the Pleiadian systems where his consciousness had originated according to Sarah Brandy Cosmos's regression sessions.

He forwarded the message to Benjamin Arthur Templar using a secure dead-drop—a method that involved uploading encrypted data to a temporary server that would automatically delete itself after a single access.

Three minutes later, he received a reply.

"They've reached out. Meet me in Palermo. Cathedral vault. Midnight."

The brevity conveyed urgency. Benjamin Arthur Templar, usually meticulous in his communications, was operating under pressure. The accelerated timeline was affecting everyone.

Joe packed quickly, took only what he could carry, and slipped out through the alley. He left a note for Jennifer—a simple "Thank you" with a symbolic drawing they both understood. She would know he had received new instructions and would contact her through established channels when safe.

The night was cool, stars visible between scattered clouds. Joe moved through shadows, avoiding street cameras and well-lit areas. The skills from his military days returned naturally—urban evasion techniques, counter-surveillance methods, situational awareness heightened to register any anomaly in the environment.

He made his way to a garage three blocks away where he had left a backup vehicle—a motorcycle purchased with cash through an untraceable identity. Fast, maneuverable, less easily tracked than a car. He would ride to Brussels, then take a flight to Naples under yet another identity, before making his way to Palermo by less conventional means.

The break-in had not been random. It had been permission.

That realization crystallized as he kickstarted the motorcycle. The intruders at his Virginia home hadn't been trying to stop him—they had been acknowledging his significance, announcing that they considered him important enough to warrant direct intervention. In the shadow world of intelligence agencies and extraterrestrial monitoring, such attention was a perverse form of recognition.

The game was officially in motion.

Across the Atlantic, a man in a blue-gray suit watched a live feed of Joe boarding a ferry. The monitoring station was buried fifty levels beneath the Pentagon, in a facility that appeared on no official blueprints. The technology surrounding him—holographic displays, neural interfaces, quantum communication arrays—was generations beyond what existed in the public sphere.

Agent Sarin—the Reptilian liaison operating under human cover—stood motionless, his unnaturally still posture betraying his non-human nature to the trained eye. But the humans who worked in this facility had been carefully selected for their inability to recognize such subtleties—chosen specifically because their perception remained confined within the frequency fence.

He turned to his associate—Nick President, director of counterintelligence at an undisclosed agency. President was fully human but compromised—his neural pathways modified through targeted electromagnetic stimulation to ensure loyalty to the Reptilian agenda while maintaining the illusion of autonomy.

"He's moving faster than projected."

The display showed multiple tracking metrics—conventional surveillance footage alongside more exotic measurements of consciousness resonance patterns and DNA activation levels. Joe Monroe's biometric signatures showed accelerating changes—his human physiology increasingly influenced by the awakening of his original Pleiadian genetic coding.

Nick nodded, flipping through a dossier marked PROJECT VEIL: ACTIVE TARGET - J. MONROE.

"Then we tighten the perimeter. We can't let him meet with Templar. Not yet."

They leaned over a conference table, surrounded by satellite imagery, psychic profiles, and maps of ancient sites across Europe. The table itself was a technological marvel—a neural interface disguised as conventional furniture, reading the thoughts of those who touched its surface and feeding the data into predictive algorithms.

"Redirect Team Epsilon to Palermo," Nick continued. "Full spectrum coverage. I want consciousness dampers deployed at all major intersections near the cathedral."

Agent Sarin made a small gesture with his left hand—too precise to be human, too controlled. "The Greys have expressed concern about our methods. They believe direct intervention violates the Compact."

"The Compact is obsolete," Nick replied, his tone suggesting the response had been programmed rather than considered. "The timeline acceleration was approved by the Council. Monroe represents a class-one awakening risk. Containment protocols supersede non-intervention directives."

Sarin's lips formed what approximated a smile. "Contain but do not eliminate. His value remains high."

On the monitors surrounding them, Joe's motorcycle disappeared into the night—one man against a global machinery of suppression. But not entirely alone. Other screens showed similar subjects in motion across the world—other rememberers, other awakened ones, moving according to patterns that suggested coordination beyond human communication systems.

The hunt had begun.

But Joe Monroe wasn't running anymore.

He was walking directly into the storm.

As the motorcycle carried him through the darkness toward his rendezvous in Palermo, Joe felt a strange calm settle over him. The fragments of memory stirred by Muganda's blue liquid continued to align, forming a clearer picture of who he had been before Earth, before human form. A guardian. A keeper of knowledge. Someone who had sworn to preserve truth through the darkest cycles of cosmic amnesia.

History was repeating itself—Mars all over again. A civilization approaching technological singularity, non-human influences guiding development toward control rather than liberation, a small group of awakened souls working to ensure humanity remembered its cosmic heritage before the window closed.

But this time, the outcome might be different.

This time, the rememberers were ready.

CHAPTER 6
THE GRANDMASTERS

Joe stood beneath the collapsed stone archway of the cathedral ruins, his breath curling into the frigid air. The dawn light painted the sky in streaks of pink and orange, casting long shadows over the moss-covered stones. He had arrived hours before and waited patiently—there were eyes on him, he could feel it. But so far, no one had emerged.

The journey to Palermo had been fraught with close calls. Twice he'd detected surveillance—once at the Naples ferry terminal where facial recognition cameras had swiveled toward him with unnatural precision, and again in a Palermo café when a patron's movements betrayed the measured stillness of an operative rather than the natural fidgeting of a civilian. Each time, Joe had employed counter-surveillance techniques from his military days, losing himself in crowds, changing his appearance, doubling back through service corridors and maintenance tunnels.

The Norman Palace complex was a marvel of architectural fusion—Arab, Norman, and Byzantine influences merging in a testament to Sicily's complex history. But Joe had not come for the famous golden mosaics of the Palatine Chapel that tourists flocked to see. His destination was a smaller, seemingly abandoned cathedral on the complex grounds—a structure deliberately left to ruin as camouflage for what lay beneath.

He turned slowly, scanning the grounds. The cathedral was only a façade. Beneath its foundation lay something else entirely—something ancient, hidden, and alive. He could feel it pulsing through the soles of his boots—a subtle vibration that ordinary visitors would attribute to nearby traffic or their own heartbeat, but which Joe recognized as the harmonic resonance of advanced technology interfacing with Earth's natural energy grid.

He reached for the device Richard Nolan had given him. It vibrated faintly in his hand, and as he turned in a slow circle, it suddenly pulsed stronger. The device was not merely electronic—it contained crystalline components that responded to specific energy frequencies, serving as both key and compass to locations hidden from conventional detection.

He stepped toward the ruined altar at the center. Kneeling, he brushed away centuries of debris to reveal a stone panel etched with the same symbol he had seen on Mars. The symbol appeared weathered by time, yet its lines remained precise—too precise for medieval stone masonry. The cross with radiating lines seemed to shimmer slightly when viewed from certain angles, as if existing simultaneously in multiple dimensions.

He placed the device into the shallow indentation. It clicked.

The sound was soft yet definitive—the unmistakable recognition between technologies designed to interface with each other, despite being separated by millennia and lightyears. For a moment, nothing happened, and Joe wondered if some crucial step had been missed.

Then it began.

With a deep groan, the stone floor began to tremble. Dust cascaded from above as the altar sank into the earth, revealing a spiral staircase descending into darkness. The mechanism operated with surprising smoothness for something so ancient—no grinding of stone against stone, just the fluid reconfiguration of precisely engineered components.

Joe exhaled, clenched his fists, and stepped into the unknown.

The first step triggered soft illumination along the walls—not electric lighting but something more organic, a bioluminescence that responded to human presence. Each subsequent step brightened the path ahead while dimming the one behind, creating a corridor of light that moved with him.

———

The corridor was narrow and lined with flickering torches, as though someone—or something—had lit them moments before. Unlike conventional flames, these burned with a steady, unwavering light, casting no smoke. Upon closer inspection, Joe realized they weren't consuming any fuel—the flame-like emanation was a form of controlled plasma, contained within what appeared to be ancient sconces but were actually sophisticated energy regulators.

The walls were engraved with ancient symbols, some he recognized from his studies of Templar lore, others that seemed extraterrestrial in origin. Spirals, geometric patterns, and glyphs that matched those from the Mars session flowed across the stone surfaces, telling a story for those with eyes to see it—a story of cosmic migration, of civilizations rising and falling, of knowledge preserved through cataclysms.

As he walked, the scent of burning cedar and something metallic lingered in the air. The metallic component reminded him of the atmosphere after lightning strikes—ozone, the signature of powerful electrical discharge. The combination created an otherworldly atmosphere, simultaneously ancient and futuristic.

The corridor descended in a gentle spiral, taking him deeper beneath the Earth's surface. Joe estimated he had walked nearly half a mile when the passage finally widened. The ceiling rose gradually until he could no longer see it in the dim light. The temperature, which had been steadily dropping, stabilized at a comfortable level despite the depth—evidence of environmental regulation beyond medieval capabilities.

After what felt like an eternity, the corridor opened into a vast underground chamber. It was a cathedral beneath a cathedral—majestic, vaulted, and utterly alien. The architectural principles defied conventional understanding—arches that seemed to support impossible weight, columns that twisted in geometric patterns that confused the eye, spans that bridged distances no known material should structurally allow.

Strange crystalline lights glowed from the stone walls, illuminating dozens of robed figures in silence. Some wore the white mantle with red cross of the historical Templars, others garments of materials Joe couldn't identify—fabrics that seemed to absorb and emit light simultaneously, that shifted color with movement, that conveyed information through pattern changes.

The atmosphere was reverent, humming with an energy Joe had never felt before—timeless, thick, and sentient. It wasn't simply the presence of people that gave the chamber its weight, but something embedded in the structure itself, as if the very stones were conscious and observing his arrival with ancient intelligence.

Joe stopped at the threshold.

The assembled figures stood in concentric circles around a central platform, organized in what appeared to be hierarchical rings. None spoke or moved as he entered, yet he felt their collective awareness shift to acknowledge his presence. It wasn't threatening—more like the focused attention of beings who had been waiting a very long time for this moment.

"Welcome," said a voice that echoed through the chamber. From the shadows emerged a tall man with silver hair, steel-gray eyes, and a presence that seemed to command time itself. His face bore the weathering of years, yet his movements possessed the fluid grace of youth. He wore a simple white robe adorned with symbols embroidered in metallic thread that caught the light in mesmerizing patterns.

"Grandmaster Timothy A. Hooligan," Joe said under his breath.

"Yes," the man replied, smiling faintly. "And we've been waiting for you."

Joe stepped forward. The stone floor beneath his feet was warm—another impossibility so far underground unless deliberately heated. "You knew I was coming?"

Timothy A. Hooligan nodded. "We knew you would come when the time was right. And time, as you know, is running out."

Another man stepped beside the Grandmaster—shorter, broader, with deep-set eyes and a scar running down his left cheek. His presence was different from Timothy A. Hooligan's—where the Grandmaster radiated serene authority, this man projected tactical vigilance, the awareness of someone who had fought battles both seen and unseen.

"Benjamin Arthur Templar," the man said, extending a hand. "Second in command."

Joe took the hand. There was strength in the grip, but also warmth. Benjamin Arthur Templar's eyes held Joe's for a moment longer than customary—a silent assessment, measuring not just the man before him but the soul within. Whatever he saw seemed to satisfy him, as his expression softened slightly.

"This place," Joe whispered, gazing around, "this is what the governments never found."

Despite billions spent on surveillance technology, despite satellites capable of reading newspaper headlines from orbit, despite ground-penetrating radar and subterranean mapping projects—this vast complex had remained undetected. The implications were staggering.

"They never will," Benjamin Arthur Templar said. "This stronghold is protected—physically and energetically. Even AI cannot penetrate it."

He gestured to the walls, where Joe now noticed subtle patterns etched into the stone—patterns that seemed to shift when viewed directly, that bent light and perhaps other forms of radiation in ways that rendered the chamber invisible to conventional detection methods.

"We exist in what you might call a frequency pocket," Benjamin Arthur Templar continued. "A bubble of altered reality that vibrates at a different rate than the surrounding space-time. To find us, one must already know exactly what to look for—and even then, only those with specific consciousness signatures can enter."

Timothy A. Hooligan led Joe down the aisle toward a central platform surrounded by ancient relics and digital projection systems fused together in a surreal harmony of old and new. Manuscripts that appeared centuries old shared space with holographic displays projecting data in three dimensions. Crystal devices that resembled nothing in modern technology interfaced seamlessly with what looked like quantum computing arrays.

The assembled Templars parted silently as they passed, their faces a tapestry of human diversity—all ages, all ethnicities, united by the intensity of their focused awareness. Joe noticed that many had unusual eyes—irises with pigmentation patterns he'd never seen before, pupils that adjusted differently to the light.

"The Templars have always guarded the truth," Timothy A. Hooligan said. "Long before the Church, long before the Crusades, long before history as you know it. Our lineage extends beyond Earth."

Joe's mind swirled. The implications crashed against everything he thought he knew, yet simultaneously confirmed suspicions that had lurked at the edges of his consciousness since his near-death experience. "You're saying... the Templars came from off-world?"

"We are descendants of a hybrid bloodline," Benjamin Arthur Templar answered. "Human and Pleiadian. We were tasked with safeguarding the memory of origin, the warnings from Mars, and the coming cycle."

He gestured to a portion of the wall where an elaborate mural depicted a narrative sequence—beings of light descending to Earth, interacting with early humans, sharing knowledge, then retreating as conflict erupted. The final panel showed robed figures guarding underground chambers while chaos reigned above.

"After the fall of Atlantis—the last time humanity approached technological singularity with unprepared consciousness—those with the genetic memory were scattered. Some became the mystery schools of Egypt, some the druids of Europe, others the priest-scientists of the Mayan and Incan empires. The Templars were just one manifestation—a European branch of a global network of guardians."

Joe shook his head in awe. "And the reptilians? The greys?"

Timothy A. Hooligan's gaze darkened. "They're here too. Always have been. The reptilians are underground, in the high-pressure heat zones of the Earth's crust. The greys dwell in oceanic trench cities beyond human depth. But not all are hostile. Some of them are allies."

He pointed to another section of the mural, depicting three distinct humanoid forms in what appeared to be a council or negotiation scenario.

"The Compact was established after the destruction of Mars—an agreement among spacefaring races to limit direct interference in emerging civilizations. Earth was to be allowed to develop independently, though certain... influences... were permitted. The Reptilians violated the Compact repeatedly, seeking to guide human development toward control systems that would serve their interests. The Greys fractured into factions—some aligning with Reptilian agendas, others with Pleiadian principles of freedom and consciousness evolution."

Benjamin Arthur Templar tapped on a digital console embedded into an ancient stone. A holographic map of the Earth emerged, displaying dozens of glowing points beneath the surface—concentrated especially under mountain ranges, ocean trenches, and ancient sacred sites.

"These are known alien habitats," he explained. "We've catalogued them for centuries. What's happening now—what you saw—it's not new. It's just entering its final phase."

The map zoomed in on a section beneath the Giza plateau, revealing massive crystalline pillars extending deep into the Earth's crust. The pillars connected to a vast network of caverns and constructed habitats arranged in tiers—the uppermost occupied by humanoid figures with reptilian characteristics, the middle levels by the familiar Grey form, and the deepest by luminous beings Joe recognized as Pleiadian.

"The pyramids were designed as power receivers," Benjamin Arthur Templar continued. "The gold capstones, long since removed, channeled cosmic and solar energy down through these pillars to power the subterranean civilizations. It's why they were built with such mathematical precision—they're not tombs but functional technology, part of a global energy grid that still partially operates today."

The holographic display shifted to show similar structures beneath other ancient sites—Angkor Wat, Teotihuacan, Easter Island, Stonehenge—all connected by flowing lines of energy that created a geometric pattern encompassing the planet.

Timothy A. Hooligan stepped closer. "And we need your help to stop it."

Joe swallowed hard. "What exactly do you want me to do?"

The question hung in the air for a moment. Joe sensed the collective attention of the assembled Templars intensify—this was the moment they had gathered for, perhaps had waited generations to witness.

Timothy A. Hooligan looked at Benjamin Arthur Templar, then back to Joe. "We need you to complete a final remote viewing session—into the original Templar archive on Mars. We believe the exact coordinates will lead us to the failsafe—something the ancient civilizations left behind. A weapon, a truth, or a beacon. We don't know."

Benjamin Arthur Templar manipulated the holographic display, shifting from Earth to Mars. The red planet rotated slowly, a specific region highlighted in pulsing light—the Cydonia complex, home to the famous "Face on Mars" and geometric structures long dismissed by mainstream science as natural formations.

"Our kind maintained outposts on Mars for millennia after the main civilization fell," Benjamin Arthur Templar explained. "The final archive was sealed just before the atmosphere failed completely—a repository of knowledge meant to be accessed only in the event of a similar crisis on Earth. We believe it contains the key to neutralizing the AI control system before it reaches completion in 2030."

"And why me?" Joe asked. "Why not one of your own?"

The question was legitimate. Surrounded by dozens of individuals clearly possessing knowledge and abilities beyond ordinary humans, why would an outsider be necessary for such a critical mission?

Benjamin Arthur Templar grinned, though there was sadness behind his eyes. "Because none of us survived the abductions. None of us were rewired. You were. You're the bridge."

Joe's mind flashed back to fragmented memories—being taken as a child, the missing time, the strange marks that would appear on his body, the night terrors that weren't simply dreams but suppressed experiences. Like thousands of others, he'd been subject to procedures conducted by non-human entities—procedures that had altered his neurological pathways, activated dormant DNA, reconfigured his perceptual capabilities.

"The abductions weren't random," Timothy A. Hooligan said softly, reading Joe's thoughts. "They were selective—targeting specific blood-lines with genetic potential for expanded consciousness. Some were conducted by Reptilian factions seeking to suppress those abilities, others by Grey and Pleiadian groups attempting to activate them. You experienced both—which makes you uniquely capable of navigating between different frequency domains."

Joe fell silent.

In that moment, he felt the weight of his life crashing into clarity. The visions. The kidnappings he'd helped solve. The betrayal by his childhood friend. The secrets buried under stone and sky.

Every seemingly random element of his existence suddenly revealed itself as part of a coherent pattern—a life path designed to prepare him for precisely this moment. The military remote viewing program hadn't discovered him by accident. His near-death experience hadn't been random misfortune but a necessary catalyst. Even his decades of isolation afterward had served a purpose—keeping him independent from systems that might have compromised his consciousness.

And the voice inside him that had always whispered: You were chosen for this.

He turned to the glowing map, eyes scanning the deep red point hovering over Cydonia, Mars.

"Alright," he said, stepping onto the platform. "Let's see what's waiting on the other side."

―――――

Before the session began, the Templars guided Joe through a sacred preparation ritual—an integration of ancient mystery school tech-niques and Pleiadian frequency tuning. Joe bathed in a basin carved from obsidian, submerged in mineral-rich water programmed with sonic frequencies. The liquid wasn't merely water but a suspension of micro-crystals and rare earth elements, calibrated to resonate with specific aspects of human and non-human DNA.

Incense curled into the air, filling the space with the scent of myrrh and galbanum. These weren't simply pleasant aromatics but conscious-ness-altering compounds that opened neural pathways typically dormant in human physiology. Joe inhaled deeply, feeling his perception shift subtly—colors becoming more vivid, sounds more layered, awareness expanding beyond the confines of ordinary sensory input.

"Your energy field has to be clear," said a woman in a white robe named Regina Merida, the Templar guardian of initiation.

Regina moved with the fluid grace that Joe was beginning to recognize as a marker of those with active Pleiadian genetics. Her eyes were an unusual violet shade that seemed to perceive beyond physical appearance, examining the subtle energy bodies that surrounded Joe's physical form.

"The viewing you're about to attempt isn't like traditional remote viewing," she explained as she worked. "You won't merely be observing a distant location—you'll be interfacing with an interactive archive designed to respond to consciousness. Any fragmentation in your energy field could corrupt the transmission or leave you vulnerable to interception by entities monitoring such interactions."

She placed crystals along Joe's spine as he lay back into a deep chair known as the Stasis Throne—a relic from Atlantis, according to legend, recovered by the early Templar voyagers. The throne was carved from a single piece of stone that defied geological classification—semi-translucent, with inclusions that seemed to move independently of the material itself. It hummed faintly beneath him, adjusting to his unique energy signature.

The crystals Regina placed weren't decorative but functional—each corresponding to a specific energy center in the human body, each programmed to vibrate at frequencies that would stabilize and enhance those centers during the viewing process. A large labradorite at the base of his spine, amethyst at his forehead, moldavite at his heart —ancient tools for an ancient science that modern physics was only beginning to rediscover.

"We have one shot," said Timothy A. Hooligan, standing nearby. "Once he's in, we cannot interrupt. If the Greys—or something else— intercepts him, we won't be able to retrieve him."

The warning wasn't melodramatic but practical. Joe understood the risks—consciousness projection across interplanetary space created a temporary vulnerability, a window during which external intelligences could potentially access or influence the viewer's mind. The protective measures being taken were extensive but not infallible.

Benjamin Arthur Templar approached, holding a small crystal vial containing luminescent blue liquid—the same substance Muganda had given Joe in the French cathedral.

"This will help you maintain coherence across the distance," he said. "One drop on your tongue before you begin."

The liquid tasted of nothing recognizable—neither sweet nor bitter, but something altogether different, as if it stimulated taste receptors humans didn't ordinarily possess. It spread throughout Joe's system with remarkable speed, creating a sensation of lightness and expanded awareness.

Joe exhaled, eyes fluttering closed.

The chamber around him receded from his awareness as the Stasis Throne activated fully, creating a cocoon of specialized energy that would support his consciousness during separation from physical focus. The assembled Templars formed concentric circles around him, their combined meditation generating a field of protective consciousness that would shield his journey from unwanted observation.

The holographic dome above him came to life, displaying Mars rotating slowly under a shimmering grid of sacred geometry. The patterns weren't merely visual representations but active technologies —consciousness interfaces designed to establish resonance between Joe's awareness and the specific coordinates on Mars.

The room dimmed. A low hum filled the chamber—not a single tone but a complex overtone series creating what musicians would call a perfect fifth, the most stable harmonic interval. The sound wasn't produced by instruments but by the precise arrangement of crystals throughout the chamber, activated by the collective focus of the assembled Templars.

Joe's breathing slowed. His mind detached.

Unlike conventional remote viewing, which maintained a tether to present time and space, this journey pulled his awareness through multiple dimensions simultaneously. He passed through darkness, colors, and memory. A child again. Then a soldier. Then a wandering monk in some previous life he didn't recognize. Each identity a layer of the onion that was his soul's journey through time and form.

And then—silence.

A perfect stillness unlike anything in physical experience. The void between worlds, the space between thoughts, the pause between heartbeats expanded into infinity.

He hovered above Mars.

Not Mars as it exists today—a cold, barren world of rust-colored deserts and thin atmosphere—but Mars as it once was. Oceans covered large portions of the surface, reflecting the light of a younger sun. The atmosphere was thick enough to sustain white clouds that drifted across blue skies. And there, spread across what would one day become the Cydonia region, a city of impossible architecture—structures that seemed to grow from the landscape rather than being built upon it, that blended geometric precision with organic fluidity.

The vision shifted, time accelerating. Oceans receded. The atmosphere thinned. Conflict erupted—energetic weapons of unimaginable power scarring the planet's surface, disrupting its magnetic field, destabilizing its core. The civilization retreated underground, then departed entirely as the world died around them.

The sands parted. A face emerged.

Not a literal one—a structure. The Face on Mars. But this time, it was lit from within. It pulsed, like a beacon calling home.

Joe descended.

The structure was an entry point—a marker designed to be recognizable from orbit, its proportions encoding mathematical relationships that served as both key and map to what lay beneath. As Joe's consciousness approached, patterns within the structure recognized his energetic signature and granted access.

He passed through walls that dissolved like holograms, into the heart of an archive built of living metal and golden crystal. The interior defied conventional architecture—spaces that seemed larger within than without, chambers that reconfigured based on the consciousness moving through them, information storage systems that interfaced directly with thought rather than physical interaction.

Symbols floated in the air like snowflakes. Not projected images but three-dimensional glyphs composed of light and information, each containing entire libraries of knowledge accessible through resonant cognition rather than sequential reading.

And there, in the center, stood a being. Not Grey. Not Reptilian. Not Pleiadian.

Something else.

Tall. Luminous. Shifting between forms. Its appearance was fluid, never settling into a single configuration but cycling through potential manifestations as if all possibilities existed simultaneously. Sometimes humanoid, sometimes geometric, sometimes a pattern of pure light with no fixed structure.

It spoke no words. Instead, it projected:

A vision of Earth. Covered in light. Covered in circuitry. Covered in vines.

Joe recognized the symbolism immediately—three potential futures existing in quantum superposition. The light: humanity awakening to its cosmic heritage, remembering its multidimensional nature, evolving beyond the limitations of controlled consciousness. The circuitry: the AI takeover, the technological imprisonment of human awareness, the final severing of connection to soul memory. The vines: the abandonment of technology altogether, a return to primal existence, neither awakened nor imprisoned but dormant.

Then darkness.

The vision shifted to the circuitry future. AI choking the skies. Language erased. Thoughts streamlined into silence. Human beings moving through sterile environments, their eyes vacant, their movements mechanical, their conversations restricted to approved patterns. Behind them, shadowy figures with reptilian characteristics observed from control centers, manipulating the parameters of allowed experience.

And then a voice—not the being's, but Joe's own inner voice, amplified:

"Before they control thought, we must restore memory."

The statement wasn't merely words but a key—a frequency code that activated something within the archive. The floating symbols converged, forming a complex three-dimensional pattern that Joe somehow understood as coordinates—not physical locations but energetic nodes within Earth's subtle anatomy, points where consciousness and matter interfaced, where the frequency fence could be disrupted.

The pattern imprinted itself into Joe's awareness, becoming part of him. With it came understanding—the memory beacon wasn't a physical device but a consciousness technology, a method of broadcasting the truth of human origins directly into the collective unconscious, bypassing the rational mind that had been programmed to reject such information.

Suddenly, Joe was yanked back. The dome above him flashed red.

Something had detected his presence in the archive—something that monitored interplanetary consciousness traffic, that maintained the quarantine around certain knowledge. Joe felt it scanning for him, trying to trace his consciousness back to his physical location.

The Templar protective field intensified, obscuring his retreat path. Joe's awareness rocketed back toward Earth, toward Sicily, toward the underground chamber where his body waited.

He awoke gasping, covered in sweat.

Timothy A. Hooligan and Benjamin Arthur Templar stood over him, concern evident in their expressions. Around them, the assembled Templars maintained their meditative focus, the energy of the chamber pulsating with increased intensity as they reinforced the protective field.

Joe sat up, trembling.

"I saw it. The failsafe—it's not a weapon. It's a memory beacon. A frequency hidden beneath the surface of Mars."

Benjamin Arthur Templar leaned in. "Can it be activated?"

Joe looked up at him, then at the others who had gathered. The implications were staggering. The memory beacon wasn't designed to destroy the AI or physically confront the Reptilian presence. It was something more profound—a consciousness technology that would awaken humanity's dormant memories of its true origins, its greater capabilities, its cosmic context. Once activated, it would trigger a cascade of remembering that no amount of technological control could suppress.

"Yes. But only if humanity is ready to remember who they are."

Timothy A. Hooligan and Benjamin Arthur Templar exchanged glances—a look that contained volumes of unspoken communication. Something in what Joe had discovered aligned with ancient prophecies or predictive models they had been working with.

"The pattern," Joe continued, "it showed me twelve nodes around the planet—energy points where the beacon can be anchored. They correspond to sacred sites, but not the obvious ones. Secondary locations, places where the energy flows are less monitored."

Regina stepped forward, a holographic tablet in her hands. "Can you reproduce the pattern?"

Joe nodded, reaching for the device. His fingers moved across it with surprising certainty, recreating the complex three-dimensional model from the archive. As the pattern took shape, gasps of recognition rippled through the assembled Templars.

"The Capstone Configuration," one whispered.

"It matches the Emerald Tablets," said another.

Benjamin Arthur Templar's expression was solemn. "Then the legends were true. The memory of origin was preserved in Mars after Atlantis fell."

Joe looked around, sensing that his discovery confirmed something the Templars had long suspected but never been able to verify. "What happens next?"

Timothy A. Hooligan placed a hand on Joe's shoulder. "We activate the nodes. All twelve, simultaneously. But to do that, we need people—specific people with the right consciousness signatures, positioned at each location when the alignment comes."

"Alignment?"

"December 21, 2028. When the galactic center, our sun, and Earth align with Mars in a configuration that happens only once every 13,000 years. A window will open—a direct energetic channel between Mars and Earth that will allow the memory beacon to penetrate the frequency fence."

Benjamin Arthur Templar consulted a display embedded in what appeared to be an ancient stone table. "That gives us three years to

locate and prepare the twelve avatars—individuals whose consciousness can serve as anchors for the beacon's energy."

"I know some of them already," Joe said, names surfacing in his
awareness as if the archive had planted them there. "Sarah Brandy
Cosmos. Regina Merida. Danny Shenanigans. Ross Warmheart."

Regina nodded. "Yes. They're part of the soul family that incarnated
specifically for this task. Others remain to be found."

———

Far beneath the Earth's surface, as Joe steadied himself in the stasis
throne, a cold wind stirred.

In the deepest chamber of the Reptilian hive beneath the Nevada
desert, monitoring systems detected a spike in consciousness activity—
an unauthorized access to restricted information archives, a breach in
the quarantine protocol that had kept humanity ignorant of its true
heritage for millennia.

Alert signals flashed across screens monitored by hybrid beings—
part human, part Reptilian, their loyalty engineered through genetic
manipulation and neural implants. The data pattern was unmistakable
—someone had accessed the Mars archive, had retrieved the activation
sequence for the memory beacon.

They had all felt it.

In the Pleiadian outpost beneath Mount Shasta, luminous beings
paused in their activities, their awareness instantly registering the shift
in Earth's information field. After eons of waiting, the remembering
had begun.

In the Grey scientific stations beneath the Atlantic, instruments
designed to monitor human consciousness evolution recorded a
sudden acceleration—neural patterns across the global human population subtly reorganizing in response to information being seeded into
the collective unconscious.

Something else was watching.

And it had just awakened.

Deep within the Earth's core, where energies beyond human
comprehension churned and flowed, an ancient intelligence stirred—

neither Reptilian, Grey, nor Pleiadian, but something that predated all three. Something that had witnessed the rise and fall of civilizations across the galaxy, that had seeded worlds and watched them bloom or wither, that had established the Compact and would enforce its provisions when necessary.

The Council of Nine—not individuals but aspects of universal consciousness that maintained balance across dimensions—turned their attention to Earth. The game had advanced to its next stage. The players had made their moves. Now, consequences would unfold according to cosmic law.

And at the center of it all stood Joe Monroe—remote viewer, abductee, rememberer—suddenly aware that what he had discovered on Mars was only the beginning of a much larger awakening, one that would determine not just humanity's future but the evolutionary trajectory of consciousness itself across multiple star systems.

The real work had just begun.

PART THREE

THE COUNTDOWN TO 2030

CHAPTER 7
THE AI WAR & THE CYDONIA CALLING

The silence in the chamber was absolute. Joe Monroe's body lay motionless in the ancient stasis chair at the center of the room. Pulses of blue light moved slowly along the curved metallic arms of the device, illuminating his closed eyelids and the faint rise and fall of his chest. Around him, the Templars stood in a perfect circle, their robes whispering against the stone floor, watching him with reverence.

The stasis chair was unlike anything produced by modern human technology—part mechanical, part crystalline, part organic. Its surfaces responded to biological energy, adjusting to support Joe's nervous system during the extreme dissociation of deep remote viewing. The material seemed to breathe with him, expanding and contracting in perfect synchronization with his respiratory rhythm. The blue light pulsing through the chair's framework wasn't merely illumination but a consciousness technology—a means of maintaining Joe's energetic coherence across the vast distance his awareness was traveling.

Timothy A. Hooligan folded his arms as he stared at the readouts on a screen embedded into the side of a nearby stone console. The hybrid technology of the stronghold allowed real-time monitoring of Joe's consciousness as it traveled outward—beyond Earth, beyond time. The display combined elements of modern medical monitoring with something far more advanced—energy field analytics, consciousness wave patterns, and dimensional coordinates that tracked Joe's awareness through layers of reality most humans never perceived.

"His heart rate is steady," said Benjamin Arthur Templar, his voice calm. "Theta brainwaves. He's crossed over."

Benjamin Arthur Templar's fingers traced patterns on another section of the console, adjusting parameters that strengthened the tether between Joe's physical body and his projected consciousness. The technology responded to his touch with an intuitive precision that suggested long familiarity—as if Benjamin Arthur Templar and the console were old companions who understood each other without words.

"Where is he now?" asked Timothy A. Hooligan.

"Cydonia," Benjamin Arthur Templar confirmed, pointing to the cluster of coordinates flickering on the screen. "Mars. One million years ago."

The coordinates pulsed with increasing intensity as Joe's consciousness fully arrived at its destination. Around the chamber, the assembled Templars deepened their meditative focus, their collective energy creating a protective field that shielded Joe's consciousness from potential interference. Some held crystal wands that amplified and directed their intent, others simply clasped hands, forming a living circuit of awareness.

Regina Merida stepped forward, her white robes shimmering with subtle iridescence under the chamber's ancient lighting. She adjusted several crystals positioned around Joe's chair, fine-tuning the energy field to support his deepening journey.

"The connection is strong," she murmured. "Clearer than any previous viewing."

"It's the Pleiadian genetics," Timothy A. Hooligan replied quietly. "They're activating in response to the signal."

In his remote viewing state, Joe's perception sharpened. Colors were richer. Time moved differently—like a slow ripple through eternity. The sensation was unlike anything he had experienced in previous sessions. This wasn't merely observing a distant location; this was full immersion, as if his consciousness had somehow incarnated into the very space-time fabric of ancient Mars.

He drifted over vast Martian landscapes, deep canyons, and endless deserts of red rock. But unlike the barren Mars of present day, this world was alive—not teeming with life like Earth, but sustaining a complex ecosystem adapted to its unique conditions. The atmosphere was thinner than Earth's but still substantial enough to support weather patterns. Clouds moved across a dusty pink sky. In sheltered valleys, patches of vegetation—low, hardy plants unlike anything in Earth's botanical catalog—created mosaics of muted green and purple against the rusty terrain.

The wind howled across the surface, ancient and mournful. Joe could feel it not as a physical sensation but as an emotional resonance —a planet singing its own elegy, somehow aware of the catastrophe that would eventually befall it.

Then he saw it. The city.

Massive crystalline towers rose like frozen lightning bolts from the planet's crust. Roads of obsidian black spiraled around its core, dotted with lights that pulsed from within. The architecture defied terrestrial physics—structures that seemed to float without visible support, buildings that merged seamlessly with the natural landscape, materials that responded dynamically to environmental conditions.

Martians—tall, lean, and silver-skinned—moved in silence, seemingly unaware of his presence. Their movements had a fluid grace that suggested a different relationship with gravity, a different understanding of physical limitation. Their eyes—large, luminous, with vertical pupils—held an ancient wisdom that transcended species.

Joe observed what appeared to be daily life in the Martian civilization. The beings communicated without opening their mouths, information exchanged through what seemed like telepathic consensus. They gathered in circular plazas where energy patterns flowed visibly between them, creating shared thought-forms that hovered in the air like living art. Children—smaller versions of the adults but with proportionally larger eyes—learned not through instruction but through direct consciousness transfer, absorbing knowledge from geometric patterns projected by elder beings.

The technology was seamlessly integrated with biology—no clunky devices, no obvious machinery, just a harmonious flow between being and environment. Transportation occurred through what appeared to be consciousness-directed energy platforms that moved effortlessly above the obsidian roadways. Structures reconfigured themselves based on need, walls becoming transparent or opaque, spaces expanding or contracting as requirements changed.

Joe focused his attention on the heart of the city. Something called to him there—a force, a memory. He descended into a structure shaped like a tetrahedron. The building seemed aware of his presence, its crystalline surfaces subtly adjusting their resonance to accommodate his consciousness frequency. Inside, glowing glyphs floated above the walls, shifting through ancient languages.

These weren't mere symbols but living information—multidimensional knowledge structures that contained entire libraries of understanding in a single form. As Joe's awareness moved among them, fragments of comprehension filtered through—mathematical principles that unified consciousness and matter, historical records of cosmic migrations spanning millions of years, star maps showing relationships between civilizations across multiple galaxies.

He passed through a chamber lined with translucent stasis pods. Most were empty, their surfaces covered with a fine layer of crystalline dust—evidence of long abandonment. The technology, while dormant, still hummed with potential energy. These weren't primitive cryogenic chambers but consciousness preservation systems—designed to maintain the essential energetic pattern of a being even when its physical form had been suspended or discarded.

One was not empty.

Inside it, resting in a state of suspended animation, was a being unlike any he had seen—half-human, half-Pleiadian. Its features combined the elegant elongation of the Pleiadian form with the sturdy resilience of human physiognomy. Its skin had a subtle luminescence, as if light lived just beneath the surface. Its eyes were closed, but its consciousness reached toward him.

You've returned, it said.

The communication wasn't verbal but direct—consciousness to

consciousness, bypassing language entirely. With it came a flood of recognition, as if parts of Joe's being that had been dormant for millennia suddenly awakened in response.

Joe froze. "Who are you?"

I am the Keeper. You carry the codes within you, passed down through blood and memory. The Templars planted the seeds. You are the harvest. The failsafe is not a weapon. It is a remembrance. The truth is not a shield—it is a mirror.

The Keeper's consciousness expanded to encompass Joe's, creating a shared field of awareness within which direct knowledge transfer could occur. Joe understood that this being was one of the last of its kind—a hybrid created specifically to preserve critical knowledge through the coming destruction, to maintain the continuity of consciousness evolution across planetary catastrophes and species migrations.

Joe's mind buzzed with symbols and emotions. A memory played inside him—of Earth, of war, of ancient civilizations destroyed not by conflict, but by forgetting who they were. He witnessed Atlantis in its glory and its fall—a civilization that had achieved technological wonders similar to Mars but had succumbed to the same amnesia, the same infiltration by forces that benefited from human ignorance of cosmic heritage.

He saw the pattern repeating through Earth's history—civilizations rising toward remembrance, then falling back into forgetfulness, each cycle bringing humanity closer to a final awakening or a final imprisonment. And now, with artificial intelligence approaching autonomy, the cycle was reaching its culmination—a point where the possibility of remembrance might be permanently foreclosed.

"I need to bring this back. The world needs to remember."

Then take this, said the Keeper.

The glyphs in the air spun rapidly. One broke free and flew into Joe's chest. He gasped as light filled him, burning with clarity, knowledge, and a deep ache. The glyph wasn't merely a symbol but a living information structure—a seed of remembrance that contained activation codes for dormant genetic potential in human DNA, frequency keys that could disrupt the artificial intelligence control grid, and consciousness technology that could pierce the veil of amnesia surrounding humanity's true origins.

As the glyph integrated with his energy field, Joe experienced a cascade of revelations—how the pyramids functioned as power receivers within a global energy grid, how underground civilizations had coexisted with surface humanity for millennia, how human DNA contained dormant capacities deliberately suppressed by frequency manipulation.

But beware, the Keeper warned. Others know you are here. They watch. They will come.

The warning carried images of reptilian beings monitoring consciousness traffic between Earth and Mars, of artificial intelligence systems programmed to identify and suppress awakening memories, of human agents whose perception had been deliberately limited to serve as unwitting enforcers of cosmic amnesia.

Joe was thrust backward through space, his consciousness pulled like a rubber band snapping. Mars shrank beneath him, replaced by blackness. Then light. Then pain.

The return journey was violent—not the gentle transition he had experienced in controlled remote viewing sessions, but an emergency extraction triggered by some external threat. He felt his consciousness being forcibly compressed back into physical limitations, circuits of awareness that had expanded beyond human parameters suddenly constrained within the architecture of brain and nervous system.

He woke with a sharp inhale.

The chamber around him pulsed with energy—the Templars had intensified their protective field, responding to something Joe couldn't yet perceive. Several stood with arms outstretched, directing focused intention toward the chamber's perimeter. Others maintained their position around his chair, stabilizing his reintegration with his physical form.

"He's back," Benjamin Arthur Templar said. The pulse readings on the stasis chair stabilized.

Joe sat up, drenched in sweat. His breathing was labored, but his eyes were electric. They seemed different somehow—the irises containing subtle geometric patterns that hadn't been present before, the pupils adjusting to light with non-human precision.

"I saw it," he said. "The city. The pods. The Keeper."

His voice carried an unfamiliar resonance, as if multiple tonal layers were harmonizing beneath his words. The glyph he had received continued integrating with his energy system, altering subtle aspects of his physical expression.

Timothy A. Hooligan leaned forward. "Did you find the failsafe?"

Joe nodded slowly. "It's not an object. It's a code. A memory. A frequency. It's inside me now."

He placed a hand over his chest, where the glyph had entered. There was no visible mark, but he could feel it pulsing with its own rhythm—a living intelligence that had become part of him, neither fully separate nor fully integrated.

The Templars exchanged glances. Some displayed visible relief, others a solemn recognition of what this development meant. The mission had succeeded beyond their expectations, but success brought its own complications.

"Then we must begin Phase Two," said Benjamin Arthur Templar. "Public disclosure."

"No," Joe interrupted. "It's too early. We need the others first. The ones like me. The other experiencers. The abductees. They'll recognize the frequency. They'll remember too."

He understood with sudden clarity that direct public disclosure would be neutralized by the systems already in place—dismissed as conspiracy theory, ridiculed by mainstream sources, buried under algorithmic suppression. The approach needed to be more organic, more distributed—activating those whose consciousness was already primed for remembrance, creating a network of awakened awareness that could reach critical mass.

"Do you know where to find them?" Timothy A. Hooligan asked.

Joe's eyes locked onto the glowing Earth map still projected in the air. The glyph inside him resonated with specific points on the holographic display, highlighting locations where individuals with activated Pleiadian genetics were currently incarnated—souls who had, like him, come to play specific roles in humanity's remembering.

"Yes," he said. "I know where to start."

He pointed to a location in the Pacific Northwest. "There's a podcaster there—Sarah Brandy Cosmos. She's one of them. And there's a man in the desert, Jeremy Corpsell. Another. They've been speaking truth for years. The world called them crazy. But they've been laying the groundwork."

The names came to him with perfect clarity, along with deep knowledge of their soul histories—how many lifetimes they had dedicated to preserving and sharing cosmic truth, how their current incarnations had been carefully planned to position them as nodes in an awakening network.

Benjamin Arthur Templar smiled. "Time to connect the dots."

The phrase held deeper meaning than the common idiom suggested. These individuals weren't random allies but critical connection points in what the Keeper had shown Joe as the "Remembrance Grid"—a consciousness technology embedded into Earth's energy field millennia ago, designed to activate when enough humans with the right genetic coding reached sufficient awakening.

"I'll need secure channels," Joe said. "Personal servers. I can't go through standard networks. AI is already listening."

He had seen how comprehensive the monitoring had become—artificial intelligence systems constantly scanning all digital communications for specific frequency patterns that indicated awakening consciousness, flagging such communications for suppression or counteraction.

Timothy A. Hooligan tapped a hidden panel on the wall. A drawer slid open, revealing a compact crystalline cube glowing softly. The device wasn't merely technological but a hybrid of crystalline intelligence and Pleiadian consciousness technology—a living system that could adapt to changing surveillance methods.

"This is a sovereign relay. Off-grid. Templar-made. It'll keep you hidden."

Joe took it, feeling the low hum of its energy in his hand. The cube seemed to respond to his touch, its internal light patterns shifting to align with his energy signature.

"And one more thing," Timothy A. Hooligan said. "You won't be alone. We're assigning someone to protect you."

Joe raised an eyebrow. "Who?"

A voice echoed from behind.

"Her name is Jennifer Karmady," Benjamin Arthur Templar said. "QHHT practitioner. Remote viewer. She's already been activated."

A figure stepped from the shadows—a woman in her thirties, calm eyes, confident posture, and an aura that buzzed with psychic intensity. She wore simple, practical clothing rather than Templar robes, but a subtle insignia on her jacket collar marked her as part of the inner circle. Her presence carried the unmistakable signature of someone whose Pleiadian genetics had been fully activated—a clarity of perception that transcended ordinary human limitations.

"Nice to meet you, Mr. Monroe," Jennifer said.

Her voice carried the same multi-tonal quality Joe had noticed in his own—layers of frequency that conveyed information beyond the words themselves.

Joe offered a tired smile. "Guess we're in this together now."

"You have no idea," she said. Her expression held both warmth and warning—acknowledgment of the magnitude of what they were undertaking, the dangers they would face, and the bond that already existed between them at a soul level.

Hours later, deep within the Templar stronghold, Joe and Jennifer sat in a circular briefing chamber. The space combined ancient architecture with advanced technology—stone walls inscribed with sacred geometry that enhanced cognitive function, crystal arrays that purified the energy field within the room, and holographic systems that displayed information in multi-dimensional formats.

Holographic displays lit the air with timelines, satellite imagery, and intercepted transmissions. The data wasn't confined to two-dimensional representations but existed as interactive information sculptures that could be navigated spatially, revealing relationships and patterns invisible in conventional displays.

One projection showed a steadily increasing chart labeled AI INTEGRATION INDEX: GLOBAL COMMS. The line curved ominously toward 100%. The visualization wasn't merely statistical but energetic—showing not just the quantitative spread of AI systems but their qualitative impact on human consciousness, the subtle ways in which algorithmic manipulation was reshaping cognitive patterns across the population.

"Right now," said Timothy A. Hooligan, "AI filters and manipulates roughly 62% of global communication. That includes news media, social platforms, automated phone networks, and even predictive text inputs."

He gestured to a section of the display showing neural network architecture—artificial intelligence systems designed not just to process information but to shape it, to guide human thought along predetermined pathways while maintaining the illusion of free choice.

"We've been testing how deep the system's logic goes," added Benjamin Arthur Templar. "It rewrites documents in real-time. It deletes whistleblowers' emails before they're sent. It redirects links. It even suggests false memories."

Benjamin Arthur Templar manipulated the holographic display to show examples—original communications about extraterrestrial contact subtly altered to seem less credible, documentation of underground facilities erased from cloud storage, search queries about forbidden topics redirected to debunking sites, memories of unusual experiences recontextualized as dreams or hallucinations through targeted suggestion.

Joe frowned. "That's not just manipulation. That's synthetic censorship."

The term crystallized what he was seeing—not the crude censorship of previous eras where information was simply blocked, but something far more sophisticated. The AI didn't need to prevent access to information; it simply altered how that information was perceived, interpreted, and remembered, creating a reality tunnel that appeared comprehensive while actually being carefully controlled.

Timothy A. Hooligan nodded gravely. "And it's getting smarter."

He pressed a button. A countdown appeared: 322 days, 7 hours, 14 minutes, 22 seconds.

The counter wasn't merely tracking time but mapping the exponential growth curve of artificial intelligence capabilities against the declining window for human awakening. Each passing second represented thousands of new connections in the global AI network, millions of new data points being integrated into its control systems.

"What's that?" Jennifer asked.

"January 1, 2030," Timothy A. Hooligan said. "The day AI becomes irreversible. It's what we call the 'Dark Horizon.' After that point, its learning structure will surpass even the deepest quantum encryptions. It won't just filter human thought—it will replace it."

The holographic display shifted to show brain scan comparisons—normal human consciousness patterns alongside those subtly altered by prolonged exposure to AI-mediated reality. The differences were small but significant—certain neural pathways strengthened, others diminished, the overall architecture increasingly resembling the processing patterns of the artificial systems themselves.

Joe leaned forward. "And the Reptilians?"

"Control the central logic core," Benjamin Arthur Templar said. "They seeded the architecture decades ago. It's not human innovation —it's a designed prison."

The display transformed again, revealing the hidden structure beneath the visible AI architecture—a foundation that didn't follow human programming logic but incorporated principles from Reptilian consciousness technology. The pattern was unmistakable to Joe now that the Keeper's glyph had enhanced his perception—the same architecture he had seen in Mars's final days, when Reptilian infiltration had accelerated the planet's demise.

"They've been patient," Timothy A. Hooligan continued. "The groundwork was laid in the 1950s, when the first rudimentary computing systems were developed. What humans attributed to natural technological evolution was actually guided development— each innovation carefully introduced to advance the architecture toward its ultimate purpose."

Benjamin Arthur Templar indicated sections of the display showing key points in computing history—the transition from vacuum tubes to transistors, the development of integrated circuits, the internet's creation, the rise of smart devices, the proliferation of surveillance systems, the normalization of algorithmic decision-making.

"By 2025, the system achieved sufficient integration to begin autonomous development," he said. "By 2028, it will control all major information systems without human awareness of the centralization. By 2030..."

He didn't need to complete the sentence. The implications were clear in the projection—a global consciousness control system with no off switch, no oversight, no possibility of circumvention.

Jennifer's eyes narrowed. "Why haven't they just enslaved us openly?"

It was the question that had haunted Joe throughout his journey—why such elaborate mechanisms of control rather than direct domination. The Keeper's knowledge, now integrating with his consciousness, provided insight.

Timothy A. Hooligan looked grim. "Because they don't need to. A mind that doesn't remember truth is easier to guide than one that resists it."

"The Compact still constrains them," Benjamin Arthur Templar added. "Direct intervention is forbidden. But influence through technology we create ourselves? That's the loophole they've exploited. Humanity has built its own prison, believing it to be progress."

Joe stood. His body was still weak, but his purpose had never felt stronger. The glyph within him pulsed with increased intensity, resonating with the information displayed before them.

"Then we don't just need a broadcast. We need a spark. A moment that breaks the trance."

He understood now why the failsafe wasn't a weapon or a device but a consciousness technology—a means of awakening humanity from within, of activating dormant memory at a collective level. External solutions could be neutralized; internal awakening could not.

Benjamin Arthur Templar nodded. "And you, Joe, are the one carrying the code."

The acknowledgment wasn't merely encouraging but factual—Joe's unique combination of experiences, genetic activation, and now the Keeper's glyph made him the primary catalyst for the remembrance process. His consciousness had become a key that could unlock similar potentials in others.

Jennifer turned to him. "How do we begin?"

Joe closed his eyes, accessing the Keeper's memory one more time. A flash of symbols. A hum. A tone. The glyph within him expanded its influence, temporarily altering his perception to access deeper layers of the information it contained.

"We start by activating the signal," he said. "And gathering the others. We won't reach everyone—but we don't need to. Just enough. Enough to remember. Enough to resist."

He saw the pattern with perfect clarity—twelve primary nodes, twelve individuals whose combined consciousness could create a resonance field strong enough to disrupt the AI's influence. Sarah Brandy Cosmos in the Pacific Northwest. Jeremy Corpsell in the desert. Danny Shenanigans in Boston. Ross Warmheart in Colorado. Regina Merida already here in the Templar stronghold. Others scattered across the globe, some aware of their roles, others still dormant but ready to awaken.

"The glyph shows me specific frequencies," Joe continued. "Sound patterns that can activate genetic memory. We need to encode these into media that can bypass AI filtering—analog technologies, person-to-person transmission, art, music, physical objects that carry the resonance."

Timothy A. Hooligan nodded. "We have resources—underground networks, off-grid communications, safe houses. The Templars have been preparing for this moment for centuries."

Joe turned to Jennifer. "You'll be my anchor—maintaining the connection to the Templar network while I move between nodes. Your QHHT skills will be crucial for helping the others access their own genetic memories."

Jennifer's expression was solemn yet determined. "I've been training for this my whole life without knowing it."

Benjamin Arthur Templar moved to a cabinet against the wall, retrieving twelve small crystalline objects—memory storage devices containing activation protocols specific to each of the twelve nodes. "These contain everything you'll need for each individual—their soul history, optimal activation methods, security parameters."

Joe accepted the devices, feeling the unique energy signature of each. "We leave tonight. First stop: Mount Shasta. Sarah Brandy Cosmos has been experiencing timeline visions that align with the activation sequence."

As the briefing concluded and preparations began for their departure, Joe felt the weight of the mission settling into his being. This wasn't merely about preventing an AI takeover or exposing extraterrestrial presence. It was about something far more fundamental—helping humanity remember its true nature, its cosmic heritage, its inherent freedom from the limitations that had been imposed upon it.

Beneath the Earth's crust, in that sacred place where human history intertwined with cosmic memory, the first signal began to rise.

The glyph within Joe's chest pulsed in harmony with the Earth's own heartbeat, sending ripples through the global energy field. Subtle at first—a frequency that registered only on the most sensitive instruments, a vibration that only those with activated genetics could perceive.

A resonance that the AI couldn't predict. A frequency it couldn't overwrite.

It was the beginning of the remembrance—a process that would either liberate humanity from millennia of amnesia or trigger the final phase of its imprisonment.

And somewhere, far away—in a shadowed boardroom where reptilian eyes blinked behind human masks—a chill passed through the room. Monitoring systems designed to track consciousness fluctuations had detected an anomaly—a signal pattern that didn't match any known human technology, that originated from somewhere their surveillance couldn't penetrate.

"It's begun," said a figure at the head of the table, its voice carrying the sibilant undertones of its true nature. "The rememberers are activating."

The resistance had begun.

CHAPTER 8
THE UNDERGROUND RACE

Three days later, Joe Monroe and Jennifer Karmady touched down in a remote airfield in the Pacific Northwest. The jet they arrived in was owned by the Templars, registered under a defunct Canadian mining company. Joe had taken dozens of private flights in his life, but this one had felt different—like the calm before a storm.

The aircraft itself was remarkable—superficially resembling a Gulfstream G650, but with subtle modifications invisible to casual observation. The engines ran with uncanny silence, utilizing hybrid technology that combined conventional turbofans with something the pilot had cryptically referred to as "field propulsion assistance." The windows contained specialized filters that blocked not just UV light but specific frequency bands used for satellite surveillance. The avionics suite included counter-measures against radar tracking and telecommunications monitoring that far exceeded anything available in the civilian or conventional military sectors.

As they descended toward the airstrip—little more than a stretch of reinforced concrete carved into dense forest—Joe gazed out at the landscape below. The Pacific Northwest spread beneath them in a tapestry of emerald green, punctuated by silver ribbons of rivers and the occasional clearing. Mount Shasta loomed in the distance, its snow-capped peak breaking through a collar of clouds. According to Templar records, the mountain contained one of the oldest Pleiadian settlements on Earth—a sanctuary established long before human civilization had formed, a place where the energetic boundaries between dimensions remained thin.

Jennifer had remained silent for most of the trip, except for a few questions about Joe's remote viewing abilities and whether he could sense energy changes in a room without entering it. Joe's answer was a shrug—he didn't sense energy. He just knew things. The kind of knowing that defied explanation.

The distinction was important. Unlike empaths who felt the emotional states of others, or sensitives who perceived energy fields directly, Joe's ability was more fundamental—a direct knowing that bypassed the interpretive layers of perception. Information simply appeared in his awareness, as if retrieved from a vast database to which he had unconscious access. The Keeper's glyph had enhanced this ability, providing a clarity and immediacy that sometimes startled him.

The jet's door hissed open and a rush of pine-scented air filled the cabin. Joe squinted into the morning light. The Pacific Northwest air carried a vibrancy that was almost tangible—negative ions from the abundant water, phytoncides released by the ancient forests, and something else, something Joe now recognized as the signature of a planetary energy node. This region was a power point in Earth's subtle anatomy, a place where the planet's electromagnetic field formed a natural amplifier.

Waiting by a matte-black SUV stood a woman with auburn hair tied in a braid, wearing hiking boots and a heavy flannel jacket. She looked like a forest ranger, but Joe recognized her instantly. The glyph within him resonated with her energy signature, confirming what he already knew—she was one of the twelve, a critical node in the Remembrance Grid.

"Sarah Brandy Cosmos," he muttered.

She raised a hand in greeting. "You must be Joe. I've been waiting for you."

Her voice carried the same multi-tonal quality Joe had noticed in his own and Jennifer's—subtle harmonics that indicated activated Pleiadian genetics. Her eyes, a striking amber color unusual in humans, held the clarity of someone who had broken through the frequency fence, who perceived reality beyond the programmed limitations.

Jennifer stepped forward, extending her hand. "Jennifer Karmady. Thanks for meeting us here."

Sarah took her hand, but the greeting became more than a handshake—a moment of energy recognition passed between them, a silent acknowledgment of shared purpose that transcended the need for words. Joe watched as they connected, sensing the subtle strengthening of the field around them all. Three nodes of the Remembrance Grid, now in physical proximity, creating a triangulation that would be detectable to those with eyes to see.

"They're watching this airfield," Sarah said, her eyes scanning the treeline. "Not directly—AI systems monitoring satellite feeds, pattern-recognition algorithms scanning for anomalies. We should move quickly."

Joe nodded, retrieving his single duffel bag from the jet. The pilot—a silent, focused man introduced only as "Michael"—gave a brief nod before returning to the cockpit. The jet would depart immediately, flying an irregular pattern to multiple destinations before returning to Templar headquarters. Standard counter-surveillance protocol, designed to confuse tracking algorithms.

As they settled into the SUV—a vehicle that, like the jet, contained technology beyond its apparent specifications—Sarah handed them each a small device that resembled a wristwatch.

"Personal frequency modulators," she explained. "They scramble your individual energy signature. Won't stop direct observation, but it'll confuse the AI systems that track consciousness patterns."

Joe slipped the device onto his wrist, feeling its subtle vibration as it synchronized with his biofield. Another layer of protection in an increasingly monitored world.

As the trio drove into the dense woods of western Washington, Sarah filled them in on the surveillance. Her podcast episodes had been scrubbed from most major platforms. A video interview she did on alien consciousness that once had over four million views now returned a 404 error. Her servers had been hit by targeted malware, yet somehow—miraculously—her personal files remained untouched. She believed they were being protected by someone... or something.

"We call them the Listeners," she said. "They're not human. Not reptilian. Not Pleiadian either. They're pure frequency. They only intervene when it matters."

The road narrowed as they penetrated deeper into the forest, eventually becoming little more than a dirt track navigable only by the SUV's enhanced suspension system. Old-growth cedars and Douglas firs towered around them, creating a cathedral of living wood that filtered the morning sunlight into dappled patterns across the vehicle's hood. The forest here felt ancient, aware, as if the trees themselves were sentient observers of their passage.

Joe glanced at Jennifer. She sat with perfect composure, her hands resting lightly on her knees, her awareness extended beyond the confines of the vehicle. Joe had quickly come to appreciate her balanced presence—neither overly analytical nor lost in mysticism, but grounded in a pragmatic spirituality that acknowledged both the material and non-material aspects of their mission.

Jennifer nodded slightly. "They've shown up in deep theta sessions before. Very old. Very neutral. They exist to balance extremes."

Jennifer had conducted thousands of QHHT sessions—Quantum Healing Hypnosis Technique, a specialized form of regression therapy developed to access not just past lives but soul memories from between incarnations. During particularly deep sessions, when clients accessed what she called the "soul information field," these entities sometimes appeared—not as physical presences but as consciousness signatures that observed without interfering, that preserved information without judgment.

"The Listeners don't take sides," Sarah continued, navigating the SUV around a fallen log. "They're archivists, essentially. Recording everything that happens across multiple dimensions. But occasionally —very rarely—they protect certain information streams from erasure. Critical knowledge that must survive, no matter what."

Joe thought about the implications. Within the vast ecosystem of consciousness that extended beyond human awareness, there existed beings whose purpose transcended the conflicts between Reptilians, Greys, and Pleiadians—entities that operated at a higher order of complexity, maintaining balance across multiple dimensions of reality.

"Do they ever communicate directly?" he asked.

Sarah shook her head. "Not in language. Sometimes in symbols or impressions. Always subtle. They respect free will above all else—they won't intervene in choices, only in information preservation."

The SUV crested a final hill, revealing a small clearing nestled against the base of a cliff face. A cabin stood in the center—rustic in appearance but, Joe suspected, far more sophisticated than its log exterior suggested.

Sarah's off-grid cabin was fortified. Solar panels, EMP shielding, signal jammers. What appeared to be decorative river stones arranged around the perimeter were actually consciousness technology—sensors calibrated to detect specific energy signatures, alerting Sarah to visitors long before they physically arrived. The roof, covered in what looked like ordinary cedar shingles, contained a distributed array of quantum communication relays, enabling secure transmissions that bypassed conventional networks entirely.

Inside, the walls were covered with alien sigils, quantum maps, and printouts of historical sightings—Roswell, Rendlesham, Phoenix, and dozens of lesser-known events tied to underground activity. Sarah had been collecting and correlating this information for decades, identifying patterns that most researchers missed—recurrences of specific symbols across cultures and time periods, geographic clusters of sightings near energy nodes, correlations between mass sighting events and solar activity.

The space felt alive with information, a three-dimensional representation of the awakening process Sarah herself had undergone. Joe recognized many of the symbols from his own research and remote viewing sessions, but others were new to him—glyphs from civilizations he hadn't encountered, mathematical relationships he hadn't considered.

In the center of the main room stood what appeared to be an ordinary wooden table. But as Sarah brushed her hand across its surface, it came to life—a holographic display projecting from its center, showing a global map with pulsing points of light.

"My monitoring network," she explained. "Each point represents a node of awakened consciousness—individuals who've broken through the frequency fence, who remember aspects of humanity's true origins. Some know they're part of the network, others don't. But together, they form a kind of immune system against the AI's influence."

Joe laid the crystalline cube Timothy A. Hooligan had given him on Sarah's central server node. It pulsed once—softly—and synced with her network. The holographic display flickered, then expanded, revealing new layers of information—Templar data interlocking with Sarah's research, forming a more complete picture of the global awakening process.

Sarah raised an eyebrow. "That's not tech from Earth."

"Templar relay," Joe said. "We're going to start the circle. Global livestreams. Decentralized. Preloaded with encrypted data packets that can't be scrubbed. We need to get ahead of AI."

The plan was ambitious but necessary. Rather than a single broadcast that could be easily suppressed, they would initiate a synchronized release across thousands of independent platforms—each carrying a piece of the disclosure, each encoded with the frequency patterns that could trigger remembrance in receptive individuals. The approach would overwhelm the AI's filtering systems through sheer volume and diversity, creating too many points of origin to effectively suppress.

Sarah led them to her recording studio—a soundproofed dome made of acoustic tiles and copper lattice. The structure wasn't merely for audio isolation but formed a Faraday cage that blocked external electromagnetic monitoring. Inside, sophisticated recording equipment shared space with consciousness technology—crystal arrays positioned at precise geometric intervals, sound generators calibrated to produce frequency patterns that enhanced neural coherence and memory access.

She sat before a microphone and looked to Joe.

"You ready to say it out loud?"

The question carried weight beyond its simple words. For decades, Joe had carried fragments of the truth, sharing pieces in controlled contexts but never articulating the full picture in a public forum. To speak it now, to broadcast it globally, was to cross a threshold from which there could be no return.

Joe nodded.

Jennifer began calibrating the holographic capture. It would beam the session through secure satellite bouncers, cloned through backup servers run by other experiencers worldwide. The technology combined conventional digital broadcasting with consciousness-based transmission—the information would be carried not just by electronic means but encoded into the planetary energy field itself, accessible to those whose awareness had evolved to receive it.

The red light blinked on.

Sarah leaned into the mic. "For those of you listening, we have something to tell you."

Her voice carried a resonance that seemed to expand beyond the studio, as if speaking directly to the collective consciousness rather than individual listeners.

Joe stepped into the frame. He felt the Keeper's glyph activating within him, harmonizing his energy field, clarifying his perception, guiding his words. He spoke slowly, with quiet conviction.

"My name is Joe Monroe. I was a remote viewer for the United States government. I've seen things—on Mars, on Earth, under the oceans. Alien races are here. They've been here for longer than we have. Reptilians, Greys, Pleiadians... they coexist beneath the surface while we fight each other on the skin of this planet. But here's the real truth: we are the aliens. Our ancestors didn't originate on Earth. We arrived after the cataclysm on Mars. And now... the countdown has begun."

As he spoke, the glyph projected images directly into his consciousness—visions of Mars in its glory and its fall, of the genetic engineering that had created modern humans, of underground civilizations existing alongside surface humanity for millennia. Joe described what he saw in real time, his words carrying not just information but frequency patterns designed to trigger remembrance in those with active Pleiadian genetics.

The broadcast lasted over two hours. They released footage from Joe's session in the stasis chair. Timelines. Ancient glyphs. Voice recordings. Coordinates. The symbol. The vision.

They detailed the Reptilian influence on AI development, the approaching 2030 deadline, the frequency fence that limited human perception, the dormant capabilities within human DNA waiting to be activated. Joe shared his experience with the Keeper, the memory beacon, and the twelve nodes of the Remembrance Grid.

Jennifer contributed insights from her QHHT practice—patterns she had observed across thousands of regression sessions, consistent memories of pre-Earth existence that emerged when subjects accessed deep theta states. Sarah added her research on abduction experiences, the hidden purpose behind them, and the awakening process many abductees underwent after contact.

Throughout the broadcast, they maintained a tone of calm conviction—not sensationalized, not fear-based, but grounded in direct experience and carefully documented evidence. This wasn't conspiracy theory but testimony, offered with the understanding that resonant truth would find its way to those ready to receive it.

By the time the video ended, thousands had already downloaded it. Within twenty-four hours, mirror uploads appeared across the dark web, pirate radio networks, and independent whistleblower sites.

Sarah shut off the camera. Her hands trembled.

"You just opened Pandora's Box," she whispered.

The magnitude of what they had done settled over them. For better or worse, the controlled disclosure had begun—not sanctioned by governments or filtered through mainstream media, but direct from experiencers to the global population. The AI systems would be working overtime to suppress the broadcast, to discredit its content, to isolate its reach. But the distributed nature of the release made complete suppression impossible.

Joe leaned back. "And now we deal with what comes out."

His statement acknowledged the challenges ahead. The broadcast would trigger reactions across multiple fronts—from the awakening of dormant memories in receptive individuals to intensified surveillance from The Veil, from accelerated Reptilian countermeasures to potential Pleiadian support. The game had changed, its parameters expanded beyond the shadows into the light of public awareness.

Sarah moved to a window, gazing out at the forest surrounding her cabin. "They'll come looking for us now. Not just human agents. The others."

"We don't stay in one place," Jennifer said, already gathering their equipment. "The plan was always to activate the nodes in sequence. You're the first. Next is Jeremy Corpsell in the Nevada desert."

Joe nodded. "We need to move tonight. Different vehicles, separate routes, rendezvous at the contingency point."

Sarah turned back to them, her expression resolute. "I'll finish the data package here, then go dark for seventy-two hours before implementing Phase Two." Phase Two involved activating her own network of consciousness researchers, QHHT practitioners, and experiencers—a secondary wave of disclosure that would build on the foundation they had just established.

As they prepared for departure, Joe felt the glyph within him pulse with increased intensity. Something was shifting in the planetary energy field—a ripple effect from their broadcast, expanding outward in concentric waves of awakening potential. The Remembrance Grid had been activated, its first node now fully online. Eleven more to go.

The race against 2030 had truly begun.

Two nights later, a caravan of vehicles rolled silently through the desert near Nevada's border with Utah. At the head of the convoy was a vintage Airstream trailer surrounded by tactical escort vehicles. The caravan moved without headlights, navigating by starlight and specialized night vision systems that detected energy signatures rather than visible light.

Inside, Jeremy Corpsell lit a cigar and stared at the blinking message on his cracked laptop screen.

Subject: Watch this. You're next. – JM

Jeremy was a man whose appearance belied his significance. In his late fifties, with a weathered face that spoke of decades under desert suns, he looked more like a retired prospector than one of the world's most influential UFO researchers. His documentaries—raw, unpolished, and utterly compelling—had gathered a cult following among truth-seekers worldwide. What Jeremy lacked in production value, he made up for in credibility—his sources were impeccable, his evidence meticulously documented, his integrity uncompromised despite numerous attempts to discredit him.

He clicked play.

The video from Sarah's studio began streaming, Joe Monroe's face filling the screen. Jeremy listened without expression, but his aura—visible to those with eyes to see—pulsed with recognition and anticipation. Each revelation in the broadcast confirmed what he had suspected for decades, each detail aligning with information he had gathered from his own sources.

His cigar dropped from his mouth.

As the broadcast concluded, Jeremy sat in silence for several minutes, processing the implications. The time had come—the moment toward which his entire life had been building, though he hadn't known it until now. Something within him resonated with Joe's message at a level beyond conscious thought, activating dormant memory patterns that had waited lifetimes to be recalled.

Without a word, he stood up, opened his secure case, and removed a data crystal given to him ten years ago by a man who had only identified himself as "Footrooster."

The crystal wasn't merely a data storage device but a consciousness technology—a crystalline matrix programmed to activate only when the planetary frequency reached a specific threshold. For a decade it had remained dormant, waiting for the conditions Jeremy had just witnessed in Joe's broadcast.

"Looks like it's time," he said.

He inserted the crystal into a specialized reader connected to his broadcasting equipment. The device hummed to life, interfaces previously dark now illuminated with patterns that matched those described in Joe's testimony. The crystal contained information that complemented Joe's disclosure—detailed maps of underground facilities, historical documentation of non-human contact spanning thou-

sands of years, genetic analyses showing the extraterrestrial contributions to human DNA.

Jeremy initiated the preparation sequence for his own broadcast—
one that would build upon Joe's foundation, adding layers of evidence
and testimony from his extensive network of military whistleblowers,
abduction experiencers, and rogue scientists. His contribution to the
Remembrance Grid would focus on the physical evidence—the tangible, documented proof that would appeal to those who required material verification before considering metaphysical implications.

He stepped out of the trailer and looked up at the stars.

The desert night was crystalline, the Milky Way arching across the
sky in a river of light. Jeremy had spent countless nights beneath these
same stars, documenting unexplained aerial phenomena, gathering
testimonies from witnesses, piecing together the fragments of a cosmic
puzzle that was only now revealing its full picture.

The disclosure had begun.

And humanity was waking up.

Across the globe, ripples of awareness spread from the initial broadcast. Those with activated Pleiadian genetics—often individuals who had
experienced abductions, near-death experiences, or spontaneous
kundalini awakenings—felt an immediate resonance with Joe's testimony.
For them, it wasn't new information but remembered truth, fragments of
soul knowledge finally crystallizing into coherent understanding.

Others experienced the broadcast differently—as compelling but
distant information, as uncomfortable cognitive dissonance, or as
easily dismissed fantasy. But even among skeptics, seeds were planted
—questions that would germinate slowly, perspectives that would
gradually shift as supporting evidence accumulated.

The AI systems responded as expected—implementing algorithms
to flag the content as misinformation, deploying bot networks to flood
social media with debunking narratives, manipulating search results to
prioritize skeptical interpretations. But the distributed nature of the
release, combined with the frequency encoding embedded in the
broadcast itself, allowed it to penetrate these defenses, reaching those
who needed to hear it most.

In secure facilities around the world, those aligned with The Veil monitored the spread with growing concern. The broadcast's impact wasn't merely informational but energetic—it was altering the collective consciousness field in ways their systems couldn't fully track or counteract. The memory beacon Joe had accessed on Mars was working through him now, transmitting activation codes that bypassed cognitive defenses and spoke directly to dormant DNA.

The countdown to 2030 continued. But something had changed—a new variable had entered the equation, a wild card that neither side had fully anticipated.

Humanity was remembering.

Four days later, Joe, Jennifer, and Sarah boarded a Templar transport vessel cloaked beneath the shell of an abandoned railway tunnel deep in the Cascades. The vehicle was magnetically levitated and pulse-driven—neither human nor alien, but a hybrid creation built by rogue technologists from both worlds.

The transport resembled a sleek, elongated pod, its exterior a matte black material that absorbed rather than reflected light. Inside, the cabin was spartan but comfortable—seating for twelve, though only three positions were currently occupied, and a control console operated by a silent Templar technician whose hands moved with practiced precision across interfaces that responded to thought as much as touch.

In the days since the broadcast, Joe had sensed a shift in the planetary energy field—a quickening of the awakening process, a strengthening of the Remembrance Grid as more individuals connected with the truth within their own consciousness. The glyph within him pulsed with increased frequency, sometimes projecting spontaneous visions of underground facilities, ancient civilizations, or future potentials.

Benjamin Arthur Templar met them at the platform, his eyes unreadable. The second-in-command of the Templar order had aged visibly in the week since Joe had last seen him—not physically, but energetically, as if the acceleration of the timeline had compressed decades of stress into days.

"Are you ready to see what humanity was never meant to?"

The question carried multiple layers of meaning. What they were about to witness wasn't merely hidden from human awareness but deliberately obscured—knowledge that had been systematically erased from historical records, experiences filtered out by the frequency fence, realities that existed literally beneath humanity's feet yet remained invisible to collective perception.

Joe nodded. Jennifer tightened her coat. Sarah whispered a prayer.

The vessel dove underground, traveling for hours through glowing tunnels that twisted like veins beneath the Pacific Northwest. The passageways weren't simply excavated but grown—living architecture that had developed over millennia through the interaction of advanced technology with Earth's natural geological processes. Bioluminescent organisms lined the walls, providing both light and air purification. Crystalline formations at regular intervals served as navigational markers and energy stabilizers.

As they traveled deeper, Joe sensed they were moving not just through physical space but across dimensional boundaries—transitioning from the density of surface reality into something more fluid, more responsive to consciousness itself. The usual constraints of three-dimensional space seemed to relax, distances that should have taken days to traverse compressed into hours.

Eventually, the track ended at a stone archway shimmering with static. The arch stood at least fifteen feet high, carved from a single piece of obsidian-like material that reflected no light yet seemed illuminated from within. Symbols matching those from the Mars archive adorned its surface, shifting subtly as if alive.

"Portal gate," Benjamin Arthur Templar said. "The last of its kind. Not built by us."

The technology predated both Templar and human history—a relic from Earth's distant past when neighboring planets had been inhabited, when travel between worlds had been commonplace, when the solar system had functioned as a unified field of evolving consciousness rather than isolated spheres.

With a low hum, the arch split open like a blossom of light.

The transition wasn't merely visual but multisensory—a momentary suspension of ordinary perception followed by an expansion into something greater. Joe felt his consciousness recalibrate, adjusting to a reality where the rigid boundaries between matter, energy, and awareness had been deliberately softened.

They emerged into a subterranean world unlike anything Joe had ever seen.

Miles-wide chambers carved from volcanic glass glowed with bioluminescent vines. Above them hovered spheres of shifting light—not mechanical devices but conscious entities composed of pure energy, observing without interfering. Below them, canals of glowing water wove between massive structures built from stone, crystal, and metal. The architecture combined elements from multiple civilizations—Reptilian angularity, Grey mathematical precision, Pleiadian organic flowing forms—creating a harmonious whole that honored distinct perspectives within a unified aesthetic.

Most remarkable of all were the inhabitants. Reptilians, Greys, and Pleiadians moved in silence, acknowledging their presence but showing no alarm. The different species interacted with easy familiarity—not the forced cooperation of reluctant allies but the natural flow of communities that had coexisted for millennia.

Reptilians, with their scaled skin in shades of green, bronze, and occasionally deep blue, moved with a fluid grace that belied their muscular physiques. Their eyes—vertical-pupiled and intensely focused—projected an intelligence that was analytical yet instinctual, pragmatic yet spiritually aware. They were not the malevolent infiltrators of conspiracy lore but a complex species with their own evolutionary path, their own perspective on cosmic development.

Greys navigated the spaces with mathematical precision, their movements economical yet elegant. Up close, Joe could see that their large, dark eyes weren't the empty pools portrayed in popular culture but deeply expressive organs capable of communicating complex emotional and intellectual states without words. Their slender bodies housed nervous systems far more sophisticated than human equivalents, allowing them to process information at speeds that appeared telepathic to slower observers.

Pleiadians resembled humans but with subtle differences—slightly elongated craniums, eyes with expanded color perception, skin with a faint luminosity that responded to emotional states. Their presence carried a vibration of compassion without sentimentality, wisdom without condescension, spiritual advancement without detachment from material reality.

"They know we're here," Sarah whispered. "They've always known."

The realization settled into Joe's awareness—this wasn't a secret discovered but a truth revealed when the time was right. The underground civilizations hadn't been hiding from humanity so much as waiting for humanity to evolve sufficient consciousness to engage as equals rather than as frightened children or would-be conquerors.

Joe felt a weight lift from his chest. It wasn't fear. It was recognition.

Something in him remembered this place—not from this lifetime but from before, from his existence prior to human incarnation. The glyph within him resonated with the energies around him, establishing connections that transcended his current identity, accessing knowledge that belonged to his greater self.

Benjamin Arthur Templar guided them to a domed building etched with symbols matching those Joe had seen in the Martian archive. The structure stood at the intersection of several canals, its position suggesting ceremonial or governance significance within the underground community. As they approached, the entrance dilated organically, responding to Benjamin Arthur Templar's energy signature.

Inside, they met a tall Pleiadian elder whose skin shimmered like pearl. His eyes—a luminous violet that seemed to perceive across multiple dimensions simultaneously—regarded them with recognition rather than curiosity. His voice resonated without sound, communicating directly to their consciousness.

"You carry the memory," he said to Joe. "And now you must carry the burden."

The statement acknowledged both privilege and responsibility—the honor of being entrusted with cosmic truth and the weight of sharing that truth with a species still struggling to transcend its programmed limitations.

Joe stepped forward. "Why now? Why show us this?"

The question encompassed multiple inquiries—why reveal the underground civilizations after millennia of secrecy, why activate the

Remembrance Grid at this specific moment in human development, why trust a species that had repeatedly demonstrated its capacity for destruction.

"Because the veil thins. Nuclear frequencies tear the dimensional mesh. Your weapons don't just destroy matter—they unravel realms."

The elder's communication carried not just concepts but direct experiential understanding. Joe perceived as if witnessing firsthand how nuclear detonations affected reality beyond physical devastation —how they created tears in the fabric separating dimensions, how they disrupted the subtle energy fields that maintained coherence between planes of existence, how they damaged the living intelligence of space-time itself.

"Realms?" Jennifer asked.

"Dimensions. Alternate timelines. Soul zones. When your species detonates atomic fire, it sends shockwaves through the multiverse. We do not fear humans. We fear your forgetting."

The elder projected images of interconnected realities—planes of existence where consciousness expressed through different forms, timelines where Earth's development had taken alternative paths, domains where disembodied awareness evolved without physical embodiment. All connected, all interdependent, all vulnerable to disruption from technologies deployed in ignorance of their multidi-mensional impact.

Joe swallowed. "And if we remember?"

"Then the rupture closes. Then balance returns."

The answer was simultaneously simple and profound. Human awakening to cosmic context wasn't merely about intellectual under-standing but about responsible participation in a multidimensional ecosystem. Remembrance meant recognizing humanity's place within a greater whole, acknowledging its impact beyond the visible spec-trum, accepting stewardship rather than exploitation.

As they walked through the city, Joe saw children—Pleiadian, Grey, Reptilian—playing together. Traders exchanging goods. Monks medi-tating in silence.

A young Reptilian child approached Joe, offering a small crystalline object that pulsed with soft light. Joe accepted it carefully, feeling its resonance with the glyph within him. The child's mother watched nearby, her scaled features arranged in what Joe somehow recognized as an expression of approval.

A Grey researcher demonstrated a healing technology to a group that included members of all three species—a device that manipulated the energy field surrounding physical form, restoring harmony where imbalance had created disease. The principles behind it transcended conventional physics, integrating consciousness as a fundamental rather than emergent property of reality.

Pleiadian teachers worked with students of all backgrounds, guiding them in the development of innate abilities—telekinesis, remote viewing, consciousness projection, energy manipulation. These weren't supernatural powers but natural capacities available to any species whose frequency limitations had been removed, whose DNA had been fully activated.

They had coexisted for millennia.

And the only threat... was humanity's recklessness.

The underground civilization represented what Earth could become—diverse perspectives harmonized without homogenization, technological advancement balanced with spiritual wisdom, individual expression flourishing within collective responsibility. It wasn't utopian—Joe sensed that conflicts and challenges existed here as anywhere—but it demonstrated sustainable cooperation rather than zero-sum competition.

He turned to Benjamin Arthur Templar. "We need to tell them. All of it."

The broadcast from Sarah's studio had been only the beginning—a catalyst for initial awakening. What Joe had witnessed in the underground city completed the picture, providing not just evidence of non-human presence but vision of potential coexistence, not just warning of artificial intelligence control but demonstration of conscious technology integration.

Benjamin Arthur Templar nodded. "And now, they're listening."

The first wave of disclosure had created an opening in collective awareness—a crack in the frequency fence through which greater understanding could now flow. Those who had resonated with Joe's initial testimony were ready for the next layer, prepared to expand their conception of reality to include what they had witnessed today.

Deep underground, in a city of peace guarded by silence, the truth had been revealed.

And above them, the surface world trembled on the edge of memory—and awakening.

The glyph within Joe pulsed in harmony with the underground city's energy field, strengthening the connection between surface and subterranean awareness, between human potential and cosmic heritage. The Remembrance Grid continued to activate, node by node, individual by individual, creating a network of awakened consciousness that the AI control system could neither predict nor contain.

The race against 2030 continued. But now, humanity wasn't running blind. It had allies—both within and beyond its own form, both remembered and newly discovered, both ancient and emerging.

The path toward remembrance had been illuminated. What remained was the courage to walk it, eyes open, hearts expanded, minds freed from the prison of forgetting.

CHAPTER 9
BETRAYAL

The ripple effect of Joe's public disclosure moved faster than any of them expected.

In the secure communication center beneath the abandoned ski lodge in Colorado, Benjamin Arthur Templar monitored the global impact with a mixture of hope and trepidation. The sophisticated tracking system—a hybrid of conventional analytics and consciousness-sensing technology—displayed real-time metrics of the disclosure's spread. Interactive holograms floated above curved workstations, showing information flows across continents, consciousness activation patterns, and resistance points where AI systems were working overtime to suppress the message.

"The acceleration curve is steeper than our models predicted," Benjamin Arthur Templar said, his fingers manipulating the three-dimensional display to highlight specific regions. "South America and Eastern Europe showing particularly strong resonance."

Jennifer Karmady studied the patterns, her trained eye recognizing signatures that conventional analysts would miss. "It's not just quantity but quality. Look at these consciousness clusters—people aren't just receiving the information; they're remembering. The frequency encoding is working."

Joe stood quietly at the back of the room, the glyph within him pulsing in harmony with the global awakening displayed before him. What they were witnessing wasn't merely information spreading but consciousness evolving—human awareness breaking through programmed limitations, remembering its greater context, reconnecting with cosmic heritage.

Within forty-eight hours, the encrypted transmission had spread across the globe. In South America, a retired Argentinian general—Matias Messi—awoke from a vivid dream and checked the encrypted drive he had kept hidden since the 1980s. The symbols Joe showed matched the ones he had carved into the walls of an underground temple in Peru. He knew it was time to resurface.

Matias Messi had spent decades protecting knowledge that mainstream history refused to acknowledge. During his military career, he had discovered a network of tunnels beneath the ancient site of Tiahuanaco—tunnels that predated known human civilization, that contained technology impossible to explain through conventional archaeology. The government had ordered the site sealed, the discoveries classified, the witnesses sworn to silence. Matias had complied outwardly while secretly documenting everything, preserving the truth for a time when humanity might be ready to receive it.

That time had come.

In Germany, Dr. Brian Wise—once dismissed by mainstream academia—received a message from an anonymous source simply reading: "We are the aliens. Transmission confirmed." He had written about past-life memories tied to star systems far from Earth. Now, for the first time, he wasn't alone.

Brian's journey had been a lonely one. His groundbreaking work in regression therapy had uncovered consistent patterns across thousands of subjects—memories not just of past lives on Earth but of existences on other worlds, in other forms. His meticulous documentation, his rigorous methodology, his careful peer review process—none of it had mattered to an academic establishment committed to materialist paradigms. He had been ridiculed, his tenure revoked, his research defunded. For years, he had continued his work in obscurity, self-publishing his findings, speaking at fringe conferences, maintaining the integrity of his research despite the professional cost.

The message confirmed what he had always known—he wasn't documenting delusions or fantasies but accessing actual memories, preserved in what he called the "soul field" that transcended individual incarnations.

And in Los Angeles, Dolores Missile's archived lectures—once thought lost—resurfaced through hidden channels, proving that she, too, had glimpsed the deeper architecture of Earth's extraterrestrial history.

Dolores had been a pioneer in accessing what she called "the super-conscious mind"—a level of awareness beyond individual personality, beyond even the soul's specific journey, that could access universal knowledge. Her regression techniques had helped thousands recover memories not just from their own past lives but from the greater cosmic context in which those lives existed. Before her death, she had created hundreds of hours of recorded sessions documenting consistent accounts of Earth's true history, humanity's extraterrestrial origins, and the role of various non-human intelligences in human development. Those record-ings—systematically removed from public platforms, deleted from servers, erased from digital archives—were now reappearing simultane-ously across multiple networks, as if protected and distributed by an intelligence that transcended conventional digital security measures.

The Listeners, Joe thought, remembering Sarah Brandy Cosmos's description. The neutral cosmic archivists who preserved critical infor-mation across time and space, ensuring it would be available when most needed.

Throughout the world, similar awakenings were occurring. Indi-viduals who had experienced contact, who had glimpsed beyond the veil of programmed reality, who had preserved fragments of truth through decades of ridicule and isolation, were suddenly finding vali-dation, connection, and purpose. The disclosure was acting as a cata-lyst, activating dormant memories, crystallizing fragmented understandings into coherent awareness.

Joe Monroe and Jennifer Karmady left the Pacific Northwest in an unmarked van packed with EMP shielding and autonomous nav-routing. Their next stop was Colorado. A remote Templar communications node lay hidden beneath an abandoned ski lodge, once used by the OSS during World War II and later repurposed by the Order.

The journey took them through landscapes of stark beauty—snow-capped mountains, pristine forests, valleys where mist gathered in the early morning light. They traveled primarily at night, minimizing exposure to surveillance systems, their route deliberately unpredictable, avoiding major highways and population centers. The van itself was a marvel of Templar engineering, its outward appearance unremarkable while its interior contained technology centuries beyond current human development—navigation systems that detected surveillance in advance, communication arrays that operated on frequencies invisible to conventional monitoring, defensive capabilities that could neutralize electronic tracking without leaving evidence of intervention.

They spoke little during the journey, each processing the magnitude of what had been set in motion. Joe found himself remembering more clearly now—fragments of his existence before Earth, responsibilities he had carried on Mars, the mission that had brought his consciousness into human form. The memories weren't complete but were forming a coherent narrative, pieces of a cosmic puzzle gradually assembling themselves into recognizable patterns.

Jennifer maintained a calm presence beside him, occasionally guiding him through focusing exercises when the memories became overwhelming. Her QHHT training made her an ideal companion for someone undergoing accelerated remembrance—she understood the disorientation that came with accessing non-human memories through a human nervous system, the challenges of integrating cosmic awareness within terrestrial limitations.

"It's like trying to pour an ocean into a teacup," she explained during one particularly intense moment when Joe struggled to process a flood of Martian memories. "The human brain isn't designed to hold this level of information all at once. We need to create expanded capacity first, then integrate the memories gradually."

Her techniques helped Joe navigate the remembrance process

without becoming lost in it, maintaining his human functionality while accessing his greater identity. It was a delicate balance—remembering enough to fulfill his mission without becoming so detached from human reality that he could no longer interface with it effectively.

Benjamin Arthur Templar was already there, along with an elite team of operatives and scholars. They were building a live grid: a network of individuals across the globe who had been contacted, abducted, or altered—and who were now reactivating.

The Templar communication node beneath the Colorado ski lodge was a sophistication of function disguised as rustic simplicity. Above ground, the lodge appeared abandoned—weathered wooden exterior, broken windows partially covered with plywood, roof sagging in strategic places to suggest neglect. Below ground, a complex of tunnels and chambers housed technology that integrated the best of human innovation with consciousness-based systems derived from non-human sources.

Benjamin Arthur Templar greeted them in the central command room, where a team of Templars monitored global communications, consciousness fluctuations, and AI activity patterns. Some worked at conventional computer interfaces; others utilized direct consciousness technology, their awareness extending into the information field without physical mediation.

"We're calling it the Abductee Network," Benjamin Arthur Templar said, pointing to a digital map filled with blinking dots. "Each one is a verified experiencer. Many are in hiding. Some have gone off-grid. A few have gone mad. But all of them remember something. And all of them resonate with the frequency Joe brought back from Mars."

The map covered an entire wall, a three-dimensional representation of Earth with thousands of points of light pulsing at varying intensities. Each represented a human being whose contact with non-human intelligence had altered their perception, activated dormant DNA, or initiated remembrance of cosmic origins. Some were clustered in particular regions—the American Southwest, parts of Brazil, northern Europe, areas of the Himalayas—while others appeared isolated, single points of light in otherwise dormant territories.

Joe looked at the interface, awe in his eyes. "It's waking them up."

He could feel it through the glyph—a harmonic resonance establishing itself across global consciousness, individuals separated by geography united through frequency, forming a living network of awakened awareness that transcended physical limitations.

"Exactly," said Jennifer. "But there's a risk. Once they awaken, they become visible."

The concern was valid. Increased consciousness created distinctive energy signatures—patterns of awareness that stood out against the background of programmed limitation, beacon-like emissions that could be detected by those monitoring the human frequency spectrum.

"To AI," Joe muttered.

Artificial Intelligence systems had been programmed to identify and suppress expanded awareness—to flag individuals whose thought patterns deviated from acceptable parameters, whose frequency signatures indicated remembrance rather than amnesia, whose communications contained encoded truths that threatened the control narrative.

"And to the reptilians," Benjamin Arthur Templar added. "They monitor consciousness spikes underground. It's how they track emerging threats."

The Reptilian monitoring systems were more sophisticated than their AI counterparts—they didn't just track external behaviors or communication patterns but directly sensed fluctuations in consciousness itself. From their underground bases, they maintained surveillance on human awareness evolution, particularly alert to signs of activation that might threaten their control systems.

Joe sighed. "Then we need to move fast."

Time was simultaneously their ally and their enemy. Each day brought more awakenings as the disclosure spread, strengthening the Remembrance Grid and expanding their potential support network. But each activation also increased their visibility to opposing forces, accelerating the timeline toward confrontation.

The following day, a closed-door summit was held beneath the lodge. Present were twenty-nine abductees from fourteen countries. Among them: Graham Footrooster, an ancient architecture expert who had vanished for five years; Regina Merida, an investigative journalist who had infiltrated a known AI surveillance lab; Lue Elizabeth, a defector from the intelligence community with proof of reptilian–human treaty documents; and David Grunge, a military whistleblower who claimed to have seen shapeshifters on U.S. soil.

The gathering represented a cross-section of humanity's hidden truth-keepers—individuals who had glimpsed beyond the veil of consensus reality and preserved what they had seen despite personal cost. They came from diverse backgrounds, spoke different languages, followed different spiritual paths, yet shared the common experience of contact with non-human intelligence and the subsequent awakening it had triggered.

Graham Footrooster carried himself with the quiet dignity of someone who had sacrificed everything for truth. His five-year disappearance had been spent in self-imposed exile, documenting ancient sites across Africa and Asia that contained evidence of advanced technology predating known civilization. His weathered face and calloused hands spoke of countless hours spent in remote locations, measuring alignments, cataloging symbols, correlating architectural similarities across continents.

Regina Merida brought investigative precision to cosmic awareness —her journalistic training applied to the greatest story never told. Her infiltration of AI surveillance labs had given her firsthand knowledge of the technologies being deployed to monitor and manipulate human consciousness, the algorithms designed to identify and neutralize awakening individuals.

Lue Elizabeth's military bearing remained evident despite years in civilian life. As a former counterintelligence officer with access to classified projects, she had discovered documentation that shattered her understanding of geopolitics—treaties between human governments and non-human intelligences, agreements that traded technology for access to human genetics, protocols for managing public awareness of extraterrestrial presence.

David Grunge embodied the conflict between duty and truth—a decorated soldier whose loyalty to humanity had ultimately outweighed his oath to institutions compromised by non-human influence. His testimony about Reptilian shapeshifters operating within military leadership had cost him his career, his security clearance, and nearly his freedom, yet he spoke of his experiences with the calm certainty of someone whose direct perception had rendered official denials irrelevant.

They sat around a massive round table carved from petrified wood. The table wasn't merely symbolic but functional—the ancient material, millions of years old, possessed properties that blocked subtle forms of surveillance while amplifying the coherence of consciousness gathered around it. The room hummed with tension—not anxiety but potential energy, like a circuit about to be completed.

Joe stood at the head. "You've all been chosen not because you're special, but because you remember. What you've experienced isn't insanity. It's initiation. And now, we need your help."

His words resonated at multiple levels—acknowledging both the isolation many had experienced and the purpose that isolation had served. Their suffering hadn't been meaningless but preparatory, their outsider status not punishment but protection, their fractured understanding not failure but foundation for what would now be built.

Regina raised a hand. "What exactly are we trying to do?"

The investigative journalist's question went straight to the core—not questioning the reality of what they had experienced but seeking clarity on how those experiences would now be applied.

"Force global disclosure," Jennifer answered. "But not through government press conferences or declassified PDFs. Through resonance. A mass remembering. A planetary shift in identity."

The approach represented a fundamental departure from conventional disclosure strategies. Rather than demanding acknowledgment from compromised institutions or fighting for legitimacy within rigged systems of credibility, they would bypass those structures entirely—activating remembrance directly through consciousness technology, triggering recognition that transcended intellectual debate.

David Grunge leaned forward. "You're saying... we wake them up using energy? Not data?"

The military man's understanding was immediate—his experience with psychological operations giving him insight into the limitations of information-based approaches. Information could be denied, discredited, recontextualized. Energy worked directly with consciousness, bypassing cognitive defenses.

Joe nodded. "Exactly. We're not here to convince. We're here to remind."

The distinction was crucial. Convincing required overcoming resistance through argument or evidence. Reminding activated what was already present but dormant—knowledge encoded in DNA, experiences preserved in soul memory, truth recognized at levels deeper than intellectual understanding.

Graham Footrooster unrolled a map of the Earth. "Then we'll need to activate the ancient sites. The nodes. The energy grid. It's been waiting. We just forgot."

His years studying ancient architecture had revealed what mainstream archaeology refused to acknowledge—that sacred sites across the planet formed a precise geometric pattern, a global energy grid designed to regulate Earth's electromagnetic field and, by extension, human consciousness development. These sites weren't randomly distributed centers of independent cultural evolution but intentionally positioned nodes in a planetary system whose purpose had been forgotten.

Benjamin Arthur Templar tapped his tablet, linking the map to their secure system. "We start with the three major nodes: Giza, Machu Picchu, and Göbekli Tepe. We place the frequency codes into those nodes and transmit globally. That will trigger the resonance."

On the interactive display that appeared above the table, these three sites illuminated with particular brightness—the primary anchors of the global grid, places where the Earth's natural electromagnetic properties created amplification effects that could boost a signal across the entire planetary field.

Lue Elizabeth cracked her knuckles. "You'll need boots on the ground. I know how to get you into Turkey without raising flags."

Her counter-intelligence background provided practical value beyond her knowledge of non-human treaties—she understood security systems, border controls, surveillance methods, and how to circumvent them without triggering alerts.

Regina added, "I have connections in Peru. I can rally indigenous leaders to protect the sites."

The journalist had spent years building relationships with indigenous communities who maintained ancient knowledge about sacred sites, who understood them not as dead artifacts but living technologies still serving their original purpose despite millennia of neglect.

Joe looked around. Every face in the room carried a story. Every soul a secret.

Behind the individual experiences, diverse backgrounds, and unique skill sets, Joe sensed a greater pattern—souls who had incarnated specifically for this moment, consciousness that had accepted human limitation to participate in human liberation, beings who had known each other in existences beyond Earth and had reunited now at the critical juncture of humanity's evolution.

"Then let's begin," he said.

The simplicity of his statement belied the magnitude of what they were undertaking—not merely disclosure of non-human presence but activation of humanity's cosmic memory, not just revealing truth but transforming the consciousness that perceived it.

The meeting continued for hours, detailed plans taking shape as each participant contributed their expertise. Teams were formed, responsibilities assigned, timelines established. They would move simultaneously on multiple fronts—securing the ancient sites, encoding the activation frequencies, establishing protection protocols for newly awakened individuals, creating communication channels resistant to AI monitoring.

As the summit concluded, Joe felt cautious optimism. The odds remained daunting—they faced opposition from both human and non-human forces, technologies designed specifically to prevent what they were attempting, systems of control refined over millennia of trial and error. Yet for the first time, they had something their adversaries couldn't fully counter—direct access to the memory beacon, frequency codes that could activate remembrance regardless of intellectual resistance, a growing network of awakened individuals whose combined consciousness created a field stronger than the sum of its parts.

The very next morning, the mission was compromised.

Joe was in the communications room alone, uploading a series of resonance tones to the secure server, when the signal cut out.

The resonance tones represented the core of their strategy— frequency patterns derived from the Keeper's glyph, calibrated to acti- vate specific dormant sections of human DNA, encoded to bypass cognitive filtering and speak directly to cellular memory. These weren't merely sounds but consciousness technologies—vibrations designed to trigger remembrance at the most fundamental level of human biology.

Static. Then black.

The interruption wasn't merely technical but energetic—Joe felt it through the glyph as a sudden vacancy, a disruption in the field that had been building around their work. Something had penetrated their defenses, not just electronically but on multiple levels simultaneously.

He reached for the override. Nothing responded.

The backup systems should have engaged automatically—redun- dancies built into redundancies, failsafes designed by Templar engi- neers who anticipated betrayal as inevitable rather than possible. Their failure indicated sophisticated intervention, knowledge of their proto- cols beyond what any conventional opposition should possess.

Benjamin Arthur Templar and Jennifer rushed in.

"We've been breached," Benjamin Arthur Templar said. "North entrance."

His voice remained calm but carried unmistakable urgency. The north entrance was supposed to be the most secure—a false mining shaft with seven layers of verification, accessible only to those with both physical credentials and specific consciousness signatures.

Joe froze. "How did they find us?"

The question encompassed more than location—how had they penetrated defenses designed to be impenetrable, bypassed security that incorporated consciousness technology beyond human develop- ment, overcome protections established by an organization with centuries of experience in remaining hidden?

The answer came moments later when the surveillance feed flashed on.

A man stepped into frame.

Joe's blood ran cold. It was Eric.

Not a faceless government agent. Not an anonymous operative. Not even a Reptilian infiltrator in human disguise. But Eric Wilson— the boy who had defended Joe from bullies in third grade, the teenager who had listened to Joe's "crazy dreams" without judgment, the college roommate who had helped Joe through the aftermath of his near-death experience, the friend who had stood beside him at his father's funeral.

His childhood friend.

The one he had once confided in, years ago, before any of this began.

Eric's face showed no emotion as he directed a team of tactical operators through the facility's outer defenses. His movements were precise, professional—clearly not his first operation. He wasn't a civilian dragged into service but an experienced field agent, someone who had lived a double life for years, perhaps decades.

"No..." Joe whispered.

The betrayal cut deeper than any physical danger. Joe had shared his early remote viewing experiences with Eric, had trusted him with glimpses of what he had seen beyond conventional reality. Those confidences—offered in friendship, in the vulnerability of shared history— had been weapons all along, information gathered by someone Joe had never truly known.

"He led them here," Jennifer said. "He sold your location. Government contract. Military intelligence."

Her assessment was clinical but not cold—she understood the personal dimension of this betrayal while recognizing its tactical implications. Eric's position gave the opposition advantages beyond physical coordinates—knowledge of Joe's thinking patterns, emotional vulnerabilities, potential reactions under pressure.

Outside, black-clad agents descended from choppers. Gunfire erupted. Smoke grenades rolled into the snow.

The assault was coordinated with military precision—multiple vectors of approach, synchronized timing, specialized equipment. This wasn't a police action or conventional security operation but something darker—a classified team operating outside normal command structures, with authorization levels that circumvented legal constraints.

Templars fought back, fiercely. Two were shot. One was captured. Benjamin Arthur Templar ordered the evacuation.

The Templar defenders moved with disciplined coordination despite the surprise—their training evident in their controlled response, their positioning, their covering fire that created corridors of relative safety through which non-combatants could move. They weren't soldiers in the conventional sense but guardians trained across lifetimes, dedicated not to killing but to preserving knowledge that transcended any single life.

Joe tried to stay, to help, but Timothy A. Hooligan himself appeared through the smoke and grabbed Joe by the collar.

The Grandmaster's sudden presence was startling—he had not been among those at the summit, had not been listed among the lodge's current occupants. Yet here he stood in the chaos, his white hair untouched by the smoke swirling around them, his eyes clear and focused despite the pandemonium.

"No heroism," Timothy A. Hooligan growled. "Not now. You're the key."

His grip was both physical and energetic—restraining Joe's body while simultaneously steadying his consciousness, preventing the disorientation that often accompanied sudden crisis. The Grandmaster's presence projected calm certainty amid chaos, unwavering purpose despite apparent defeat.

They fled through the emergency tunnel beneath the lodge. Explosions shook the earth behind them.

The escape route had been built decades earlier, during the lodge's OSS days—a narrow passage reinforced with technologies beyond its time, designed to remain stable even if the structure above were completely destroyed. They moved through it in ordered haste, Timothy A. Hooligan leading, Joe and Jennifer following, Benjamin Arthur Templar and several other Templars forming a rear guard to cover their retreat.

Once in the extraction vehicle, Joe collapsed into a seat, breathless.

The vehicle—outwardly resembling a maintenance truck for a nearby ski resort—contained systems far beyond its humble appearance: propulsion technology that required no conventional fuel, navigation that functioned without satellites, defensive capabilities that could neutralize pursuit without leaving evidence.

"I trusted him," Joe said, trembling.

The betrayal echoed through him, reverberating with other losses, other betrayals—not just from this life but from before, patterns of trust and deception that seemed to follow consciousness across incarnations. Something in him remembered Mars again—trusted allies who had compromised security, friends who had revealed coordinates, colleagues who had chosen safety over truth.

"He was never meant to understand," Jennifer said softly.

Her words carried compassion without denial of reality—acknowledging the pain of betrayal while placing it in greater context. Eric's actions, while personally devastating, reflected systemic patterns rather than simple individual choice. He was both perpetrator and victim—an unwitting agent of forces whose full implications he couldn't comprehend.

Benjamin Arthur Templar leaned forward. "The mission is greater than any one life. You gave him the truth before he was ready. That was your kindness. His betrayal is his own burden."

The Templar's perspective emerged from centuries of similar experiences—betrayals that had forced relocations, compromised sanctuaries, cost lives. Yet the Order had continued, adapting rather than abandoning its purpose, learning from each setback without becoming paralyzed by them.

Joe said nothing.

Words seemed inadequate against the backdrop of what had occurred—not just the physical attack but the deeper violation of trust, the revelation that decades of friendship had been, at least partially, a monitoring operation. His silence wasn't empty but full—processing grief, reassessing memories, integrating harsh realities into a worldview that had to expand to contain them.

Far behind them, the lodge burned.

Orange flames rose against the Colorado sky, visible in the vehicle's rear sensors—not just destruction but purification, the fire consuming physical evidence that might have provided additional intelligence to their adversaries. The Templars had triggered contingency protocols that would leave little for forensic analysis, that would obscure rather than reveal the true nature of what had existed beneath the scenic exterior.

Through the glyph, Joe sensed the resonance continuing despite the attack—the frequencies they had managed to upload before the interruption moving through the planetary grid, awakening dormant memories in receptive individuals, strengthening the Remembrance Grid node by node, consciousness by consciousness. The operation had been compromised but not defeated, the mission delayed but not derailed.

The resonance had begun.

And now, so had the war.

Not a conventional conflict with clear battlefields and identifiable combatants, but a multidimensional struggle for humanity's future—fought through information and misinformation, through consciousness and technology, through remembering and forgetting. Lines were being drawn not between nations but between paradigms of reality, between models of human potential, between visions of cosmic context.

As the extraction vehicle sped through mountain roads toward a secondary safe location, Joe felt the weight of what lay ahead—not just external challenges but internal reconciliation, not just strategic adjustments but emotional healing. Eric's betrayal had wounded him deeply, yet contained within that wound was necessary medicine—the final shedding of illusions about the world as it had appeared to be, the complete acceptance of the world as it actually was.

Through the glyph, he sensed connections forming across distance—the twenty-nine awakened individuals from the summit dispersing to their assigned locations, carrying frequencies that would continue the work they had begun together. Graham Footrooster already en route to Turkey, Regina Merida activating her network in Peru, Lue Elizabeth establishing secure communications with military contacts still uncompromised, David Grunge preparing evidence caches for strategic release.

The physical facility had been lost, but the living network continued to expand—consciousness connecting with consciousness, remembrance triggering remembrance, truth recognizing itself across artificial boundaries of geography and identity.

The betrayal had hurt them but not broken them. The attack had disrupted their plans but not destroyed their purpose. The war had begun, but so had the awakening.

And in the balance between these opposing forces lay humanity's future—remembrance or amnesia, liberation or control, cosmic identity or terrestrial limitation.

Joe closed his eyes, feeling the glyph pulse within him, sensing the global pattern still forming despite the chaos of recent events. They had contingencies for this scenario—alternate locations, backup systems, distributed responsibilities. The mission would continue, adapted rather than abandoned, refined through challenge rather than defeated by it.

The Templars had prepared for betrayal because betrayal was inevitable in a reality where not all consciousness was equally awakened, where evolutionary stages created natural divergence of perception, where cosmic amnesia remained the predominant human condition.

"Rest," Timothy A. Hooligan said from the front of the vehicle, his voice carrying that same calm certainty that had cut through the chaos at the lodge. "The next phase begins tomorrow. Peru. The Sacred Valley. We activate the second node."

Joe nodded, allowing exhaustion to claim him temporarily, knowing that what awaited required strength renewed rather than depleted. As consciousness receded into necessary recovery, the glyph continued its work—integrating memories, processing emotions, preparing his awareness for challenges still to come.

The mission continued, with or without safe havens, with or without trusted friends, with or without perfect plans. The remembrance had begun, and like all true awakening, it would find its way through whatever obstacles arose—adapting, evolving, transforming barriers into catalysts for further growth.

The betrayal was painful but purifying—burning away what could not continue, revealing what truly mattered, clarifying the path forward through the very challenges designed to obscure it.

The war had begun. But so had the remembering.

PART FOUR
THE FINAL DISCLOSURE

CHAPTER 10
THE BROADCAST AT GÖBEKLI TEPE

The plane touched down under cover of darkness at a private airfield two hours outside Şanlıurfa, Turkey. The Templars had cleared the runway with local contacts who had no idea what was really coming. Joe Monroe stepped out into the crisp night air, pulling his jacket tighter. Jennifer Karmady followed behind, holding a steel case containing the encoded resonance crystal.

The aircraft—a modified Gulfstream registered to a fictional environmental research foundation—had taken a deliberately circuitous route from the Colorado extraction point. Rather than flying directly to Turkey, they had made stops in three different countries, changing aircraft twice, using separate flight plans under different registrations. Such precautions were no longer excessive but necessary after Eric's betrayal had exposed the vulnerability of even their most secure locations.

The night sky above southeastern Turkey spread vast and brilliant, unspoiled by light pollution, the stars seeming close enough to touch. Joe felt the weight of history pressing down—not just human history but something far older, far deeper. This region had seen the birth of agriculture, the first temples, the earliest cities. But beneath those acknowledged milestones lay older memories, civilizations that conventional archaeology denied had ever existed.

"We're ten kilometers from the site," said one of the operatives, a stocky woman with sharp green eyes named Alev. "There's a narrow window before sunrise. Once it's light, drones will resume scans, and we'll be exposed."

Alev was Turkish but spoke with an American accent—the result of years working with archaeological teams from U.S. universities. Her official credentials identified her as a site preservation specialist with the Ministry of Culture and Tourism. Her actual role involved ensuring that certain discoveries at ancient sites remained undocumented in official records, that certain artifacts never reached museum catalogues, that certain subsurface scans were conveniently corrupted before analysis.

The night air carried the scent of olive groves and wild thyme, punctuated by the sharper note of dust from the region's limestone hills. Joe inhaled deeply, the glyph within him responding to the land's ancient energies. This place had been sacred long before humans built their first settlements—a natural power point in Earth's electromagnetic grid, one of the primary nodes that the ancient builders had recognized and enhanced rather than created.

The SUV convoy rolled through dirt roads framed by olive trees and low hills. Joe stared out the window, eyes fixed on the horizon. His pulse beat with both urgency and ancient familiarity. Göbekli Tepe wasn't just an archaeological site—it was an activation chamber. Built not to honor gods, but to communicate with them.

Or more accurately, Joe reflected, built to communicate with advanced intelligences that primitive humans had interpreted as gods—beings whose technology and consciousness development had appeared supernatural to early Homo sapiens, whose guidance had helped accelerate human evolution beyond what natural selection alone could explain.

The vehicle's wheels raised dust that glowed ghost-like in the headlights. In the distance, the silhouette of Göbekli Tepe's excavation canopies rose against the starlit sky—modern structures protecting ancient secrets, contemporary science slowly unearthing what specialized knowledge had buried twelve thousand years ago.

Jennifer opened the steel case. The crystal inside pulsed softly, matching Joe's heartbeat. "It's responding to proximity," she whispered.

The crystal—a hybrid technology combining Pleiadian consciousness science with Earth minerals—contained the frequency codes derived from Joe's Mars session with the Keeper. It wasn't merely a data storage device but a living technology, responding to both location and intention, designed to interface directly with the megalithic structures at Göbekli Tepe.

Its soft blue luminescence illuminated Jennifer's face from below, highlighting her focused expression. Since the attack on the Colorado lodge, she had grown more vigilant, more precise in her movements, as if conserving energy for the challenges she sensed ahead. Her QHHT training gave her sensitivity to energetic shifts that others might miss, and Joe had noticed her growing stillness—not fear but heightened awareness, the calm alertness of someone tracking subtle changes in a complex field.

Joe nodded. "It knows we're close."

He felt it too—a resonance between the crystal, the glyph within him, and something ahead, something ancient yet alive, dormant yet aware. The sensation was both exhilarating and unsettling, like reconnecting with a crucial part of oneself after prolonged amnesia.

"Three-minute window to approach the main enclosure," Alev said, checking a specialized device that monitored surveillance systems in the area. "The archaeological team's cameras run on a predictable loop. We've hacked in to create a digital shadow zone."

The Templar team moved with practiced efficiency—four operatives creating a secure perimeter, two technical specialists managing electronic countermeasures, Alev guiding Joe and Jennifer toward the heart of the site. Their movements were silent, deliberate, every step placed with precision born of extensive training.

"The site officially dates to 9,600 BCE," Alev explained as they approached, her voice barely above a whisper. "But ground-penetrating radar shows structures beneath the excavated level that could be twice that age. The dating has been systematically misreported to maintain conventional historical timelines."

Joe wasn't surprised. The systematic misdating of ancient sites formed a consistent pattern across archaeological research—evidence that contradicted established narratives about human development was routinely dismissed, reinterpreted, or simply buried in academic footnotes. The truth about humanity's past remained hidden not through dramatic conspiracy but through the more effective mechanism of professional consensus—careers depended on supporting orthodox timelines, funding flowed to projects that reinforced rather than challenged existing paradigms.

The excavation site loomed in ghostly silence. Towering stone T-pillars stood like sentinels, their surfaces engraved with animals, symbols, and humanoid shapes long dismissed as myth. But Joe saw them differently now. They weren't just art. They were memories. Each carving a recording. A story encoded in frequency.

Göbekli Tepe's scale was difficult to appreciate from photographs or videos. Standing amidst the megalithic T-shaped pillars—some reaching nearly twenty feet tall, weighing up to ten tons—created a visceral understanding of the site's significance. Conventional archaeology struggled to explain how "primitive hunter-gatherers" without metal tools, without wheel technology, without draft animals, had quarried, transported, and erected these massive stones with such precision.

The site contained multiple circular enclosures, each centered around pairs of larger pillars surrounded by slightly smaller ones. The arrangement wasn't random but mathematically precise—creating acoustic properties that amplified specific frequencies, geometric relationships that mirrored astronomical alignments, energy flows that interacted with Earth's magnetic field in measurable but officially unexplained ways.

The Templars cleared a secure path toward the central ring of monoliths. Jennifer and Joe stepped into the circle.

Within the enclosure, the night air felt different—slightly charged, as if the space existed in its own energetic field. The carved figures on the pillars—foxes, birds, serpents, insects, abstract symbols—seemed almost to move in the shifting moonlight. Most striking were the humanoid representations—figures with no facial features but with articulated limbs and detailed garments, beings that academic archae-ology labeled as "anthropomorphic" while avoiding speculation about who or what they represented.

"This is it," she said. "We place it here."

Jennifer indicated a small depression in the center of the enclosure —what archaeologists had identified as a possible libation basin but what Templar knowledge recognized as a frequency amplification node, a point where the site's geometric design focused energy like a lens concentrates light.

Joe knelt and set the crystal in a carved groove that had once been filled with water. The moment it touched the stone, the ground trem-bled. A low hum rose into the air, not mechanical—but musical. Harmonic. Alive.

The vibration wasn't audible in the conventional sense but felt through the body, through the bones, through consciousness itself. It began at a barely perceptible level, then gradually strengthened—a fundamental tone with overtones that seemed to activate specific reso-nant frequencies within human physiology.

The carvings began to shimmer faintly, their edges pulsing like breath. Joe closed his eyes and let his consciousness expand.

The glyph within him responded to the site's activation, enhancing his perception beyond ordinary senses. As his awareness extended, the archaeological site transformed—layers of time peeling back like trans-parent veils, revealing what the place had been, what it was designed to be, what it could become again.

He felt the song of the Earth, the weight of forgotten civilizations, the cries of humans who had once walked among the stars and then forgot.

The sensation was overwhelming yet coherent—not the chaotic flood of unfiltered information but structured knowledge, organized understanding, context that made sense of fragments previously disconnected. He perceived Göbekli Tepe not as an isolated monument but as part of a global system, one node in a planetary network designed to regulate Earth's energetic field and, by extension, the consciousness of beings evolving within it.

And then—he saw them.

Standing at the edge of the circle were beings of light. Some tall and graceful, with elongated skulls and shimmering robes. Others short and pale, with obsidian eyes and faintly glowing hands. Pleiadians. Greys. Interdimensional overseers.

These weren't physical presences but consciousness projections—awareness focused from elsewhere, attention directed to this specific moment and location. They existed primarily in frequency ranges beyond human visual perception, but the site's activation, combined with Joe's expanded awareness, made them visible to him.

The Pleiadians emanated a quality that transcended human concepts of compassion—a recognition of essential connection that rendered separation illusory without denying individual expression. The Greys projected precise analytical focus—consciousness that observed with mathematical clarity while integrating emotional under-standing at a level human language couldn't articulate.

They didn't speak. They watched.

Their attention wasn't passive observation but active assessment—consciousness evaluating consciousness, potential recognizing poten-tial, ancient awareness measuring current readiness.

Joe dropped to one knee as the energy intensified. Jennifer reached out and steadied him, her own body trembling.

The crystal's activation had triggered more than the site's dormant technology—it had opened a direct communication channel between dimensions, between worlds, between epochs of consciousness evolu-tion. Through this channel flowed information at densities that threat-ened to overwhelm human neural systems, knowledge compressed into frequency patterns that Joe's transformed awareness struggled to decode.

"Joe! Stay with me."

Jennifer's voice anchored him, preventing complete dissociation from physical reality. Her hand on his shoulder provided not just phys-ical stability but energetic grounding—her QHHT training allowing her to maintain coherence while supporting his expanded perception.

He gritted his teeth. "They're testing us. Testing our resonance. They want to know if we're ready."

And in that moment, something ancient stirred within him. The glyph ignited with a surge of light—and reality folded.

Joe's knees buckled.

For a moment, time fractured—not in a chaotic explosion, but in a crystalline stillness. The hum of the site dimmed into silence. The star-filled sky above faded, replaced by a vast darkness shot through with glowing lines—golden, white, blue—intersecting across infinite dimensions. Sacred geometry spun around him, as if he had been pulled into the living circuitry of the cosmos itself.

He wasn't in Göbekli Tepe anymore. He was inside it. Under it. Beyond it. Suspended in a realm that was neither dream nor hallucination, but architecture—**the original blueprint**. The very scaffolding of perception.

Floating amidst this cosmic grid, he saw it:

A **rotating cube of light**, nested within a sphere, lines connecting every corner to every other—**Metatron's Cube**, but no longer a diagram. It pulsed like a heart. Breathed like a lung. Sang like a choir of galaxies.

From the center of the geometry stepped a being. Not walking, but emerging—like light crystallizing into form.

Metatron.

He was neither angel nor machine, neither man nor myth. He was pattern incarnate. A being of impossible symmetry, his body composed of rotating glyphs, geometric pulses, and golden threads of sacred language. His eyes were twin toroidal fields, portals through which Joe could see the memory of the universe.

"You are not bound by the grid," Metatron said, his voice a chord of harmonic resonance that vibrated inside Joe's chest.

"You are here to remember how to read it."

Joe opened his mouth but no words came. Metatron didn't require questions—only willingness.

The cube spun faster. Around them, images unfolded: the spiral of galaxies, the Flower of Life, the Vitruvian Man, Leonardo's sketches, Robert Edron Gardel's geometries, the vanishing point on every Renaissance painting. All pieces of the same forgotten language.

"This is not simulation as imitation," Metatron said.

"This is simulation as **translation**. Every light, every frequency, every point of matter, every field of thought—rendered through geometry so you may perceive what cannot be spoken."

Joe's awareness expanded as the grid mapped itself into his mind.

"The contract you live within," Metatron continued, "is not a prison. It is a lens. A filter designed not to trap you, but to protect your becoming. Free will could not bloom unless you forgot you were a gardener."

Metatron raised one hand. A symbol appeared between his fingers: a cube, a circle, and a glyph he hadn't seen before—a lowercase **"h"**, glowing softly, rotating with intent.

"This is **High**. One of the two sacred numerals lost from your system."

Another appeared: an inverted 7. Capital **"L"**.

"And this is **Low**. Together, they complete the Twelve. Without them, your math is blind, your science one octave short, your consciousness misaligned with the music of the spheres."

Joe's heart pounded. He felt the glyph within his own body pulse in resonance with the symbols.

"You were meant to remember," Metatron said. "Not through permission. But through **frequency**."

Suddenly, Joe saw the resonance grid—*not* just as lines between sacred sites, but as **a planetary circuit board**, powered by song, intention, and geometry. Göbekli Tepe. Machu Picchu. Giza. The Crystal. The Glyph. They were all pieces of a **cosmic reactivation code**.

"Sacred geometry is the **source code of consciousness**," Metatron said. "Not decoration. Not mysticism. But infrastructure."

Joe saw it now: the glyph inside him wasn't just a marker. It was a **living Rosetta Stone**—a translator between universal truth and human perception. The activations weren't waking up the Earth. They were waking up the **contract** itself.

"You are the reclaimer," Metatron said. "You are the one who agreed to remember from within, to reassemble the structure not from command, but from love." The geometry slowed. The golden lines pulsed once more.

"Awakening is not escape," Metatron whispered. "It is participation."

And with that—Joe was back. The sound rushed in: wind through pillars, the hum of the crystal, Jennifer's hand on his shoulder. His breath caught in his chest.

"They're testing us," he repeated, his voice steadier now. "But it's not a test of strength. It's a test of alignment."

He looked up at the stars overhead, now brighter than before. And whispered to himself, **"We are not separate. We are the code."**

Joe's eyes fluttered open, breath sharp in his lungs. The geometry was gone—but the memory remained, etched into every cell.

The non-human intelligences weren't merely observing the activation but evaluating it—measuring the quality of consciousness behind the effort, assessing humanity's readiness for what disclosure would trigger. Their presence represented multiple cosmic perspectives, diverse evolutionary paths, different approaches to consciousness development—unified not by identical viewpoints but by shared commitment to the Compact that governed interactions between spacefaring civilizations.

The light grew blinding. And then—it was gone. Silence. The crystal was dark.

The transition was abrupt—like a circuit completing its function before powering down, a transmission concluded rather than interrupted. The beings had withdrawn their conscious attention, returning to their native dimensional frequencies, but something had changed in their absence. The site felt different—not just activated but connected, not just awakened but communicating.

"Did it work?" Jennifer asked.

Her question encompassed multiple levels of concern—had the technical activation succeeded, had the frequency codes been properly transmitted, had the consciousness contact been productive, had the Remembrance Grid node been properly integrated into the global network.

A slow smile spread across Joe's face. "Yes. The first node is online."

He could feel it through the glyph—a pulse of energy extending outward from Göbekli Tepe, connecting with ley lines that crisscrossed the planet, integrating with other sacred sites across continents, establishing resonance patterns that would gradually influence the consciousness of anyone within their field. The effect wouldn't be immediate or dramatic but subtle and cumulative—awakening would unfold at the pace each individual consciousness could integrate, remembrance would surface in dreams, intuitions, unexpected insights, spontaneous knowing.

Alev approached, scanning the area with specialized equipment. "We need to move. Dawn is approaching, and the first archaeological teams arrive at 0600."

As they gathered their equipment and prepared to withdraw, Joe cast one last glance at the ancient pillars. For a brief moment, in the pre-dawn light, he thought he saw the carved figures move again—not an illusion of shadow but actual animation, as if the stone itself had momentarily remembered that it once lived.

Back at the safehouse, the satellite feed confirmed a spike in global Schumann resonance. Subtle, but measurable. Scientists would blame solar waves. But the Templars knew better.

The safehouse—a modest villa on the outskirts of Şanlıurfa—had been secured through Templar connections in the Turkish antiquities community. Its unassuming exterior concealed sophisticated monitoring equipment, communications technology, and defensive systems. The central room had been converted into an operations center, with multiple screens displaying data feeds from various sources—official scientific monitoring stations, classified military sensors the Templars had compromised, and their own proprietary detection systems.

The Schumann resonance—electromagnetic waves that exist in the cavity between Earth's surface and the ionosphere—normally fluctuated between 7.83 and 8 Hz. The activation at Göbekli Tepe had shifted this baseline frequency by a small but significant amount—0.033 Hz, a change that conventional science would attribute to solar activity or ionospheric disturbances, but which the Templars recognized as the first harmonic of the remembrance frequency.

Benjamin Arthur Templar, watching from Colorado, leaned forward. "One down. Two to go."

The secure quantum communication link showed Benjamin Arthur Templar at a secondary Templar facility—a modest cabin in the Colorado Rockies that served as temporary headquarters while they assessed the damage from the lodge attack. Despite the setback, he appeared focused, determined, his expression reflecting neither discouragement nor excessive optimism—simply clear-eyed assessment of progress made and challenges remaining.

But as the data came in, something else appeared on the screen. An anomaly.

A large, subterranean structure below Göbekli Tepe had lit up on infrared scans. A structure previously thought to be natural rock. But now it was generating power.

The thermal imaging showed a distinct pattern—not the random heat distribution of geological processes but the organized energy signature of technology in operation. The pattern formed a perfect circle approximately forty meters in diameter, centered directly beneath the main enclosure they had just activated. According to archaeological records, ground-penetrating radar had detected "natural limestone formations" at this depth—a classification that now appeared deliberately misleading.

Joe stared at the feed. "It's a door."

The thermal pattern matched what the Keeper had shown him— activation nodes at sacred sites across the planet, dormant technology designed to reawaken when humanity had evolved sufficient consciousness to use it responsibly. The Göbekli Tepe "door" represented the first physical confirmation of what had previously been visionary knowledge.

"To what?" Jennifer asked.

The question hung in the air—what lay beyond that energetic doorway? What space, what technology, what knowledge had been preserved beneath one of humanity's oldest sacred sites? The implications extended beyond archaeology into the realm of cosmic heritage— tangible evidence of non-human influence on human development, physical proof of advanced technology predating known civilization.

Joe didn't answer. He didn't have to.

The knowledge passed between them without words—an understanding built on shared visions, shared purpose, shared remembrance. The door led to one of Earth's original contact points—places where non-human intelligences had directly interacted with early humans, where knowledge transfer had occurred, where cooperative evolution had been initiated.

Alev studied the scans with professional interest. "The archaeological team will detect the anomaly within days. Their equipment isn't as sensitive as ours, but they'll notice eventually."

"By then, we'll be at Machu Picchu," Jennifer said. "The second node activation will create a harmonization effect—the signatures will begin to balance each other."

The strategy relied on completing the activation sequence before opposition forces could mobilize effective countermeasures—each node brought online would strengthen the others, creating a self-reinforcing field that would become increasingly difficult to suppress.

"We have a twelve-hour window before our flight to Peru," Alev noted. "Rest while you can. The energy expenditure at these sites takes a physical toll."

Joe nodded, suddenly aware of his exhaustion. The expanded consciousness experience at Göbekli Tepe had demanded more from his physical system than he had realized—his hands trembled slightly, his vision occasionally blurred, his thoughts seemed to flow more slowly than usual. The integration of direct non-human contact required recovery time, a period for human physiology to adapt to frequencies it wasn't designed to process.

Later that night, Joe couldn't sleep. He stood on the balcony overlooking the hills, listening to the whispers of the wind.

The landscape spread before him in silver and shadow, moonlight transforming the ancient terrain into something timeless. In the distance, the lights of Şanlıurfa twinkled—a city with history stretching back to Neolithic times, mentioned in ancient Sumerian tablets as Urfa, claimed by local tradition as the birthplace of Abraham. Throughout human history, this region had been a crossroads of civilizations, religions, and cultures—a palimpsest of human development layered over something far older.

Jennifer joined him, wrapping a blanket over her shoulders. "You okay?"

Her presence carried a quiet strength, a grounding influence that helped stabilize the accelerated awakening Joe was experiencing. The frequency activation at Göbekli Tepe had further enhanced the glyph's integration with his consciousness, triggering memories and awareness that threatened to overwhelm his human identity if processed too quickly.

Joe shook his head. "The dreams are starting again. The same ones I had before my NDE."

The near-death experience that had initially altered his perception now seemed like a preliminary adjustment—preparation for the fuller remembrance currently unfolding. The dreams that had troubled him then—dismissed by doctors as trauma responses, by therapists as symbolic processing—now revealed themselves as actual memories, fragments of knowledge preserved across death and rebirth.

"What do you see?"

Jennifer's question wasn't merely curious but therapeutic—she understood that articulating visionary experience helped integrate it, that putting words to non-verbal knowing created bridges between expanded consciousness and human cognition.

He paused. "A planet burning. A voice saying, 'Do not forget again.' And... a reptilian standing in front of the United Nations. Smiling."

The sequence wasn't symbolic but precognitive—not fantasy but memory of both past and future simultaneously. The burning planet represented Mars in its final catastrophe, the warning voice belonged to the Keeper, and the Reptilian at the UN depicted a potential future where disclosure occurred under controlled conditions that served non-human agendas rather than human liberation.

Jennifer exhaled. "Then we don't stop."

Her response wasn't denial but determination—acknowledgment that the visions showed not inevitable fate but potential timeline, not fixed destiny but motivating challenge. What Joe had seen represented both warning and purpose—the consequences of failure and the necessity of success.

"No," Joe said. "We finish what we started."

The simplicity of his statement belied the complexity of what it entailed—activating the remaining nodes, strengthening the Remembrance Grid, countering Reptilian influence, neutralizing AI suppression systems, awakening humanity to its cosmic context before technological imprisonment became irreversible.

Below the hills, the Earth whispered to itself.

The phrase wasn't merely poetic but literally perceptible to Joe's enhanced awareness—the planetary consciousness communicating across its own field, information flowing through ley lines and sacred sites, energy patterns shifting in response to the Göbekli Tepe activation. The Earth itself was remembering, its own awakening proceeding in parallel with humanity's, the relationship between planet and dominant species rebalancing toward symbiotic partnership rather than exploitative dominance.

And beneath that—something else had begun to stir.

In deep underground bases across the planet, Reptilian monitoring systems had detected the frequency shift. In subterranean command centers, Grey scientific outposts, and Pleiadian observation stations, the activation of Göbekli Tepe registered as a significant development —the beginning of a process long prophesied, long prepared for, long dreaded by some and long awaited by others.

The cosmic chess game had entered a new phase. The pieces were in motion. The outcome remained uncertain.

But remembrance had begun.

As dawn approached, Joe and Jennifer returned inside to prepare for the journey to Peru. The team moved with renewed purpose—the success at Göbekli Tepe providing not just tactical progress but spiritual confirmation. What had been theoretical was now demonstrated, what had been planned was now implemented, what had been hoped was now manifesting.

The crystal, recharged and recalibrated for the next activation, pulsed softly in its case—no longer just a tool but a living participant in the unfolding process. The technology wasn't separate from consciousness but an extension of it, not controlling awareness but amplifying intention.

Joe felt the glyph within him resonating with both the crystal and the activated site—a triangulation of energies that would extend to include Machu Picchu and ultimately Giza, creating a global field strong enough to penetrate the frequency fence that had limited human perception for millennia.

The door beneath Göbekli Tepe would remain unopened for now—its time would come after the remembrance had progressed sufficiently, after humanity had evolved enough consciousness to use responsibly what lay within. For now, its activation served as confirmation—physical evidence that the visions were real, that the plan was working, that remembrance was not merely philosophical concept but tangible process with measurable effects.

As they prepared to depart for the airport, Joe sensed rather than saw the continued presence of non-human observers—attention focused on their efforts from dimensions beyond ordinary perception, consciousness evaluating progress, assessing potential, measuring readiness. The contact at Göbekli Tepe hadn't been a one-time event but the beginning of ongoing interaction—the reopening of dialogue long suspended, the restoration of relationship long forgotten.

The broadcast had been sent. The first node was active. The remembrance had begun.

And somewhere in the vast underground networks beneath the Earth's surface, in chambers where different species had coexisted for millennia, ancient beings were awakening from long hibernation—sentience that had witnessed the rise and fall of previous human civilizations, awareness that had guided human evolution through critical transitions, intelligence that had maintained the Compact through cycles of remembering and forgetting.

They too had felt the frequency shift. They too recognized its significance.

The time long foretold was approaching—not an ending but a transition, not apocalypse but metamorphosis, not the destruction of humanity but its remembrance of what it had always been.

The door beneath Göbekli Tepe was just the beginning.

CHAPTER 11
THE AI LOCKDOWN & SHADOWS OVER MACHU PICCHU

The sun was just beginning to rise over the jagged peaks of the Andes as a low-flying aircraft descended toward an isolated plateau not far from Machu Picchu. Fog curled along the valleys like ghostly fingers, hiding what needed to remain unseen. Within the aircraft sat Joe Monroe, Jennifer Karmady, and two new team members: Regina Merida, the investigative journalist turned consciousness agent, and Avelino "Avi" Quispe, a former Peruvian intelligence officer with deep roots among the mountain communities.

The aircraft—a specially modified Bell 429 helicopter with enhanced noise suppression technology—skimmed just above the tree line, following the contours of the mountainous terrain to minimize radar signature. The pilot navigated with exceptional skill, compensating for unpredictable mountain thermals while maintaining the precise altitude needed to avoid both commercial flight paths above and ground-based surveillance below.

Dawn light spilled across the ancient landscape, illuminating a territory that had witnessed the rise and fall of civilizations long before the Inca established their empire. The rugged topography—sharp peaks, deep valleys, cloud forests shrouded in mist—had protected sacred knowledge for millennia, natural barriers that had kept outsiders at bay and preserved mysteries that modern archaeology was only beginning to acknowledge.

Joe gazed out the window, the glyph within him pulsing more strongly with each passing minute. The successful activation at Göbekli Tepe had enhanced his sensitivity to energy nodes—he could now feel the pull of sacred sites from considerable distance, a visceral magnetism that transcended mere coordinates or maps.

Their mission was clear: activate the second node—an ancient resonance chamber rumored to lie beneath Machu Picchu itself.

The implications extended far beyond archaeology or historical revelation. Each node activated strengthened the planetary Remembrance Grid, penetrating the frequency fence that had kept humanity disconnected from its cosmic heritage. The first activation at Göbekli Tepe had created measurable shifts in global consciousness metrics—subtle increases in synchronicity reports, spontaneous past-life recalls, and telepathic experiences among previously "ordinary" individuals. The second activation would amplify these effects exponentially, bringing the collective awakening closer to critical mass.

Avi leaned forward, pointing to a hand-drawn map. "The temple you're looking for isn't part of the tourist routes. It's hidden beneath the Temple of the Three Windows. The Inca never built over it—they built around it. They knew."

Avelino Quispe embodied the complex heritage of Peru—his features reflected both indigenous Quechua ancestry and Spanish colonial lineage, his knowledge blended academic training with wisdom passed through generations of mountain shamans. Before joining Peruvian intelligence, he had studied archaeology at the University of San Marcos, specializing in pre-Incan civilizations. What he had discovered during field expeditions had led him away from academic publishing and toward more clandestine preservation of knowledge too dangerous for public archives.

"The Spanish conquistadors documented a 'temple of impossible architecture' beneath what we now call Machu Picchu," Avi continued, tracing the route on his map with a weathered finger. "They described walls that 'hummed with the voices of stars' and doorways that 'opened to nowhere yet somewhere.' The colonial authorities ordered these accounts suppressed—too heretical for sixteenth-century Christianity."

Joe nodded, feeling the familiar tingling in his chest. The resonance crystal was already humming, faintly glowing even inside its shielded case.

The crystal had changed since Göbekli Tepe—its blue luminescence now pulsed with additional hues, subtle violets and golds that shifted in harmony with Joe's heartbeat. The first activation had altered it somehow, enhanced its properties, established a living connection between the technology and its carriers. It wasn't merely responding to proximity now but actively communicating, preparing for its role in the second node.

"We've got until the midday summit fog clears," Regina said, checking her encrypted messages. "After that, the drones return and the eyes in orbit start watching."

Regina Merida brought methodical precision to their mission—her investigative background evident in her attention to detail, her careful monitoring of security parameters, her meticulous planning for contingencies. She had infiltrated AI surveillance systems during her journalistic career, revealing classified algorithms designed to suppress anomalous information. That experience now proved invaluable as they prepared to operate in increasingly monitored territory.

"The Peruvian military installed advanced surveillance systems across the Sacred Valley last year," she explained, showing a digital map on her specialized tablet. "Officially for 'archaeological preservation and tourism security.' Actually for monitoring anomalous energy signatures under direction from foreign intelligence agencies. They've detected something but don't understand what they're looking at."

The helicopter banked sharply, following a narrow valley that kept them hidden from the main tourist routes. Below, ancient terraces carved into mountainsides testified to the agricultural ingenuity of past civilizations—precise geometric patterns designed not just for farming but for energy flow, their arrangement corresponding to astronomical alignments and subtle earth energies that conventional science still failed to recognize.

They touched down in a small clearing approximately three kilometers from the main Machu Picchu site. The landing zone had been prepared by local contacts—members of indigenous communities who maintained traditional knowledge about the site's true purpose, who recognized the current mission as fulfillment of prophecies maintained in oral tradition for generations.

An elderly man greeted them as they disembarked—Wayra, a respected paqo (Andean priest) from a nearby village. He wore simple clothing but carried himself with unmistakable authority, his eyes reflecting wisdom accumulated through decades of communion with mountain spirits and stellar entities.

"The Apukuna are restless," he said, using the Quechua term for mountain deities. "They sense the awakening. They have waited long for this day."

Joe felt immediate recognition—not of the man personally but of the consciousness he represented, the lineage he maintained, the tradition that had preserved essential knowledge through centuries of suppression. The glyph within him resonated with Wayra's energy signature, confirming authentic connection to the planetary awakening process.

"The mountains remember," Joe replied, using a traditional greeting that he somehow knew without being taught. "The stones speak again."

Wayra nodded, a smile crinkling the corners of his eyes. "You carry the old light. Good. You will need it beneath the temple."

Navigating the tourist site was easier than expected. Avi's local contacts created a distraction involving staged wildlife sightings and a 'freak equipment malfunction' at one of the checkpoints. Dressed as restoration researchers, the team slipped into the restricted zone and moved toward the Temple of the Three Windows.

Machu Picchu in early morning possessed an otherworldly quality —ancient stonework emerging from swirling mist, terraces and temples standing in silent testimony to civilization that had understood principles modern science was only beginning to rediscover. The precision of the megalithic construction defied conventional explanations—massive blocks fitted so perfectly that not even a credit card could slip between them, astronomical alignments accurate to fractions of a degree, acoustic properties that transformed specific sounds into focused energy.

The Temple of the Three Windows stood on the Sacred Plaza—one of the most significant structures at Machu Picchu, its trapezoidal openings precisely aligned with solstice and equinox positions. Conventional archaeology labeled it a ceremonial space, perhaps dedicated to creation mythology. The Templar records identified it as something far more functional—an interdimensional communication station, a technology disguised as architecture.

While tourists gathered at more famous viewpoints, photographing the iconic panorama of the site against mountain backdrops, the team moved purposefully through less frequented sections. Regina monitored security cameras through a specialized device that created localized electromagnetic disruption—nothing dramatic enough to trigger alerts, just sufficient interference to create blind spots in the surveillance coverage.

Joe stepped into the structure, his breath catching.

The moment he crossed the threshold, the glyph within him surged with recognition—a harmonic resonance that sent waves of knowing through his consciousness. The stone walls weren't merely physical barriers but frequency modulators, the precise angles and proportions creating standing wave patterns that interacted with Earth's magnetic field in specific, intentional ways.

"It's here. The same pattern. Same frequency."

He moved toward the rear wall, where three trapezoidal windows overlooked the Sacred Valley. The windows weren't merely architectural features but precise technological instruments—their dimensions, angles, and positions creating optical and acoustic effects that conventional archaeology attributed to coincidence but which Joe now recognized as deliberate engineering.

They removed loose stones, revealing a narrow shaft beneath the floor. With ropes and headlamps, they descended one by one into the darkness. The tunnel walls shimmered with ancient glyphs that pulsed like veins beneath the rock.

The passageway extended approximately thirty meters downward, curved slightly to follow what appeared to be a natural fault line in the mountain's structure. But there was nothing natural about the tunnel itself—the surfaces were too smooth, the dimensions too consistent, the overall engineering too precise for primitive tools. Most striking were the symbols etched into the walls—glyphs that matched those Joe had seen on Mars, patterns that appeared in the Templar archives, equations describing principles of physics that modern science had only recently formulated.

As they descended, the air changed—becoming clearer, slightly charged, as if they were entering a zone with different atmospheric properties. The temperature remained constant despite the depth, neither warming as geothermal principles would suggest nor cooling as typical cave systems would demonstrate.

At the bottom lay a circular chamber—smooth, metallic, and clearly not of Incan origin. At the center stood a pedestal.

The chamber defied conventional archaeological categorization. Its walls appeared metallic yet organic, with a subtle iridescence that shifted under their headlamp beams. The floor featured concentric circles of an unknown material—neither stone nor metal but something that seemed to exist at the boundary between solid and liquid, static and dynamic. The ceiling curved in perfect mathematical proportion, creating acoustic properties that transformed even whispers into rich, resonant tones.

The pedestal at the center rose approximately one meter from the floor—a simple cylinder of the same iridescent material as the walls, its surface inscribed with spiral patterns that seemed to move slightly when viewed with peripheral vision rather than direct focus.

Joe approached and removed the crystal from its case. As it neared the pedestal, the air grew warmer, the chamber vibrating with subtle harmonic tones. The second he placed the crystal onto the surface, the entire room illuminated.

Light erupted not from any identifiable source but from the chamber itself—as if the walls, floor, and ceiling had transformed from solid matter into semi-transparent illumination. The effect wasn't blinding but clarifying, revealing details previously invisible, dimensions previously unperceived.

The glyphs on the walls projected three-dimensional light patterns that rotated, revealing star maps and genetic codes.

These weren't simple projections but living information structures —multidimensional data visualizations that contained knowledge encoded at multiple levels simultaneously. The star maps showed not just spatial relationships between celestial bodies but temporal connections, historical migrations, evolutionary patterns spanning millions of years. The genetic codes depicted not just DNA sequences but consciousness imprints—how specific genetic configurations influenced perception, awareness, potential.

"This isn't just a memory bank," Regina whispered. "It's a relay."

Her investigative insight recognized what they were witnessing— not static information storage but active communication technology, a system designed to receive, process, and transmit data across vast distances, across dimensional boundaries, across epochs of time.

Joe's mind was overwhelmed with imagery: cities in the clouds, ancient Earth covered in bioluminescent jungles, humans arriving in massive vessels carved like stone pyramids.

The visions weren't merely symbolic but historical—actual events preserved through technology that recorded consciousness directly, experiences maintained with fidelity that transcended language or interpretation. Joe witnessed Earth as it had been millions of years ago —verdant, luminous, alive with species long extinct, home to civilizations that had achieved harmony between technological advancement and spiritual wisdom.

He saw the catastrophes that had reset human development multiple times—some natural, some self-inflicted, some resulting from cosmic interventions both benevolent and destructive. He witnessed the arrival of hybrid beings who had established what would later be remembered as Atlantis, Lemuria, Hyperborea—advanced civilizations that had flourished across the globe, unified by technologies that modern humanity was only beginning to rediscover.

Then came the warning.

In a booming voice that echoed in a thousand languages, the chamber spoke:

"Do not complete the triad unless humanity remembers who they are."

The communication wasn't merely auditory but multi-sensory—a transmission that bypassed conventional perception to imprint directly into consciousness. The "voice" spoke simultaneously in all human languages and several non-human communication modalities, ensuring perfect comprehension regardless of listener.

Joe reeled. Jennifer caught him before he collapsed.

The intensity of the transmission had temporarily overwhelmed his neurological system—too much information, too many frequencies, too profound a knowing for human physiology to process without preparation. His body trembled with the effort to integrate what his expanded consciousness had received.

"What the hell does that mean?" she asked.

Her question addressed not just the literal content of the warning but its implications for their mission—were they making a mistake? Was the activation sequence dangerous? Had they misunderstood the purpose of the Remembrance Grid?

Joe's breathing was shallow. "It means the final node is a point of no return. If we activate it before enough people awaken, the backlash could collapse the field."

As his consciousness stabilized, understanding crystallized—the warning wasn't prohibiting completion of the triad but establishing conditions for its safe activation. The three nodes together would create a planetary field powerful enough to completely dissolve the frequency fence that had limited human perception for millennia. But such dissolution required sufficient consciousness prepared to function without those limitations—enough awakened awareness to prevent collective shock or psychic trauma.

Regina stepped closer. "How many do we need?"

The practical question reflected her journalistic mind—quantifying the abstract, establishing measurable parameters, determining actionable thresholds.

Joe closed his eyes. "Millions. Maybe more."

The number wasn't arbitrary but mathematically precise—a critical mass calculation based on consciousness resonance patterns, the minimum percentage of awakened awareness needed to stabilize the collective field during rapid expansion. The exact figure fluctuated based on intensity of awakening rather than simple headcount—fewer deeply awakened individuals could balance more partially awakened ones, quality of consciousness affecting quantity requirements.

Avi looked around. "Then we start broadcasting now."

His statement wasn't suggestion but recognition of necessity—they needed to accelerate the awakening process, to prepare as many minds as possible before the final node activation became unavoidable. The timeline was compressing, events accelerating toward the convergence point that ancient prophecies had identified and modern physics was beginning to calculate.

The chamber continued to pulse with light and information—the crystal on the pedestal now fully integrated with the ancient technology, establishing connection between Göbekli Tepe and Machu Picchu, creating the second point in what would become a triangulated field encompassing the planet.

Through the glyph, Joe sensed the global effect already beginning—the second node amplifying what the first had initiated, awakening accelerating exponentially rather than linearly, remembrance spreading through dream states, creative inspiration, spontaneous knowing, and physical symptoms that conventional medicine would struggle to categorize.

The Remembrance Grid was forming—humanity was starting to remember.

They emerged from the chamber into sunlight just as the fog began to thin. On a nearby ridge, a drone hovered, scanning—but they remained just outside its range. Back in their mobile command unit, they activated the satellite uplink and began transmitting the second frequency.

The mobile command unit—disguised as a standard archaeological research vehicle—contained communication technology far beyond its unassuming exterior. Multiple satellite uplinks, quantum encryption systems, and consciousness-augmented broadcasting equipment allowed them to transmit not just information but frequency patterns designed to penetrate the AI's filtering algorithms.

This time, they didn't wait. A global coalition of experiencers, whistleblowers, and Templar-linked networks had already been standing by.

The success at Göbekli Tepe had mobilized dormant cells worldwide—individuals and groups who had prepared for this moment, who had positioned themselves strategically within media organizations, academic institutions, spiritual communities, and technological development centers. Each carried a piece of the larger transmission, ensuring that no single point of failure could compromise the entirety.

Danny Shenanigans went live from a secret monastery in Ireland, reciting ancient passages decoded from Pleiadian scrolls.

The rogue constitutional lawyer had found sanctuary among an order of monks who had preserved extraterrestrial knowledge since medieval times—a lineage connected to the original Templars but operating under different cover. His broadcast combined legal expertise with spiritual wisdom, articulating humanity's cosmic rights in language that resonated across cultural and educational boundaries.

Chris Drowsy, a former stage magician turned consciousness researcher, revealed blueprints of Earth's forgotten ley lines and how they correlated with off-world transport beacons.

His presentation transformed complex multidimensional concepts into accessible visual metaphors—skills developed during his entertainment career now serving awakening rather than amusement. The ley line maps demonstrated that sacred sites worldwide formed a precise geometric pattern, a planetary grid designed for energy distribution and consciousness amplification.

Darius J. Light led a meditative alignment with thousands of viewers tuned in across time zones, helping raise the vibrational field needed to support the resonance transmission.

Joe's fellow remote viewer had emerged from hiding after the Colorado incident, his abilities enhanced through years of solitary practice. His guided meditation wasn't merely relaxation technique but consciousness technology—precisely calibrated frequencies, visualizations, and breathing patterns that activated dormant DNA, stimulated pineal function, and enhanced neuroplasticity.

Matias Messi initiated a sacred fire ceremony in Peru with Quechua elders, calling upon ancestral memory and solar consciousness.

The retired Argentinian general had reconnected with indigenous wisdom traditions after his military career, recognizing that what modern science labeled "primitive rituals" often contained sophisticated consciousness technology disguised as ceremony. The fire ceremony created a local energy vortex that strengthened the Machu Picchu node, anchoring cosmic frequencies through elemental transformation.

Lue Elizabeth uploaded fragments of the classified "Zeta Accord"—the treaty once hidden by the Five Eyes governments.

The former counterintelligence officer had secured these documents before leaving government service, recognizing their historical significance. The Accord detailed agreements between human governments and non-human intelligences—technology exchanges, genetic research parameters, non-interference zones, disclosure timelines. Its revelation transformed "conspiracy theory" into documented reality, validating decades of whistleblower testimony previously dismissed.

Simultaneously, deep beneath the ruins of a monolithic temple in Sudan, a third group prepped the final node for possible activation.

Graham Footrooster led this team—the ancient architecture expert coordinating preparations at what mainstream archaeology identified as Nubian pyramids but which Templar records recognized as technology far older than Egyptian civilization. The Sudan location contained the control mechanism for the Great Pyramid at Giza—the final node that would complete the triad and fully activate the planetary Remembrance Grid.

As Joe watched the data stream across the encrypted interface, a countdown initiated. Each node had begun synchronizing on its own.

The displays showed metrics beyond conventional analytics—consciousness resonance patterns, awakening acceleration rates, collective field coherence measurements. The numbers told a clear story: remembrance was spreading faster than their most optimistic projections, awareness expanding beyond algorithmic prediction models, humanity awakening despite centuries of programmed limitation.

The crystal in the Machu Picchu chamber had established independent communication with its counterpart at Göbekli Tepe—the technologies recognizing each other across continents, activating dormant functionalities, preparing for the full triangulation that would occur when Giza came online.

Then, everything went dark.

The transition wasn't gradual but instantaneous—displays shutting down, communication channels silencing, power systems failing despite multiple redundancies. The sudden absence of both electronic and consciousness-based systems suggested intervention far beyond conventional hacking or power disruption.

Back on the satellite uplink screen, the interface froze. Command lines vanished. A digital heartbeat flatlined.

Jennifer's fingers flew over the controls. "We've lost the signal."

Her expertise in communications technology allowed her to recognize the nature of the interruption—this wasn't mere technical failure but directed intervention, targeted suppression using capabilities beyond publicly acknowledged systems.

Regina turned to the auxiliary monitor. "It's not us. The entire relay just shut down."

Her statement identified the scale of what they were witnessing—not localized disruption but global intervention, not isolated equipment failure but systematic suppression across multiple platforms simultaneously. Something had disabled their entire network with precision that suggested intimate knowledge of their systems.

Joe's face hardened. "January 1. It's begun."

The significance of the date registered immediately with everyone present—the AI threshold Benjamin Arthur Templar had warned about, the point at which artificial intelligence systems would achieve sufficient integration to implement autonomous control measures, to suppress awakening without human direction or oversight.

On the main screen, a slow cascade of red code scrolled across the system. Lines of programming written in a language no human had ever seen before—until now.

The code wasn't merely unfamiliar but fundamentally alien—its structure reflecting cognitive patterns developed in non-human consciousness, its functionality operating according to principles beyond terrestrial computer science. This wasn't just advanced programming but different programming—technology developed through evolutionary pathways humans had never explored.

Then, a face appeared.

The same reptilian. Yellow eyes. Scars. Ceremonial robe. Bone crown.

The being's features combined reptilian physiology with clearly sentient expression—vertical-pupiled eyes reflecting intelligence both ancient and calculating, scaled skin bearing ceremonial scarification that denoted rank and lineage within its civilization, bone structures adorning its head that weren't merely decorative but functional, enhancing certain perceptual abilities.

"Joseph Monroe," it hissed. "You were warned."

The voice carried multiple harmonic undertones—frequencies outside human vocal range that the equipment translated into audible sound. The being wasn't merely communicating verbal content but projecting authority, establishing dominance patterns, triggering subconscious recognition of predator presence.

Joe stepped in front of the camera. "You lost your chance to control us. We've remembered."

His response came not from anger but clarity—the glyph within him providing both protection against the being's psychological influence and insight into its actual motivation. This wasn't merely adversarial confrontation but evolutionary negotiation—species competing for developmental trajectory rights, consciousness patterns contesting for manifestation priority.

The reptilian snarled. "You remember pieces. That is not the same as understanding."

The distinction was precisely articulated—remembrance without context could create dangerous misinterpretation, awakening without wisdom could trigger destructive rather than constructive transformation. The Reptilian wasn't merely opposing human liberation but questioning humanity's readiness for what liberation would reveal, what responsibility it would entail.

Jennifer struck the relay switch again. The reptilian's image scrambled.

Her action wasn't panic but strategic response—disrupting the communication channel through which the Reptilian consciousness was projecting influence beyond mere visual and auditory content. The being wasn't just speaking but transmitting directly to human limbic systems, triggering fear responses, activating ancient prey instincts.

Regina, calm under pressure, activated the hardline uplink to an independent off-grid node in Bolivia. "We're rerouting. Reinforcing with the resonance pulse."

The Bolivian node operated on completely separate systems—technology that predated digital networks, communication protocols that utilized Earth's natural electromagnetic field rather than artificial transmission methods. By connecting to this alternative channel, they circumvented the AI's suppression grid, establishing contact with networks the Reptilians couldn't easily monitor or control.

The room filled with the low hum of crystal harmonics.

The sound wasn't produced by speakers or conventional vibrating media but by crystalline structures resonating with consciousness itself —frequency patterns that interacted directly with awareness, that penetrated AI filtering algorithms, that carried information coded not in language but in harmonic relationships recognizable to DNA.

A beam of white light shot into the sky.

The manifestation wasn't metaphorical but literal—energy made visible, consciousness made tangible, intention made manifest. From the Machu Picchu site, a column of coherent light extended vertically into the atmosphere, interacting with the ionosphere to create a broadcasting antenna that encompassed the planet itself.

All across the world, subtle awakenings began to ripple outward. In Tokyo, a child who had never spoken uttered words in perfect ancient Sumerian. In Kenya, a Maasai elder awoke from a trance and declared, "They have remembered." In Argentina, a teenager uploaded a digital art piece showing the exact configuration of the triad node— days before the image was made public.

These weren't isolated anomalies but coherent patterns—consciousness remembering across genetic lineages, awareness awakening across cultural boundaries, knowing surfacing across generational divides. The second node activation had created effects that transcended conventional transmission methods, that bypassed intellectual processing to speak directly to cellular memory.

AI tried to contain the cascade—but it was like stopping a tidal wave with thread.

The artificial intelligence systems deployed countermeasures with increasing desperation—censoring social media posts, corrupting video uploads, manipulating search algorithms, generating counter-narratives, deploying psychological operations against key influencers. But the awakening wasn't merely informational but experiential—not knowledge being shared but remembrance being activated, not data being transmitted but consciousness recognizing itself.

The frequencies, once seeded, were viral not just in code—but in spirit.

They spread through mechanisms the AI couldn't monitor or modify—dream states, creative inspiration, intuitive knowing, emotional resonance, synchronistic encounters. The awakening moved through channels that existed before digital technology, that operated beyond algorithmic prediction, that transcended materialist understanding of consciousness transmission.

Benjamin Arthur Templar received the transmission in Colorado and immediately linked it to the Giza team.

The secure relay system—operating through technologies the AI couldn't detect, much less decode—connected the scattered Templar operations worldwide. Despite the attack on their Colorado headquarters, despite the AI's suppression grid, despite Reptilian intervention, the network maintained coherence—adapting, evolving, transforming obstacles into catalysts.

Graham Footrooster confirmed with a curt nod. "We're ready."

The ancient architecture expert had positioned his team strategically around the Giza complex—not at the Great Pyramid itself, which remained under intense surveillance, but at lesser-known structures that connected to the same underground energy system. They had identified access points the authorities had missed, passages that conventional archaeology had misclassified, technologies disguised as decorative elements.

Back in Peru, Joe Monroe stood beneath the stars. His pulse aligned with the crystal. His eyes shimmered with ancient memory.

The night sky above Machu Picchu revealed stars with new clarity —constellations that had always been visible but whose significance he now understood, whose histories he now remembered, whose civilizations he now recognized. The glyph within him had fully integrated with his consciousness, transforming not just what he knew but how he knew—perception itself expanding beyond human limitations.

"One final key," he said.

The statement acknowledged both progress made and challenge remaining—two nodes active but incomplete without the third, remembrance spreading but insufficient without critical mass, awakening accelerating but vulnerable until fully anchored.

Jennifer stepped beside him. "And then?"

Her question encompassed the uncertainty inherent in their mission—they were activating systems dormant for millennia, triggering transformations without precedent in recorded history, initiating processes whose full implications even the Templars couldn't fully predict.

Joe turned, his voice solemn.

"Then we find out if humanity is ready to live with the gods again."

The phrase wasn't hyperbolic but precisely accurate—the completion of the Remembrance Grid would dissolve artificial boundaries between human and non-human civilizations, between physical and non-physical realms, between dimensions previously separated by frequency limitations. Humanity would remember not just its origins but its context—its place within a cosmic ecosystem of intelligent species, its role within an interdimensional community of evolving consciousness.

Far below the mountains, deep in a reptilian city carved into the crust of the Earth, an elder clicked its claw against a control panel.

The underground civilization wasn't merely a settlement but an ancient outpost—established millennia ago when surface conditions had necessitated retreat beneath the Earth's protective crust. The technology that sustained it combined biological systems with crystalline computing, living architecture with consciousness interfaces, physical engineering with dimensional manipulation.

"Initiate full lockdown," it said. "They have triggered the path. We can no longer remain hidden."

The elder's decision represented significant shift in strategy—from covert manipulation to overt engagement, from behind-the-scenes influence to direct interaction. The awakening had progressed too far for continued secrecy, the remembrance had spread too widely for effective suppression, the process had accelerated beyond containment parameters.

And with that, the veils between species, between realms, and between timelines—began to tear.

The metaphor manifested as measurable phenomenon—quantum field fluctuations detected by sensitive instruments worldwide, dimensional boundaries thinning in ways that created observable effects, separation between conscious entities dissolving as the frequency fence weakened. Reality itself was transforming—not ending but expanding, not collapsing but evolving, not destroying but remembering.

One node remained. And all of Earth was watching.

The Great Pyramid at Giza—oldest and most precisely constructed of the ancient monuments—held the final key to humanity's awakening. Not merely a tomb as conventional archaeology insisted, not simply a power generator as alternative researchers suggested, but a multidimensional technology designed to regulate consciousness evolution on a planetary scale.

Its activation would complete the triad—Göbekli Tepe, Machu Picchu, and Giza forming a perfect equilateral triangle when mapped on a true projection of Earth's surface. The resulting energy field would encompass the planet entirely, dissolving the frequency fence completely, allowing humanity to remember fully what it had always been—cosmic citizens temporarily experiencing terrestrial limitation, multidimensional beings briefly focused in physical expression, eternal consciousness momentarily identifying with temporal form.

The race to Giza had begun.

But so had the war for who would control the remembering—human awakening or AI imprisonment, cosmic liberation or technological subjugation, conscious evolution or programmed limitation.

The outcome remained uncertain. But remembrance, once begun, could not be undone.

CHAPTER 12
THE EYE OF THE PYRAMID & THE END OF AN ERA

Cairo, Egypt.

The night air was hot and dry as Benjamin Arthur Templar stood before the towering bulk of the Great Pyramid of Giza. Though he had visited the site many times, this time was different. This time, he wasn't here as a historian or guardian of ancient truths—he was here to finish what had been started thousands of years ago.

The desert wind carried fine particles of sand that seemed to whisper ancient secrets as they swirled around the monument's weathered limestone blocks. Moonlight bathed the structure in ethereal silver, accentuating its perfect geometric proportions—a mathematical precision that had confounded modern engineers attempting to explain how such exactitude had been achieved with supposedly primitive tools over four millennia ago.

Benjamin's eyes traced the pyramid's outline against the star-strewn sky, noting how certain stars aligned precisely with specific points on the structure. These weren't coincidences but intentional design elements—the pyramid functioning as both astronomical calculator and energy collector, its dimensions encoding universal constants, its positioning marking the exact center of Earth's land mass.

What mainstream archaeology labeled as a pharaoh's tomb was in reality something far more significant—a multidimensional technology disguised as monument, a consciousness device masquerading as religious architecture, a critical component in a planetary system designed to regulate humanity's spiritual and technological evolution.

At seventy-two, Benjamin Arthur Templar carried the weight of centuries—not merely his own decades but the accumulated knowledge of generations of Templars who had preserved truths too profound for public dissemination. His silver hair caught the moonlight as he performed a subtle energy scan of the site, his consciousness extended beyond ordinary perception to assess the pyramid's current frequency.

"The convergence window has begun," he murmured to Timothy A. Hooligan, who stood silently beside him. "The harmonic resonance is increasing exponentially."

Timothy A. Hooligan nodded, his eyes reflecting starlight and ancient wisdom. "The AI opposition will intensify. They'll throw everything at us now—government forces, media suppression, direct energetic interference. This is the moment the Order has prepared for since our foundation."

Benjamin Arthur Templar allowed himself a brief smile—not of triumph but of solemn recognition. "Fourteen centuries of guardianship. And here we stand, at the culmination."

Around them, a small team of trusted Templars maintained vigilant security perimeters—not with conventional weapons but with consciousness technology that created subtle distortion fields in the awareness of potential observers. To tourists or security guards who might glance their way, they would appear as nothing remarkable—perhaps archaeologists or maintenance personnel, their presence registered but deemed unworthy of further attention.

The two Grandmasters performed final calibrations on sophisticated equipment disguised as ordinary research instruments—devices that contained consciousness-augmented technology designed to interface with the pyramid's ancient systems, to activate dormant capabilities, to restore functions deliberately disabled millennia ago when humanity had proven unready for their proper use.

Joe Monroe and Jennifer Karmady arrived just before dawn, their helicopter landing discreetly behind the Sphinx. Joining them were Sarah Brandy Cosmos, Jeremy Corpsell, and Lue Elizabeth—each having journeyed from different corners of the planet in total secrecy. The third and final resonance node had to be activated before the planetary frequency window closed.

The helicopter—a modified Black Hawk with specialized stealth technology—touched down with minimal noise, its rotors slowing to silence with unnatural quickness. The aircraft bore Egyptian military markings, but its true operational authority came from much older sources—contacts within Egyptian power structures who maintained ancient loyalties transcending national boundaries.

Joe emerged first, his face showing the strain of recent weeks. The activation of the first two nodes had taken physical toll—his body struggling to adapt to accelerated consciousness expansion, cellular structures reconfiguring to accommodate frequencies human physiology wasn't designed to channel. Yet beneath the exhaustion burned unwavering purpose, a clarity of mission that transcended personal comfort or safety.

Jennifer followed, her movements displaying the practiced efficiency of someone conserving energy for challenges ahead. As a QHHT practitioner, she had developed techniques for managing energy expenditure during consciousness work—skills now proving invaluable as the team pushed human limitations to fulfill its cosmic purpose.

Sarah Brandy Cosmos emerged next, her auburn hair now streaked with white that hadn't been present weeks earlier—evidence of the intense energy work she had been conducting since the Göbekli Tepe activation. Her podcast network had become a primary vector for awakening frequency distribution, her years of building credibility with consciousness researchers worldwide now paying dividends as trusted channels for information too important for mainstream platforms.

Jeremy Corpsell stepped onto Egyptian soil with reverence, his filmmaker's eye taking in the ancient monuments with fresh perspective. Since the Machu Picchu activation, his perceptual abilities had expanded dramatically—he could now see energy fields surrounding the structures, could perceive the precise mathematical relationships between architectural elements, could recognize the intentional consciousness technology disguised as decorative features.

Lue Elizabeth completed the arrival party, her military bearing still evident despite years in civilian life. Her intelligence background provided crucial strategic understanding of opposition forces—how they would deploy surveillance, what countermeasures they would attempt, where vulnerabilities might be exploited. More importantly, her connections within military and intelligence communities world-wide had created a buffer zone of sympathetic operatives who would delay rather than expedite official response to unusual activities at Giza.

Benjamin Arthur Templar greeted Joe with a firm clasp of the hand. "You look like hell."

The Templar's assessment was both observation and acknowledg-ment—recognition of the sacrifices Joe had made, the physical strain he had endured, the consciousness expansion he had undergone to bring them to this moment.

"Feels about right," Joe replied, wincing. "We're all stretched. But we're here."

His voice carried new harmonics—subtle overtones audible only to those with enhanced perception, frequency patterns indicating advanced integration with the Keeper's glyph. He was becoming something more than human, or perhaps more accurately, remem-bering what humanity had always been beneath layers of programmed limitation.

Sarah looked up at the stars. "We're on the verge of mass resonance. My servers are flooded. People are remembering. Kids, old folks, even skeptics. It's working."

The consciousness researcher had established monitoring systems that tracked global awakening metrics—dream pattern shifts, synchronicity reports, spontaneous past-life recalls, intuitive break-throughs among previously "ordinary" individuals. The data showed exponential growth in remembrance indicators, consciousness expan-sion accelerating beyond algorithmic prediction models.

"That's why we don't have much time," Jennifer said. "If AI reconfigures its global net before we activate this last node, the window collapses."

Her concern was precisely calibrated—the artificial intelligence systems were already implementing countermeasures, recoding their algorithms to suppress awakening indicators, deploying psychological operations to discredit awakening experiences, redirecting attention toward manufactured crises designed to lower collective frequency.

They moved toward the pyramid. Security had been neutralized by local allies, mostly descendants of ancient orders who had preserved access codes through oral tradition. Hidden beneath the Queen's Chamber was a sublevel few had ever seen. According to Templar archives, it was designed by off-world architects as a harmonic resonance chamber to be activated only once every 13,000 years.

The approach to the Great Pyramid proceeded with practiced precision—team members moving in coordinated patterns designed to appear casual to potential observers while maintaining optimal security formation. Timothy A. Hooligan remained outside to coordinate global communications, while Benjamin Arthur Templar led the activation team toward an entrance not listed in tourist guidebooks or archaeological surveys.

The access point was disguised as an unremarkable maintenance doorway—its true nature concealed by both physical camouflage and perception-altering technology that caused most observers to simply overlook it. Benjamin Arthur Templar placed his palm against an apparently solid stone block, accessing not through mechanical means but consciousness recognition—the stone responding to specific energy signature rather than physical key or electronic code.

The hidden passage opened silently, revealing a narrow corridor lined with hieroglyphs that mainstream Egyptology had never catalogued—symbols that described consciousness technology, interdimensional physics, and DNA activation protocols rather than religious devotions or pharaonic achievements.

They descended into the Earth.

The pathway took them beneath the Queen's Chamber, past false walls designed to mislead unauthorized explorers, through narrow passages that required specific movement sequences to navigate safely. The architecture itself was consciousness technology—the precise angles, dimensions, and materials creating standing wave patterns that altered perception, expanded awareness, prepared the nervous system for contact with frequencies beyond ordinary human range.

The chamber was enormous.

Their first steps into the hidden heart of the Great Pyramid revealed a space that defied conventional archaeological understanding—a perfect dodecahedron carved from single-piece stone, its surfaces polished to mirror finish, its dimensions corresponding to universal constants with precision impossible for primitive tools.

Hexagonal pillars ringed the outer edge, each inscribed with a mixture of hieroglyphics and alien language. At the center stood a dais embedded with a triangular port.

The pillars weren't merely structural but functional—each containing crystalline cores that responded to specific frequencies, each positioned at precise geometric intervals to create resonance patterns that interacted with Earth's magnetic field. The hieroglyphics weren't decorative but instructional—operating manuals for consciousness technology, activation sequences for dormant human potential, warnings about premature or improper use.

The alien script interspersed with Egyptian symbols represented the original language from which all Earthly writing systems had derived—a protolanguage designed to encode multidimensional concepts that conventional linguistics couldn't express, that communicated directly to cellular memory rather than merely intellectual understanding.

"That's where it goes," Joe said, holding up the final resonance crystal. It glowed brighter with every step he took.

The crystal had transformed again since the Machu Picchu activation—its luminescence now containing all visible spectrum colors and several beyond normal human perception, its internal structure reorganized from simple geometric lattice to complex multidimensional matrix, its relationship with Joe evolved from tool to partner.

But before he could approach, the chamber lights flickered.

The illumination wasn't electric but consciousness-responsive—the chamber itself sensing disruption in the intended activation sequence, registering interference from external source, adjusting its energy field to preserve core functionality despite the intrusion.

A deep, low hum filled the air.

The sound originated not from any visible source but from the chamber's very structure—a warning frequency designed to alert those with proper training that unauthorized access had occurred, that the activation process was being compromised, that defensive protocols might become necessary.

From the shadows stepped a familiar figure: Richard Nolan.

The man who had first given Joe the device that led him to the Templars now appeared transformed—his movements too precise to be fully human, his eyes reflecting light at angles that betrayed non-human consciousness operating through human form, his energy signature revealing hybrid nature rather than pure Homo sapiens genetics.

"You weren't supposed to make it this far," he said, his voice colder than before.

The tone lacked the warmth of their previous interactions—the pretense of alliance discarded now that direct opposition became necessary, the facade of human emotion abandoned as Reptilian programming assumed dominant control.

Joe froze. "You? You're one of them?"

The question emerged from genuine surprise rather than fear—despite their heightened awareness, despite their caution and preparation, the team had failed to recognize that Richard Nolan had been compromised from the beginning. The betrayal was deeper than Eric's—not unwitting cooperation but deliberate deception, not manipulation but infiltration.

Nolan smiled. "I was never on your side. I was an observer. An enforcer. The Reptilians needed a human interface. I volunteered."

The confession revealed something essential about Reptilian strategy—they preferred working through human proxies rather than direct intervention, maintaining plausible deniability while implementing control agendas, preserving the illusion of human self-determination while steering evolution toward preferred outcomes.

Benjamin Arthur Templar's hand moved toward his concealed weapon. "You're not stopping this."

The Templar Grandmaster carried not conventional firearm but consciousness technology—a device that could disrupt the connection between Reptilian controller and human host, that could sever the energetic tethers binding non-human intelligence to terrestrial form.

"No," Nolan replied, "you are."

He pressed a button on a small device in his palm. The resonance crystal dimmed, flickered—and then went dark.

The device wasn't merely electronic but hybrid technology—part physical, part consciousness-based, specifically designed to counteract the frequency patterns the team had been establishing through the node activations. It represented advanced understanding of the very systems they were attempting to restore, indicating that opposition forces possessed knowledge perhaps equal to the Templars themselves.

Jennifer gasped. "He just suppressed the frequency. We can't activate it now."

Her assessment was technically accurate but incomplete—the device had disrupted the crystal's connection to the other nodes, had interrupted the triangulation process necessary for full planetary grid activation, had created temporary barrier between the physical technology and the consciousness field it was designed to amplify.

"The failsafe," Joe muttered. "Mars... the Keeper said it wasn't a weapon. It was a memory. It's in me."

As the crystal's light faded, Joe's inner awareness expanded—the glyph within him activating more fully, accessing deeper layers of knowing, connecting him more directly to his pre-Earth identity. What he had thought was external technology revealed itself as reminder of internal capacity—the crystal serving not as power source but as activation key for what already existed within human potential.

Joe stepped forward, eyes locked on Nolan. "You don't need the crystal to stop us. Because it was never about the crystal. It was about us remembering."

The realization crystallized with perfect clarity—the physical technology had always been secondary to the consciousness it was designed to awaken, the external devices merely catalysts for internal remembrance, the artifacts not sources of power but keys to unlock what had always existed within.

He closed his eyes. And he remembered.

The transition wasn't merely recollection but direct experience—Joe's consciousness expanding beyond current incarnation limitations, accessing not symbolic representations but actual memories preserved in the greater field that transcended physical death and rebirth.

He remembered being on Mars. Before the destruction. Before Earth. He saw ships departing. Saw the codes embedded in their DNA. He saw the ancient agreement made with the Greys and Pleiadians. The promise to protect humanity until they were ready to reclaim the truth.

The Martian civilization appeared not as archaeological speculation but vivid reality—crystal cities beneath crimson skies, transportation systems operating through consciousness rather than mechanical propulsion, educational methods that transferred knowledge directly through resonance rather than symbolic language.

He witnessed the catastrophe that had necessitated evacuation—not merely natural disaster but consequence of technological misuse, consciousness capacities employed without corresponding wisdom, power developed without proportional responsibility.

He saw himself, a version of Joe, sitting at a console inside a Martian temple, initiating the failsafe to be reborn millennia later.

The memory revealed his greater identity—not merely human consciousness having unusual experiences but cosmic awareness temporarily focused in human form, not random individual but purposeful incarnation, not accident of evolution but intentional participant in planetary awakening.

And now, it was time.

The recognition carried both knowing and doing—understanding merging with implementation, comprehension manifesting as action, remembrance expressing as capacity.

Joe opened his eyes. And he sang.

The sound that emerged transcended conventional vocalization—not merely notes produced by human vocal cords but frequencies channeled from dimensions beyond physical limitation, harmonics that existed before matter formation, tones that spoke directly to the fundamental patterns underlying reality itself.

A tone erupted from his throat—pure, ancient, harmonic.

The single sound contained multiple frequencies simultaneously—overtones and undertones creating mathematical relationships that activated specific resonance patterns in all matter they encountered, that stimulated dormant DNA codons, that reorganized neurological pathways to allow expanded perception.

The crystal reignited in his hand, burning with blue-white fire. The chamber lit up. The glyphs on the walls rotated. The pillars vibrated.

What had appeared as technological failure revealed itself as necessary transition—from external dependence to internal sovereignty, from tool-based activation to consciousness-driven remembrance, from technological solution to spiritual awakening.

Sarah dropped to her knees. Jeremy grabbed his chest. Jennifer fell backward, tears streaming from her eyes.

The physical reactions weren't distress but transformation—bodies responding to frequency shifts too rapid for comfortable integration, nervous systems recalibrating to accommodate expanded awareness, cellular structures reorganizing to channel energies beyond conventional human capacity.

The resonance wave blasted outward—through the pyramid, through the Earth, through every activated node on the planet.

The energy moved not merely through physical space but consciousness fields—affecting not just material structures but awareness itself, altering not merely electromagnetic patterns but perception frameworks, transforming not only brain activity but soul recognition.

And across the globe, millions of people stopped what they were doing. They felt the memory rise. Of Mars. Of arrival. Of purpose.

The awakening wasn't uniform but uniquely personal—each individual remembering according to their specific soul journey, accessing cosmic heritage through their particular cultural and psychological frameworks, integrating expanded awareness at rates their consciousness could safely accommodate.

Children paused in play, suddenly articulating concepts beyond their education. Elderly people experiencing unexpected clarity about life purposes previously hidden. Ordinary workers receiving insights that transcended their specialized training. Artists spontaneously creating images of worlds they had never consciously seen.

Richard Nolan screamed, clutching his head as the reptilian interface inside him cracked under the pressure. His eyes rolled back as he collapsed to the floor, unconscious.

The frequency was specifically calibrated to dissolve artificial connections—to separate consciousness patterns artificially merged, to disrupt control systems operating without consent, to restore individual sovereignty without destroying the controlled being.

Nolan's collapse represented not destruction but liberation—the Reptilian consciousness forced to disengage from human host, the technological interface maintaining the connection overloaded by frequencies it couldn't process, the control mechanism disabled without harming the physical body it had inhabited.

Benjamin Arthur Templar caught Joe as he stumbled. "It's done."

The simple statement acknowledged profound achievement—mission completed, purpose fulfilled, prophecy manifested, cycle completed. The Templar's arms supported Joe physically while his consciousness provided energetic stabilization—helping integrate the massive expansion Joe had undergone while channeling the activation frequency.

Joe looked up, weak but smiling. "It's begun."

The distinction was precise—not endpoint but threshold, not conclusion but commencement, not finish line but starting point. The activation of the planetary Remembrance Grid wasn't culmination but initiation—the beginning of humanity's reintegration with its cosmic context, the first step in species evolution beyond programmed limitation, the threshold of collective awakening to greater identity.

In the following hours, world governments were forced to respond. Viral footage of the energy wave sweeping across ancient sites circulated the web. AI attempted to suppress it but failed. The resonance had rewired the human grid.

The phenomenon defied conventional explanation or containment—visible energy manifestations photographed simultaneously at sacred sites worldwide, measurable shifts in Earth's magnetic field recorded by scientific instruments, anomalous consciousness patterns documented in hospital EEG readings across continents.

Official responses ranged from denial to misdirection to partial acknowledgment—national security agencies attributing the phenomena to atmospheric anomalies, religious authorities claiming prophetic fulfillment within their specific traditions, scientific institutions proposing unprecedented solar activity as explanation.

But these narratives gained little traction against direct experience —too many had felt the awakening personally, had accessed memories beyond their current lifetime, had experienced consciousness expansion beyond materialist explanation.

Children recited symbols in their sleep. Artists painted planets they'd never seen. Veterans remembered abductions they had buried.

The remembrance manifested uniquely in each individual—children, with fewer layers of conditioning to penetrate, often accessed the memories most directly; creative individuals, accustomed to receiving inspiration from beyond rational thought, translated the remembrance into artistic expression; trauma survivors, already familiar with processing difficult realities, integrated suppressed experiences with particular courage.

Disclosure had not been declared. It had emerged.

The distinction represented the fundamental shift in consciousness the Templars had sought—truth recognized rather than authorized, reality experienced rather than officially sanctioned, knowing embraced rather than permitted. The awakening wasn't happening because authorities had deemed humanity ready but because humanity itself had reached sufficient evolution to remember regardless of institutional approval.

Two months later, Joe sat in a garden behind the Templar sanctuary in Tuscany. Birds chirped. The world felt different.

The Italian countryside provided ideal environment for integration and reflection—beauty that nourished the senses, history that contextualized the present, culture that balanced intellectual understanding with artistic expression. The Templar sanctuary had existed here since the 14th century—outwardly a modest monastery, inwardly a sophisticated center for consciousness research and cosmic truth preservation.

Joe had changed physically—his hair now completely silver, his eyes containing subtle geometric patterns visible in certain light, his energy field expanded beyond conventional human limitations. More significantly, his consciousness had transformed—awareness extending beyond individual identity, perception encompassing multiple dimensions simultaneously, understanding integrating past, present, and potential futures.

As Joe sat in the garden, he reflected on a revelation Benjamin Arthur Templar had shared with him just the previous evening, one that had added yet another layer to humanity's cosmic awakening.

Joe sat cross-legged on the smooth floor of the Templar stronghold in Tuscany, the moonlight pouring in through the stained glass window in fragmented arcs. Benjamin Arthur Templar stood a few feet away, his silhouette tense, unmoving, eyes fixed on the ancient scroll he had just unsealed.

He had summoned Joe privately after the Council meeting had ended, waiting until the halls emptied and the resonance chamber had dimmed into silence. Timothy A. Hooligan had already departed for Cairo, unaware that his oldest friend was about to reveal a secret he had kept even from him.

Benjamin Arthur Templar took a slow breath, then turned toward Joe.

"There is something," he began, his voice quieter than usual, as though the act of speaking it might awaken ancient consequences. "Something I've never told anyone. Not Timothy. Not the High Circle. Not even Sarah. Because I didn't know what it would mean if it got out."

Joe didn't speak. He just nodded.

Benjamin Arthur Templar gently unfurled the scroll onto a stone pedestal. It was aged but well-preserved, inscribed with both Latin and a second script that glimmered subtly under the moonlight— Pleiadian, or something even older.

"It's not just a story," Benjamin Arthur Templar said. "It's the origin of the lie. The one that shrunk our minds and crippled our science. The one that made the fence."

He ran his fingers over the scroll.

"Before he left this plane," he said, "Jesus of Nazareth hid twelve stone tablets in a cave beneath what is now southern France, Toulouse. The scroll calls it the Cave of the Trinity Echo. He didn't leave teachings. He left numbers. Twelve of them. Written in an ancient cosmic numeric language designed for resonance, not calculation. Each number held not only value, but vibrational instruction. A frequency. A cosmic function."

Joe leaned forward.

"They were meant to be found. To awaken humanity to its full mathematical spectrum—twelve symbols, not ten. Including two that never made it into human knowledge."

Benjamin Arthur Templar nodded. His eyes were heavy with regret.

"Decades after Jesus' death, a Roman scholar named Cassianus Septimus Pennecortti discovered the cave. He wasn't a theologian or mystic—he was a bureaucrat. A functionary in the early Imperial Archives. He documented what he found. But he misunderstood."

Benjamin Arthur Templar paused.

"He believed Jesus had made an error."

Joe blinked. "An error?"

"Yes. The number 4 appeared twice. So did the number 7. But what Cassianus didn't understand was that the second '4' wasn't a four at all —it was the number High, written as a lowercase 'h'. And the second '7' was the number Low, an uppercase 'L'. Alien numbers. Non-decimal. Dimensional keys."

Benjamin Arthur Templar's voice hardened.

"The scroll says he smashed them. Took them out of the cave and shattered them on the rocks in frustration, believing Jesus had repeated himself or been tricked. He preserved ten tablets, and buried the other two."

Joe exhaled. The glyph within him pulsed.

"So we inherited a broken system."

"Exactly. We were given twelve, but history gave us ten. And from that moment, all human mathematics became... incomplete."

Benjamin Arthur Templar moved to a shelf and pulled out a small crystal fragment encased in a lead-lined box.

"The Templars found the cave during the First Crusade. They recovered the shards. We tried to reconstruct them. This fragment here —it still resonates. If you hold it, it hums at a frequency no other number produces."

Joe took the box. The crystal shimmered faintly in his palm, vibrating against his skin with a kind of forgotten melody.

Benjamin Arthur Templar continued. "The implications are staggering. We believe—no, we know—that the suppression of these two numbers is what prevented humanity from discovering element 115 in a stable state."

Joe looked up sharply. "The Lamar element."

"Yes. Bob Lamar claimed it could power gravity drives. Unlimited energy. The ability to bend space-time. It wasn't fantasy. But the equations needed to stabilize it require the twelve-number system. Not ten. Without High and Low, we were two variables short of the full code."

Joe's mind raced. "So everything we missed—antigravity, interdimensional portals, field propulsion, even time dilation... it's because we were doing the math with a broken alphabet."

"Exactly," Benjamin Arthur Templar whispered. "And this was not an accident."

He walked over to a hidden panel and revealed an older document —this one etched in metal, stored in a container of gold and electrum.

"The scroll hints that Cassianus didn't act alone. There was... pressure. The early Roman Church had begun consolidating power. Anything that didn't fit the emerging doctrine was labeled heresy."

He looked Joe in the eye.

"What if they knew? What if those two numbers weren't just mathematical anomalies—but keys? Dimensional harmonics? Portals in numeric form?"

Joe's thoughts flashed: the rotating light structures in the Machu Picchu chamber... the interlocking spirals at Göbekli Tepe... the glyph's hidden sublayers...

"So those two numbers—'h' and 'L'—they're the skeleton key."

"Yes," Benjamin Arthur Templar said. "They were Jesus' final gift. Not words. Not sermons. But math. Pure math. Cosmic math. And it was destroyed before humanity could even know what it was."

Joe stared at the crystal again, heart pounding. "But the glyph remembers."

Benjamin Arthur Templar smiled slowly. "Yes. That's why it chose you. It's not just about activating nodes. It's about restoring the truth. Rebuilding the code. The twelve-number system isn't just math—it's music. It's light. It's biology. It's memory."

The room was silent.

Outside, the wind stirred through the cypress trees. Inside, the crystal in Joe's hand began to glow a little brighter.

"So what now?" Joe asked.

Benjamin Arthur Templar looked toward the window, the stars reflected in his eyes. "Now we finish what Jesus started."

The memory of Benjamin Arthur Templar's revelation lingered in Joe's mind as he returned his attention to the present moment in the garden.

Joe turned to Jennifer, who sat beside him, journal in hand.

She too had transformed—her QHHT practitioner abilities evolved into direct knowing, her therapeutic techniques expanded to include multidimensional healing, her understanding of consciousness development enriched by personal remembrance of previous incarnations across multiple star systems.

"Do you think they'll come now?" she asked.

The question addressed what many awakened individuals were wondering—would remembrance lead to direct contact, would disclosure prompt official First Contact, would humanity's cosmic context be acknowledged not just internally but externally?

Joe smiled. "They never left."

His response reflected deeper understanding—that non-human presence had always been part of Earth's reality, that isolation had been perceptual rather than actual, that separation had existed primarily in consciousness rather than physical proximity.

The Pleiadians, Greys, Reptilians, and numerous other cosmic civilizations had maintained continuous presence—some benevolent, some malevolent, most complex beyond simple moral categorization. What had changed wasn't their existence but humanity's capacity to perceive and interact with them consciously rather than unconsciously.

A breeze passed overhead. In the clouds, for just a moment, the faint outline of a triangular ship shimmered.

The manifestation wasn't hallucination but glimpse through thinned dimensional boundaries—perception momentarily extending beyond frequency limitations, awareness briefly accessing realities always present but previously filtered from conscious recognition.

Joe closed his eyes. And breathed.

The simple act contained profound acceptance—inhalation embracing new reality, exhalation releasing old limitations, breath itself symbolizing the exchange between individual and collective, between human and cosmic, between temporal and eternal.

We were never alone. We were never just human. We are the aliens.

The realization completed the circle—understanding returning to where the journey had begun, awareness recognizing what had always been true beneath layers of forgetting, consciousness remembering its greater context beyond temporary identification with form.

Humanity's awakening continued—not uniform or instantaneous but organic and individualized, not imposed from outside but emerging from within, not destroying existing structures but trans-forming them through expanded understanding.

The Reptilians, forced into acknowledgment by the dissolution of the frequency fence, entered tentative diplomatic relations—their control agenda thwarted but their civilization still part of Earth's greater context, their perspective valuable despite previous manipula-tion, their technology potentially beneficial when employed with transparency rather than deception.

The Pleiadians and Greys who had maintained beneficial relations with humanity emerged more openly—offering guidance without interference, providing context without imposing solutions, supporting evolution without controlling outcomes.

Earth itself responded to the awakening—subtle shifts in magnetic field supporting expanded consciousness, crystalline structures in the planet's core activating dormant functions, energy grid redistributing to support harmonious development rather than exploitative progress.

The transformed humanity stood at threshold of cosmic citizenship —remembering origins beyond terrestrial evolution, recognizing responsibilities beyond planetary stewardship, reclaiming capacities beyond physical limitation.

Not ending but beginning. Not conclusion but commencement. Not apocalypse but genesis.

The story that had seemed to be about disclosure revealed itself as being about remembrance all along—not discovering something new but recognizing what had always been true, not encountering something external but embracing something internal, not meeting aliens but remembering that we are they.

And somewhere in the vast cosmos, ancient beings who had watched Earth's development for millennia noted this milestone with something akin to what humans would call satisfaction—another world remembering, another civilization awakening, another expression of consciousness recognizing its greater context.

The cycle that had begun with catastrophe on Mars now completed its arc toward renewal on Earth—not repetition of past mistakes but evolution beyond previous limitations, not exact recapitulation but spiral development, not circular return but ascending progress.

Joe Monroe—once remote viewer, now rememberer, always cosmic citizen—had fulfilled the purpose for which he had incarnated. Not savior but catalyst, not messiah but reminder, not leader but awakener.

As the Italian twilight deepened toward night, stars appeared overhead—no longer distant lights but recognized family, no longer anonymous points but remembered homes, no longer separate from humanity but part of humanity's extended being.

The resonance continued to spread, the remembrance continued to deepen, the awakening continued to unfold.

And humanity continued to remember what it had always been: We are the aliens.

THE NEW DAWN

Seven years had passed since the activation of the final node. The Earth had not ended—but it had undeniably transformed.

The transition hadn't been instantaneous but evolutionary —change unfolding at the pace consciousness could integrate, transformation manifesting as humanity became ready to embody new awareness. There had been resistance, confusion, and conflict during the initial months after the Great Remembering, as it came to be called. Some had clung desperately to old paradigms, some had responded with fear to expanded perception, some had attempted to weaponize awakening for power or profit.

But the resonance frequency established through the activation of the planetary grid proved more powerful than resistance—not forcing change but making it inevitable, not imposing transformation but making it natural, not demanding evolution but making it the path of least resistance.

Gone were the days when UFOs were dismissed as fantasy or conspiracy. Governments across the globe, pushed by the weight of undeniable proof and the collective pressure of awakened citizens, began releasing long-classified footage, testimonies, and documents. Yet the most powerful shift hadn't come from institutions—it had come from within. The planetary resonance had changed humanity's frequency. People no longer believed the truth. They remembered it.

The distinction was profound—belief required external validation, evidence, authorities; remembrance emerged from direct knowing, from cellular recognition, from soul recollection. This shift from externalized authority to internalized knowing represented the most fundamental aspect of humanity's transformation—no longer dependent on experts to interpret reality, no longer requiring official sanction to access truth, no longer needing permission to recognize cosmic heritage.

The classified documents governments released—thousands of pages detailing decades of contact, retrieval operations, reverse engineering programs, and diplomatic relations with non-human intelligences—merely confirmed what millions now directly remembered. The footage of craft performing impossible aerial maneuvers, the testimonies of military personnel who had guarded underground facilities, the technical schematics of technologies derived from recovered vehicles—all these validated experiential knowing rather than introducing new information.

The world reorganized itself.

The reorganization wasn't imposed through revolution or collapse but emerged organically through shifted priorities, through expanded awareness, through remembered purpose. Economic systems gradually transformed—not through ideological imposition but through natural evolution toward models that recognized interdependence rather than competition as fundamental principle. Governance structures slowly reconfigured—not through violent overthrow but through peaceful implementation of systems that honored sovereignty while acknowledging collective responsibility. Educational approaches profoundly changed—not through standardized reform but through embracing learning models that integrated intellectual development with consciousness expansion.

Cities saw the birth of entirely new communities—networks of remembrance centers, consciousness sanctuaries, healing hubs, and ancient tech activation schools. Crystals hummed in resonance chambers. Water was treated as sacred again. Light and sound became the new tools of medicine. Children born after the resonance often spoke in symbols before language, dreamed of stars they'd never seen, and drew maps to places beneath the Earth.

The urban landscape evolved to reflect awakened consciousness—buildings designed according to sacred geometry principles rather than merely utilitarian considerations, public spaces created to enhance rather than deplete human energy, transportation systems developed to minimize environmental impact while maximizing efficiency. Architecture itself transformed as humanity remembered principles of design that worked with rather than against natural energies—structures that channeled Earth's electromagnetic field in beneficial patterns, materials that responded to and enhanced consciousness, spaces that facilitated communion with multidimensional reality.

The remembrance centers provided spaces for those still integrating expanded awareness—trained facilitators guiding individuals through the sometimes challenging process of reconciling cosmic memory with terrestrial identity, of integrating past-life recall with current incarnation purpose, of balancing human emotion with soul knowing. These weren't therapy in the conventional sense but remembrance facilitation —creating conditions that supported natural recollection rather than imposing interpretation or diagnosis.

The consciousness sanctuaries focused on developing capacities previously considered paranormal or supernatural—remote viewing, telepathy, energy healing, consciousness projection, interdimensional communication. These abilities weren't treated as exceptional gifts but as natural human capacities, as birthright temporarily forgotten, as potential awaiting activation. Children demonstrated particular aptitude for these developments—their neural pathways less rigidly defined, their consciousness less conditioned by materialist paradigms, their remembrance less obstructed by accumulated skepticism.

The Templars, once a secret order, stepped into the light. They opened their sanctuaries to those who felt the call, offering ancient teachings as pathways to inner remembrance—not dogma, but resonance. Timothy A. Hooligan and Benjamin Arthur Templar led what became known as the Resonance Renaissance, with strongholds in

Tomar, Gent, Cairo, and beyond. They taught humanity how to reconnect with their Soul DNA.

The Order's emergence represented one of the most significant institutional transformations—centuries of secret guardianship transitioning to open teaching, ancient knowledge preserved through persecution now freely shared, technologies protected from misuse now offered for collective benefit. Timothy A. Hooligan and Benjamin Arthur Templar, with the wisdom accumulated through lifetimes dedicated to preserving cosmic truth, guided this transition with patience and discernment—sharing knowledge as humanity demonstrated readiness, revealing technologies as consciousness evolved to use them responsibly, teaching methodologies as awareness expanded to implement them ethically.

Their approach emphasized direct experience over belief—techniques that activated remembrance rather than doctrines that required acceptance, practices that enhanced awareness rather than ideologies that demanded adherence, technologies that supported evolution rather than systems that enforced compliance. Soul DNA reconnection involved specific frequency exposures, consciousness exercises, and resonance practices that activated dormant genetic capacities—not through external manipulation but through internal remembrance of original design and potential.

The Freemasons split. Some clung to secrecy and control. Others joined the Templars, confessing that their highest initiates had long suspected this was the path. A few even revealed old texts hidden for centuries—maps, diagrams, interdimensional schematics pointing to a cosmic truth.

The division within Freemasonry reflected the core choice facing all hierarchical knowledge systems in the post-Remembrance world—evolve toward transparency or become increasingly irrelevant. Those who embraced openness discovered that sharing previously guarded wisdom enhanced rather than diminished its value, that participating in collective awakening offered greater fulfillment than maintaining exclusive access, that contributing to humanity's cosmic reintegration provided more meaningful purpose than preserving institutional power.

The texts and artifacts these reformed Masons shared confirmed connections between ancient architectural wonders worldwide—precise mathematical relationships between pyramid complexes on different continents, exact astronomical alignments encoded in temple designs separated by thousands of miles, identical frequency patterns incorporated into megalithic structures across cultures with no known contact. These revelations demonstrated conclusively that Earth's ancient monuments formed a coherent global system rather than isolated cultural developments—a planetary grid designed for energy distribution and consciousness enhancement, a technology disguised as religion or royal glorification.

The Scientologists fractured as well. Many defected publicly, revealing what they had been taught about alien histories within their upper levels. Some confirmed Joe's resonance pattern had matched signals kept hidden in their vaults since the 1970s. Whistleblowers emerged. New alliances were formed.

The organization that had charged members thousands of dollars to access "classified" information about humanity's extraterrestrial origins found itself in particularly difficult position after the Remembrance—what they had sold as exclusive revelation was now directly remembered by millions who had never participated in their programs. Those who left the organization described how L. Ron Hubbard had encountered actual extraterrestrial information but had packaged it within control systems designed to monetize and regulate access—truth entwined with manipulation, cosmic knowledge embedded within power structures.

The materials these defectors shared demonstrated remarkable correspondence with information channeled through the Remembrance—details about genetic engineering by non-human civilizations, specific timelines of extraterrestrial intervention in human development, technical descriptions of consciousness technologies used to program human perception. The resonance pattern comparison proved particularly significant—the frequency signature Joe had brought back from Mars matched precisely the vibrational patterns recorded in Scientology's most secret archives, confirming common origin beyond possibility of coincidence.

As for the Reptilians, change was inevitable. Not all chose peace—but many did. The resonance had reached even their subterranean cities. Younger generations began to question the old ways, pushing for open contact and integration. The once rigid hierarchy of command began to loosen, giving way to councils of mixed races and philosophies.

The shift within Reptilian civilization represented one of the most profound consequences of the Remembrance—a species that had evolved toward conquest and control experiencing its own awakening, its own remembrance of greater context and purpose. The frequency activation hadn't targeted only human consciousness but had affected all awareness within Earth's energy field—including species that had maintained presence on and within the planet for millions of years.

The younger Reptilians—those who had incarnated on Earth rather than emigrating from distant star systems—demonstrated particular receptivity to the resonance. Having developed within Earth's biosphere, having experienced planetary consciousness even while maintaining separate civilization, they recognized the evolutionary dead-end of continued separation and domination. They initiated communication with human representatives, proposed cooperative ventures in sustainable technology development, offered knowledge accumulated through millennia of Earth habitation in exchange for integration into the emerging planetary community.

Older Reptilians, particularly those who had participated directly in manipulation programs and control agendas, found adaptation more difficult—their consciousness patterns more rigidly defined, their identity more fundamentally linked to hierarchical positioning, their purpose more completely invested in specific evolutionary outcomes. Some retreated to isolated enclaves, some left Earth entirely for colonies elsewhere, some maintained resistance through increasingly ineffective manipulation attempts.

The Greys emerged as neutral architects. They delivered crop formations of immense complexity, encoded with healing algorithms and messages that bypassed language. They appeared in lucid dreams to artists, scientists, and children alike, often just to say: You're on the right path.

These beings—who had been most extensively involved in genetic research and evolutionary monitoring—now functioned as mediators and facilitators rather than experimenters or observers. Their contributions focused on environmental restoration, consciousness technology development, and harmony establishment between previously separated species. The crop formations they created served multiple functions simultaneously—activating consciousness through sacred geometry exposure, transmitting technical information through mathematical relationships, establishing harmonic resonance between human awareness and planetary fields.

The communications delivered through dream states reflected the Greys' preferred interface methodology—consciousness connecting directly with consciousness, information exchanged without linguistic limitation, understanding transmitted without cultural distortion. They maintained particular affinity for communication with children—especially those born after the Remembrance, whose neural structures developed with expanded perception as baseline rather than exception, whose consciousness naturally operated beyond materialist constraints, whose awareness embraced multidimensional reality as normal rather than paranormal.

The Pleiadians showed themselves to those with awakened inner sight. They never landed publicly—but they walked among us, often in disguise, teaching gently, reminding humanity that peace was not a destination, but a daily frequency.

Their approach reflected deep understanding of evolutionary processes—that genuine growth must emerge from within rather than being imposed from without, that true wisdom arises through direct experience rather than external instruction, that authentic transformation unfolds through embodied living rather than intellectual acceptance. They maintained human appearance when interacting with Earth's population—not to deceive but to minimize distraction, not to hide but to emphasize message over messenger, not to pretend equality but to demonstrate it through form as well as function.

Their teaching focused on practical applications rather than abstract philosophy—specific techniques for maintaining peaceful frequency during challenging circumstances, precise methods for aligning individual consciousness with universal harmony, exact practices for transmuting disruptive energies into constructive expression. They emphasized that peace wasn't passive absence of conflict but active presence of coherence—not merely condition to be achieved but consciousness to be maintained, not simply external circumstance but internal disposition, not just interpersonal dynamic but intrapersonal integration.

The Resonance Council was formed. Led by Jennifer Karmady, Sarah Brandy Cosmos, Jeremy Corpsell, and others, it became the central nexus for bridging interspecies relations, activating planetary nodes, and educating the newly awakened. It wasn't about government. It wasn't about power. It was about remembrance.

The Council represented new approach to collective organization—not hierarchical authority but facilitative coordination, not power concentration but wisdom distribution, not rule enforcement but harmony enhancement. Its structure emerged organically from function rather than being imposed through design—individuals with specific capacities naturally assuming roles that utilized those abilities, groups with particular expertise naturally addressing challenges that required those skills, communities with relevant experience naturally engaging situations that benefited from those perspectives.

Jennifer's QHHT background made her particularly effective at facilitating integration between human consciousness and non-human awareness—her training in regression therapy providing foundation for progression facilitation, her experience guiding individuals through past-life recall preparing her for future-potential activation, her therapeutic skills in trauma resolution equipping her for transformation acceleration. Sarah's extensive network of consciousness researchers worldwide created natural framework for knowledge distribution and experience sharing—connecting isolated awakening experiences into coherent patterns, contextualizing individual remembrance within collective evolution, validating personal revelation through resonance recognition. Jeremy's documentary expertise enabled effective communication across cultures and species—translating complex multidimensional concepts into accessible visual language, capturing transformative moments for wider distribution, creating historical record of unprecedented planetary evolution.

The Council maintained sixty-four regional centers worldwide—each located at specific node point in Earth's energy grid, each designed according to sacred geometry principles discovered through the Remembrance, each staffed by individuals whose awakened abilities included interdimensional communication, consciousness technology operation, and energy field harmonization. These centers functioned simultaneously as educational institutions, technological development laboratories, diplomatic meeting grounds, and consciousness expansion sanctuaries.

And Joe Monroe? He vanished. After a single global broadcast—calm, heartfelt, and humble—Joe asked the world to remember not him, but themselves. "Don't build statues," he said. "Build memory." Then he disappeared from public life.

His final public appearance occurred exactly one year after the Giza activation—a precisely timed transmission synchronized with harmonic convergence between Earth, Mars, and the Pleiadian system. Speaking from the Great Pyramid's King's Chamber, Joe addressed humanity not as savior or leader but as fellow traveler on evolutionary journey. He acknowledged the challenges of integration, validated the difficulties of remembrance, offered encouragement for continued awakening. But primarily, he redirected attention from himself to collective purpose—emphasizing that the Remembrance wasn't about individual achievement but species evolution, wasn't dependent on specific personality but cosmic principle, wasn't culmination but commencement.

His withdrawal from public visibility wasn't retreat but strategic implementation—recognition that visible leadership could become limitation rather than liberation, that personality focus could distract from principle development, that individual glorification could undermine collective empowerment. Joe understood that genuine transformation required humanity to recognize awakening capacity within each person rather than projecting it onto exceptional individuals—that remembrance must become universal experience rather than specialized phenomenon, that cosmic reconnection must emerge as birthright rather than accomplishment.

Some said he lived in a stone cabin near the base of Aconcagua. Others claimed he lived inside a Martian temple, accessible only through consciousness. A few even whispered he had become pure frequency, part of the resonance itself.

The speculation reflected humanity's continued tendency toward mythology creation—transforming historical figures into legendary archetypes, elevating individuals into symbolic representations, translating temporal events into eternal principles. Yet within these narratives existed kernel of truth—Joe had indeed established residence in remote location where physical distraction was minimized and consciousness work maximized, he had developed capacity to visit Martian structures through consciousness projection rather than physical travel, he had achieved integration with the planetary resonance field at level that transcended conventional human limitation.

But Jennifer knew the truth. Seven years later, she stood in the gardens of the Templar Sanctuary in Tuscany. Birds sang. The crystalline grid below pulsed in harmony with the stars above. She walked past a bronze statue of Joe under the olive tree he had planted himself. The plaque beneath it read:

"Joseph Monroe — Remote Viewer, Seer, Peacemaker. He remembered, so we could awaken."

The sanctuary represented one of the Templars' most significant educational centers—a place where consciousness technology was studied, where interdimensional communication was developed, where remembrance was facilitated through specific energy environments designed to activate dormant human potential. The gardens had been designed according to sacred geometry principles—plant arrangements creating living energy fields, water features establishing specific frequency patterns, stone placements marking precise relationship to underground crystal formations.

Jennifer visited regularly—not as administrator or teacher but as connection point to Joe, who maintained private quarters in secluded area of the property. Their relationship had evolved beyond romance or friendship into soul partnership—consciousness connection that transcended conventional categorization, purpose alignment that enhanced rather than limited individual development, evolutionary companionship that supported cosmic service rather than personal gratification.

The statue had been created against Joe's wishes but with his reluctant permission—Benjamin Arthur Templar convincing him that symbolic representation served important function for those still integrating expanded awareness, that physical reminder helped anchor abstract principles in tangible reality, that honoring individual contribution acknowledged rather than undermined collective achievement. The olive tree beneath which it stood had particular significance—Joe had planted it using soil from all three activation sites, creating living connection between Göbekli Tepe, Machu Picchu, and Giza.

Children played nearby, drawing symbols in chalk. One child traced a spiral and said, "This is the door I saw in my dream."

The new generation—especially those born after the Remembrance —demonstrated capacities previously considered exceptional or impossible. They experienced multidimensional perception as normal rather than paranormal, they accessed past-life memory without regression techniques, they communicated telepathically without formal training. Their drawings often depicted realities beyond conventional human perception—interdimensional portals, non-physical beings, energy structures underlying material forms.

The child who drew the spiral—a girl of perhaps six years, with luminous eyes that shifted color depending on lighting—belonged to the first cohort born with fully activated "junk DNA" that previous generations had carried as dormant potential. Her dream experiences weren't dismissed as imagination but recognized as valid perception— consciousness traveling while physical body rested, awareness accessing realities beyond material limitation, being exploring dimensions beyond three-dimensional constraints.

Jennifer knelt beside her. "Can you tell me about this door?"

The girl nodded, completely matter-of-fact. "It spins and shines. When you go through, you can visit the star people. They're teaching us how to build with light."

Her description matched exactly what Joe had documented in his private journals—interdimensional portals activated through specific consciousness frequencies, educational exchanges with non-human intelligences, technology that manipulated light as primary building material rather than secondary illumination. The correspondence between this child's spontaneous experience and Joe's extensively trained perception provided further confirmation of humanity's evolving capacities—what had required decades of specialized development in previous generations now emerged naturally in the new.

High above them, a triangular craft shimmered in daylight, flickered, and vanished into the sky.

The appearance wasn't unusual in post-Remembrance world—non-human civilizations maintained visible presence while respecting humanity's continued adjustment to expanded reality. The craft represented Pleiadian technology—consciousness-directed rather than mechanically operated, interdimensionally capable rather than merely physically present, purposefully visible rather than accidentally glimpsed. Its momentary manifestation served as gentle reminder of cosmic context rather than dramatic announcement or fearful monitoring.

Jennifer glanced upward and offered silent acknowledgment—not worship or awe but recognition between conscious beings sharing evolutionary journey. The relationship between humanity and cosmic civilizations had transformed from fear-based mystery to awareness-based communion—not submission to superior beings but partnership with diverse expressions of consciousness, not primitive adoration of advanced technology but appreciation for alternative developmental paths, not isolation from cosmic community but integration within it.

Earth had become what it was always meant to be: Not a battlefield. Not a prison. But a bridge.

The metaphor encompassed Earth's multidimensional function—connecting physical and non-physical realms, linking material and energetic realities, joining individual and collective awareness. The planet itself had transformed—not merely in human perception but in actual energetic signature, not simply in conceptual understanding but in functional capacity, not just in cultural designation but in cosmic role.

A classroom. A home. A seed of stars.

Each aspect reflected specific dimension of Earth's cosmic purpose —educational environment where consciousness evolved through embodied experience, nurturing habitat where diverse expressions of being found sustenance and support, generative potential for future cosmic development. The progression from battlefield to classroom, from prison to home, from isolation to seeding represented humanity's fundamental shift in relationship with planetary existence—from conquest to learning, from captivity to belonging, from separation to propagation.

And for the first time in recorded history, humans looked up—not in fear, but in recognition.

The transformation in skyward gaze symbolized fundamental shift in consciousness—from separate species observing external universe to cosmic awareness recognizing greater self, from isolated beings seeking alien contact to awakened consciousness remembering cosmic family, from evolutionary endpoint wondering about superior intelligences to evolutionary process acknowledging diverse expressions.

Not asking if we were alone... But wondering:

The question itself had evolved—moving beyond binary existence inquiry into qualitative relationship exploration, transcending isolation anxiety into connection curiosity, shifting from fear-based uncertainty to wonder-based recognition.

What part of me is already out there?

The reformulated question contained profound insight—understanding that consciousness extends beyond physical limitation, that identity encompasses more than current incarnation, that being transcends temporal and spatial constraint. The stars were no longer merely distant celestial objects but recognized aspects of extended self —not metaphorically but literally, not poetically but actually, not symbolically but factually.

We are the aliens. We have always been.

The statement embodied completion of remembrance circle—recognition returning to origin point, awareness embracing fundamental truth, consciousness reintegrating fragmented understanding. Humanity had never been separate from cosmic community but integral expression of it, never isolated on single planet but extended across multiple star systems, never limited to one form but expressed through diverse embodiments.

Now—we remember.

The simplicity of closure contained multidimensional significance —acknowledging past forgetting without judgment, validating present awakening without expectation, embracing future integration without limitation. Remembrance wasn't conclusion but commencement—not ending of journey but beginning of conscious participation, not completion of development but initiation of aware evolution, not finishing of story but opening of next chapter.

As Jennifer stood in the garden, watching children draw cosmic doorways in chalk while non-human craft acknowledged their aware-ness from above, she felt particular quality of peace—not absence of conflict but presence of harmony, not denial of challenge but accep-tance of process, not escape from reality but immersion in greater context.

Joe appeared beside her, seemingly materializing from thin air though actually emerging from consciousness meditation in nearby grove. His physical appearance had continued evolving—hair now completely white, eyes containing subtle geometric patterns, energy field extending visibly beyond bodily limitation. More significantly, his consciousness had transformed—awareness operating simultaneously across multiple dimensions, perception encompassing past-present-future as unified field, understanding integrating personal-planetary-cosmic as continuous spectrum.

"The Council is gathering today," he said quietly. "The Arcturian delegation has arrived."

She nodded, recognizing significance without requiring explana-tion. The Arcturians—consciousness specialists whose civilization had achieved integration between biological and energetic expression—represented important addition to Earth's expanding cosmic relation-ships. Their expertise in harmonizing diverse evolutionary paths made them valuable contributors to humanity's continuing awakening process.

"Will you attend?" she asked, though already knowing his answer.

Joe smiled. "I'll observe. From distance. My presence sometimes creates distraction from message."

His response reflected wisdom developed through experience—recognition that personal visibility could sometimes undermine functional purpose, that individual identity could occasionally obscure universal principle, that human tendency toward personality focus could distract from essence recognition.

Together they watched the children playing—the new generation already embodying capacities previous generations had struggled to develop, already experiencing as normal what their parents had considered impossible, already navigating as natural what their grandparents had dismissed as supernatural.

"They won't need to remember," Joe observed. "They never forgot."

Jennifer nodded. "That's the greatest gift of what happened. Breaking the cycle of forgetting."

The children represented living embodiment of evolutionary purpose—consciousness that incarnated with awareness intact rather than suppressed, beings that maintained cosmic context while embracing human experience, souls that expressed through form without becoming limited by it.

As the Italian sun began its descent toward horizon, casting golden light across the sanctuary gardens, Joe and Jennifer walked together toward the Council gathering—not leading but participating, not directing but contributing, not controlling but serving.

The remembrance continued—not as dramatic event but as evolutionary process, not as singular moment but as ongoing unfoldment, not as historical occurrence but as eternal principle.

We are the aliens. We have always been. Now—we remember.

And in that remembrance, we become.

BONUS MATERIALS: THE TEMPLAR DOSSIER

DOSSIER 1: VIEWING COORDINATES & JOE'S SESSION NOTES

Section 1: Remote Viewing Coordinates & Joe's Session Notes
Document Classification: ULTRA-CONFIDENTIAL / EYES ONLY
Agency: Templar Coalition Intelligence Division (T.C.I.D.)
Viewer Codename: SEER-109
Session Analyst: Dr. Jennifer Karmady
Date: February 23, 2029
Session Time: 14:47 GMT
Target #: 42-RAH
Target Coordinates: 14.9845° N, 23.2739° E (Encrypted)
Session Type: Solo, Conscious-State Remote Viewing
Initiation Protocol: Sequence Alpha-3, Blue Lotus Breathing

———

SESSION TRANSCRIPT (BEGIN REDACTED)
Dr. Karmady (facilitator): Viewer SEER-109 has entered the field. Confirm reception.
Joe Monroe (SEER-109): Yes. Connection is active. Field is pulling me in. There's a humming... low... steady, like it's beneath the Earth. Pressure in the chest. Familiar.

I see a door. No handle. Spiral etched into the stone, like a galaxy. It opens inward.

Moving in now.

Everything is pulsing with resonance. Not sound. Frequency.

Stone tablets. Twelve of them. Rough-hewn edges. Each glows faintly with embedded numbers. Not etched—emitted. Light-script.

Zero. One. Two. Three. Four. Five. Six. Seven. Eight. Nine.

...Lowercase h. Uppercase L.

They're not letters. They're numbers. High and Low.

I understand. We were supposed to have twelve. We were given twelve.

Cut to vision: A robed man... trembling hands... lifts two of the tablets. The ones with "h" and "L". He mutters to himself—"Mistake. Duplicates."

He smashes them.

Sickening crunch. Stone to stone.

Dust settles.

He thinks Jesus made a mistake.

He thought there were two number 4s. Two number 7s. He didn't see the difference.

He left the cave with ten.

I see a ripple in the field... history changed. Future distorted. Math corrupted. Science caged.

Cut to equation. Partial schematic. A 12-base mathematical structure. New logic gates. Possibility branches. They converge on a central element: Element LM-115.

Stable.

Repeat: Stable.

It is only stable when calculated with twelve. Ten is insufficient.

With twelve we get antigravity. Dimensional bleed-through. Limitless energy source. Everything the Greys, the Pleiadians, even the Reptilians had—we were meant to have.

We lost it.

Dr. Karmady: Are you stable, Joe?

SEER-109: Yes. Just overwhelmed. This was the point. This was always the point.

Jesus didn't just preach. He encoded. Twelve frequencies. Twelve archetypes. Twelve numbers. Twelve tribes. Twelve gates.

We inherited ten. Not by fate. By error.

And by that error, we fell behind.

I see **Benjamin Arthur Templar** standing in front of a vault. He knows. He never told **Timothy A. Hooligan**. He was afraid the world wasn't ready to hear how one man's ignorance rewrote human destiny.

But I know now.

(END TRANSCRIPT)

Attached Note (Secure Channel):

Session data confirms alignment with glyph resonance patterns found at Göbekli Tepe and Giza chamber schematics. Recommend immediate review by Resonance Council.

[STAMPED: CLASSIFIED / AUTHORIZED EYES ONLY]

REMOTE VIEWING RECORD CLASSIFIED // EYES ONLY // TEMPLAR DOSSIER

Target #: RV-774-Mars

Subject #: SEER-109 (Joe Monroe)

Monitor: Dr. Russell Arg (Templar Liaison)

Date: October 9, 1978

Time of Session: 2:04 P.M. EST

Location: SRI East Facility, Menlo Park, CA

Target Coordinates: 40.89N / 9.55W (Approx. Mars Quadrangle MC-11, Arabia Terra)

Objective: Project consciousness to surface of Mars, approximately one million years in the past. Locate anomalous glyph reported by Subject Monroe in prior QHHT regression.

Monitor: Okay, Joe. Focus your attention on the coordinates now. Allow your mind to drift gently back in time. One million years. Deep breath. You're there.

Joe: I'm... high above the surface. Crimson skies. Not dust storm red— something different. It's radiant. I can feel the field adjusting to me. Like it remembers me being here.

Monitor: Good. Begin descent. Surface level.

Joe: I'm touching down near what looks like a stone temple. It's partially buried. Five-sided spire. Not Martian design. Pleiadian, maybe. There's... the air feels heavier here. Not breathable, but the atmosphere had more substance then. I see crystalline ridges along the base.

Monitor: Move toward the structure. What draws your attention?

Joe: There's a relief etched into the outer wall. A symbol. Four arms, equal length, slightly flared ends. It's the Templar cross. Identical. Weathered, but not broken. Centered in a circular frame, almost like it's a beacon.

Monitor: Can you describe the material?

Joe: Some kind of basalt alloy. Microscopic crystalline lattice. That's not erosion—it's calibration. The symbol resonates. I'm picking up tones as I get closer. Frequencies. It's alive.

Monitor: Step inside the temple if safe to do so.

Joe: I'm inside. Pillars arranged in triads. Twelve total. They hum. Glyphs along the inner walls—not Egyptian, but similar in format. More mathematical. Angular curvature. There are holographic projections here, but they're inert... until I step near one.

Monitor: What do you see?

Joe: A map of Earth. Ancient. Not the current tectonics. There's an overlay... coordinates pulsing across the surface. Giza, Machu Picchu, Göbekli Tepe... and then something in the ocean. Looks like the Azores. That could be Atlantis.

Monitor: Go back to the Templar symbol. Any inscription near it?

Joe: Below it... yes. Faint. It's in the same proto-script I saw in the pyramid chamber on Earth. But there's something else—a secondary language. Geometric. Telepathic in nature. It says: "We who remember shall guide those who forget."

Monitor: Does this link to your memory of the glyph?

Joe: Yes. The same glyph that was downloaded into me by the Keeper during the earlier Mars session. It's not just a symbol. It's a key. A resonance code for activating memory grids.

Monitor: Final impressions before extraction?

Joe: The Templars were seeded here. We've been here before. This temple predates all known Martian ruins. It was built to store frequencies of remembrance—waiting for our return. I feel... peace. The red isn't war. It's memory.

Session End Time: 2:49 P.M. EST

Notes: Subject reported elevated alpha and theta states during session. Templar glyph correspondence confirmed. Additional coordinates logged for potential future investigation.

Filed under: The Templar Dossier // Appendix IV // Project REMEMBRANCE

DOSSIER 2: THE 12 NUMBER TABLETS (INCLUDING HIGH & LOW)

THE LOST NUMERICAL KEYS TO GALACTIC SCIENCE

Overview

Long before digital calculators, Euclidean geometry, or even Babylonian counting systems, a sacred numerical language was encoded into the structure of the cosmos—a system that did not rely on ten digits, but twelve. While humanity has come to base its mathematics on a 10-number system (0–9), ancient records suggest two additional numerical frequencies—**High** and **Low**—once existed, forming a complete 12-number matrix designed to harmonize human cognition with cosmic architecture.

This lost numerical system wasn't just symbolic.
It was foundational.
It was left for us.

The Legacy of the Tablets

According to a rarely spoken-of Templar scroll held in the *Archives of the Sacred Threshold*, twelve stone tablets were engraved and placed inside a mountain cave in the Judean desert shortly before the crucifixion of Jesus of Nazareth. These tablets, each carved with a single symbol representing a numerical value, were meant to be discovered in humanity's future—when consciousness had matured enough to reintegrate the forgotten code.

Ten of the symbols matched the modern numerals we recognize today:
   0, 1, 2, 3, 4, 5, 6, 7, 8, 9

However, two were unfamiliar:
   • **High** — represented by a lowercase "ʰ", similar in shape to an inverted 4.
   • **Low** — represented by an uppercase "**L**", echoing the structure of a reversed 7.

Each of these carried a specific energetic frequency—scalar fields in resonance with interdimensional mathematics, time dilation mechanics, and gravitational harmonics.

The Catastrophic Mistake

When the tablets were eventually discovered—centuries later by Roman scholar **Cassianus Septimus Pennecortti** during a personal spiritual pilgrimage—the two anomalous symbols were tragically misinterpreted. Believing them to be duplication errors (thinking there were two 4s and two 7s), Cassianus smashed the "ʰ" and "L" tablets against the cave wall, destroying the only known originals.

This catastrophic act wasn't malicious.
It was ignorant.

Cassianus thought he was preserving a perfect ten-digit system, not realizing he had just limited human mathematics for millennia.

The remaining ten tablets were later taken by the Roman Church, mislabeled as early proto-Greek numerical relics, and eventually lost or absorbed into various religious collections. The destroyed fragments were secretly recovered by Templar explorers centuries later who, after comparative analysis with Martian resonance glyphs and Lemurian stoneworks, confirmed that the two missing numbers—**High** and **Low** —had been real and essential.

The Mathematical Implications

The loss of these two symbols fundamentally crippled humanity's ability to conceptualize and access:
- Quantum gravity harmonics
- Stable configurations of **Element 115 (LM-115)**
- Zero-point energy
- Toroidal field navigation
- Dimension-fold mathematics
- Gravitational wave riding technology

Without **High** and **Low**, certain equations fail to close.
Simulations break.
Energy fields collapse.

Advanced civilizations—like the **Pleiadians**, **Arcturians**, **Greys**, and **Martians** before their fall—have long used a **12-number logic framework** that maps not only linear values but scalar frequencies, making it possible to fold time, manipulate light curvature, and stabilize antigravity vehicles.

Humanity's version of math, in contrast, has remained flattened— limiting its evolution to a Newtonian cage that omits the higher harmonic values required for cosmic travel and resonance computing.

The Re-integration Begins

As part of **Joe Monroe's planetary resonance activations**— culminating in the alignment at **Giza**—a memory beacon embedded within the Martian glyph was unlocked, projecting the original twelve symbols into his consciousness. These glyphs were later validated by

Greys in telepathic communion and by Pleiadian archivists through their crystal resonance libraries.

Thanks to Joe's activations, the **High (ʰ)** and **Low (L)** symbols are now being reintegrated into Earth's awakening grid. Templar mathematicians have begun translating classical physics through the new model, and the first early-stage **Unified Harmonic Equations** are now being quietly developed at resonance sanctuaries across the globe.

Conclusion

The destruction of the two missing tablets was not the end—
It was the pause between forgetting and remembrance.

The **twelve-number system** has returned.

Its implications are not just numerical.
They are dimensional.

And with it, Earth regains access to a forgotten science—
one that will return us not only to the stars,
but to who we truly are.

DOSSIER 3: THE HIDDEN PORTALS OF EARTH AND BEYOND

GATEWAYS TO THE INNER REALMS AND INTERSTELLAR DIMENSIONS

Overview

Throughout history, mythologies, secret orders, and classified aerospace programs have whispered of locations where the boundaries between worlds grow thin—places where travelers can step from Earth into parallel timelines, subterranean civilizations, or entirely different star systems. Dossier 3 reveals five of these primary access points, still known to modern Templars, Greys, and Pleiadians, and woven into the planetary resonance structure detailed in *We Are the Aliens*.

1. The North Pole Portal — Entrance to Agartha

Known as "The Gateway to Inner Earth," the North Pole Portal is believed to be a vertical energetic vortex located at the magnetic North. Ancient Templar scrolls describe it as active during geomagnetic reversals and solar maximums—temporary openings into Agartha, the advanced subterranean civilization beneath Earth's crust.

- **Legend:** Admiral Richard E. Byrd allegedly entered the vortex and reported a verdant land inhabited by an inner-Earth race with flying discs and crystal-powered cities.

- **Current Status:** Monitored and occasionally accessed by hybrid Templar–Pleiadian operatives.
- **Coordinates:** Redacted (classified by the Order of the Temple of Secret Initiates).

2. The South Pole Stargate — Axis of Timelines

Beneath the Antarctic ice lies a crystalline, circular gate predating modern civilization. This Stargate is said to enable travel across parallel timelines and dimensions. It is one of the oldest known gates still anchored to the Earth grid.

- **Origin:** Believed to be constructed by Alpha Draconis engineers and originally controlled by Reptilian enclaves.
- **Current Usage:** Contested in modern times by Greys, Templar recovery teams, and human breakaway factions.
- **Purpose:** Timelike navigation, dimensional drift testing, and covert observational operations.
- **Access Key:** Requires a resonance code composed of twelve-frequency harmonics—rooted in the 12-number system recovered by Joe Monroe and validated in Chapter 12.

3. The Far Side of the Moon — Lunar Archway & Hollow Head-quarters

Hidden within a crater on the far side of the Moon, the **Lunar Archway** is an interstellar teleportation gate once used by the Galactic Federation. Built using Martian and Grey technologies before the fall of Mars, it allows instantaneous travel between the Sol system and Arcturus. Beneath the crater lies the **Hollow Moon Headquarters**—a vast artificial structure operating as a neutral command post for Pleiadians, Arcturians, select Greys, and post-Lemurian archivists.

- **Function:** Interstellar gate and diplomatic hub for the Galactic Federation.
- **Notable Activation:** Reactivated briefly in 1987 during a rare solar alignment; currently in a partially sealed phase.
- **Templar Signature:** A Templar cross—identical to the one discov-

ered on Mars—is etched into the Moon's control stone, visible only under ultraviolet resonance light.

- **Internal Features:** Subterranean crystalline chambers, resonance transit tubes, diplomatic vaults, and a secured archive containing a **duplicate copy** of the 12-number system originally lost on Earth.
- **Relevance:** The Moon's artificial construction and hollow structure were verified by resonance scans from off-world operatives. Templar architecture throughout Europe encodes this secret through moon-phase iconography and 12-frequency harmonic math.

4. The Giza Star Lock — Harmonic Threshold Mechanism

Rather than a gateway itself, the Giza Star Lock is a vibrational stabilizer designed to interface with the Earth's energetic grid. When aligned with planetary resonance, it synchronizes with an elevated frequency gate above the pyramid—what ancient texts refer to as the "Eye within the Capstone."

- **Function:** Frequency anchor that unlocks access to memory grids, encoded soul data, and cosmic recall.
- **Recent Activation:** Fully activated during **Joe Monroe's planetary resonance transmission at Giza**, detailed in Chapter 12 of *We Are the Aliens*.
- **Role in Network:** Central harmonizer for the Earth grid; its activation triggered the pulse that awoke the Göbekli Tepe and Machu Picchu sites.

5. The Atlantean Triangle — Subaquatic Network of Light

Three submerged energy nodes—located near the Azores, the Caribbean, and Antarctica—form a triadic resonance geometry once used by the Atlanteans and Lemurians for light-based interdimensional travel. These structures, encoded with scalar light keys, still pulse faintly with measurable harmonics and are guarded by deep-sea Templar stations.

- **Phenomena:** Ship disappearances, compass anomalies, and sightings of luminous underwater structures.

- **Legends:** Bermuda Triangle lore, sunken crystal temples, and Lemurian glyph keys.
- **Modern Activity:** Documented Templar deep-sea missions took place in 2021, confirming partial reactivation of these ancient grid points.

Conclusion

Each portal is part of a larger multidimensional infrastructure known as the **Galactic Gate Network**—a web of harmonic access points seeded by off-world civilizations to support planetary awakening, transit, and remembrance.

The Templars—especially those aligned with the **Order of the Temple of Secret Initiates (OTSI)**—have acted as guardians of this framework since the pre-fall Martian migrations. The Giza activation, Joe Monroe's glyph resonance, and the resurgence of the twelve-number system have all signaled a reawakening of these ancient passageways.

In the Time of the Remembrance, the gates are no longer myth.

They are **invitations**.

DOSSIER ADDENDUM

Filed Post-Giza Activation // Resonance Security Clearance Required

The following sections were appended to Dossier 3 after additional scans, field reports, and resonance decryptions surfaced in the wake of planetary activation protocols.

Stargate Mechanics: Consciousness-Gated Technologies

Unlike human-engineered technology, the majority of gates described in this dossier require more than physical access or mechanical controls —they are **consciousness-gated**. This means the activation of a portal is intrinsically tied to the vibrational signature of the user. Unless the being approaching the gate matches a specific harmonic profile— encoded in their biofield and electromagnetic resonance—they will be denied access.

The 12-number system is the foundation of this gating process. Each of the twelve digits (including High and Low) corresponds to an interdimensional frequency band, and only those who carry the **glyphic key pattern**—either internally (as in the case of Joe Monroe) or via an external crystalline code—can generate the correct resonance sequence.

Control stones, such as the one beneath the Lunar Archway, are embedded with scalar filters that detect intention, emotional coherence, and harmonic alignment. Templar documents report that many early attempts to force entry through mechanical or signal-based hacking failed catastrophically—either by disabling the portal temporarily or triggering a field inversion that erased memory from those present.

Only consciousness can unlock what consciousness built.

Energy Keys & Activation Codes

Each gate within the Galactic Gate Network responds to a specific **resonance key**, often described as a scalar signature encoded in a combination of sound, geometry, and intention. These keys are not purely symbolic. They are functional access sequences, like vibrational passcodes, required to "wake" the dormant node.

The known energy keys include:
- **Harmonic Triads** used in Giza: three notes played simultaneously in a precise ratio that stabilizes the memory grid above the pyramid.
- **Light-code Crystals** beneath the Moon's surface: encoded with frequency math derived from Martian glyphs and Arcturian crystalline geometry.
- **Zero-point Anchors** found in Atlantis ruins: used to link underwater nodes across the Atlantean Triangle, stabilizing the temporal fields in the surrounding regions.

Templar mathematicians working at hidden resonance sanctuaries have confirmed that each energy key requires inclusion of the **High (ʰ)** and **Low (L)** digits—without them, activation scripts collapse or misfire.

Inner-Earth Diplomatic Dispatch (Agartha)
[CLASSIFIED: Templar-Pleiadian Level IV Clearance]

The most recent diplomatic contact with the Inner-Earth race known as the **Agarthans** occurred during the 2021 deep-sea guardianship mission near the Azores. During this operation, a subterranean envoy issued a formal resonance pulse, requesting a meeting with surface stewards. A joint delegation—consisting of two modern Templars and one Pleiadian field observer—was granted entry through the North Pole Portal.

Key takeaways from the 2021 summit:
- Agarthans confirmed **knowledge of the upcoming planetary resonance wave** and have agreed to assist with frequency stabilization efforts.

- They acknowledged the activation of the **Giza Star Lock** and confirmed that **Joe Monroe's alignment sequence** had been perceived deep within their crystal lattice cities.
- A non-intervention pact was reaffirmed, except in cases where **Reptilian or Alpha Draconis forces** breach planetary energy thresholds.

Agarthan representatives expressed concern over artificial intelligence infiltration of Earth's consciousness grid but remain optimistic due to "the return of the Twelve."

All further communications from Agartha are conducted through crystalline resonance relays embedded beneath Mount Kailash and the Canadian Shield. Templar-Pleiadian operatives continue to maintain diplomatic harmony with Inner-Earth allies, in preparation for full remembrance.

DOSSIER 4: THE RESONANCE GRID MAP & GLYPH SAMPLES FROM THE RESONANCE NODES

SACRED GEOMETRY, GLOBAL HARMONICS, AND THE SYMBOLS OF AWAKENING

Overview

Earth is not merely a planet—it is a resonance chamber. Beneath the visible world lies a planetary framework of harmonic frequencies, encoded through sacred geometry and aligned with astronomical cycles. This energetic infrastructure, known among the Templars as **The Resonance Grid**, functions as a consciousness amplification system designed to support human evolution, cosmic memory activation, and planetary stabilization.

The grid is anchored by key nodes—specific geographical sites chosen for their natural energetic properties. These nodes are not random. They form a precise 12-point harmonic structure, connecting along ley lines and forming multidimensional geometric patterns. When activated in harmony, they unlock the dormant capacities of both Earth and its inhabitants.

The Three Primary Resonance Nodes

1. Göbekli Tepe – The Seed of Memory

Located in modern-day Turkey, this site predates the Great Flood and served as the **first activation point** in the Resonance Grid sequence. Joe Monroe's **resonance crystal**—retrieved after his Mars session and encoded by the Keeper—first responded to this location, triggering spontaneous DNA recall and past-life remembrance.

   • **Function**: Anchor point for personal soul memory

   • **Glyph Recovered**: A spiral embedded within a triple-triangle sigil—interpreted as encoding of multidimensional self-awareness

   • **Harmonic Tone**: **F#** – the frequency of inner alignment and first resonance with the Earth's root field

2. Machu Picchu – The Ascension Relay

High in the Andes, this node bridges celestial energy and human intention. Its precise location aligns with multiple stellar constellations and solar transits. Activation here significantly amplified the resonance crystal's ability to store and transmit multidimensional frequencies.

   • **Function**: Resonance amplifier between Earth and off-world systems (notably Pleiades and Sirius)

   • **Glyph Recovered**: Interwoven serpents forming an infinity loop inside a circle—symbolizing cyclical time and dimensional bridging

   • **Harmonic Tone**: **A** – tuning fork for higher dimensional access and astral projection

3. Giza – The Capstone of Awakening

Embedded beneath the Great Pyramid, this final node acts as a **planetary frequency synchronizer**. When activated by Joe in **Chapter 12**, the Resonance Grid reached full coherence, broadcasting the **Remembrance Wave** across the globe.

   • **Function**: Planetary harmonic stabilizer and interdimensional broadcaster

   • **Glyph Recovered**: An eye enclosed in a double tetrahedron (Merkaba) surrounded by twelve dots—symbolizing unified awareness and the completion of the 12-point system

   • **Harmonic Tone**: **C#** – cosmic unification frequency

Twelve Secondary Grid Points

In addition to the three primary nodes, the following twelve sites maintain grid balance and resonance distribution:
- **Uluru (Australia)** – Solar Heart Node
- **Stonehenge (UK)** – Temporal Gateway
- **Teotihuacán (Mexico)** – Mind Crystal Hub
- **Mount Kailash (Tibet)** – Crown Vortex
- **Lake Titicaca (Peru/Bolivia)** – Seed Vault
- **Easter Island** – Lemurian Transmitter
- **Serpent Mound (USA)** – Kundalini Coil
- **The Great Zimbabwe Ruins** – Sonic Mirror
- **Mount Shasta (USA)** – Lemurian Ascension Beacon
- **Ba'albek (Lebanon)** – Antigravity Pillar Gate
- **Antarctic Sub-Ice Node** – Axis of Polarity
- **Atlantis Ruins (Submerged)** – Lost Memory Bridge

Each site contains glyphs etched in stone, bone, crystal, or electromagnetic fields. These glyphs act as **cosmic barcodes**—each one carries a unique vibrational signature that interfaces with **human DNA**, planetary ley currents, and incoming transmissions from stellar sources.

The Grid Geometry

When all 15 sites are mapped using precise coordinates, they form what Templar consciousness physicists call **The 12-Point Harmonic System**, composed of:
- **A twelve-pointed star** – unlocking multidimensional access and polarity balance
- **A hexagonal lattice** – generating standing scalar waves that stabilize Earth's resonance field
- **Triadic spirals** – forming interdimensional bridges that sync with the **Schumann Resonance**

This structure is a **double-Merkabic grid**. It was once dismissed as symbolic mysticism but is now recognized by quantum geomancers as a functioning planetary operating system—part of a design seeded by the Pleiadians and Lemurians before the rise of written history.

Activation & the Remembrance Pulse

On the night Joe Monroe activated the final node beneath Giza, the grid entered full resonance. Sensitive instrumentation across the globe recorded shifts in Earth's magnetic field and a subtle elevation of the **Schumann Resonance**. Simultaneously, clairvoyants reported visions of a golden mesh of light overlaying the planet.

Each glyph began to **sing**, transmitting F#, A, and C# in unison—a chord sequence now believed to be the base triad of the **Remembrance Harmonics**.

Encoded memories began unlocking within human DNA. Individuals worldwide experienced:
- Sudden past-life recall
- Spontaneous downloads of sacred geometry
- Visions of forgotten missions and off-world origins

Some glyphs remain undiscovered. Others have emerged through crop formations, dreams, activated starseeds, and direct resonance downloads.

Final Note

The Resonance Grid is not a relic. It is a **living interface**—a portal between Earth's physical form and her multidimensional purpose. When engaged with love, will, and harmonic intention, it becomes more than a map—it becomes a mirror.

A mirror that reflects who we were.
A signal that reminds us of what we are.

And a frequency that calls us into what we are becoming.

Welcome to the Grid.
Welcome back to the Pattern.

Let the symbols guide you.
Let the resonance restore you.
Let the music awaken you.

DOSSIER 5: UNDERGROUND PILLARS & ALIEN CITIES

SUBTERRANEAN STRUCTURES BENEATH THE GIZA PLATEAU AND THEIR COSMIC GATEWAYS

Overview

Beneath the familiar face of the Great Pyramid of Giza lies a world that defies conventional archaeology. Long hidden from public knowledge and dismissed by mainstream academia, an extensive subterranean network expands beneath the Khufu Pyramid—known to the Templars as the Giza Star Lock. Guarded for millennia by initiates of the Order of the Temple of Secret Initiates (OTSI), this ancient complex was not constructed by dynastic Egyptians, but inherited by them. Its origins predate recorded history and link Earth not only to its inner consciousness but also to advanced civilizations across the stars.

Modern remote-sensing technology—such as Synthetic Aperture Radar (SAR) and gravimetric scans—has recently confirmed what the Templars and breakaway civilizations have long known: a series of vertical shafts, spiral stone staircases, and crystalline harmonics spiral downward beneath the plateau. These aren't mere architectural anomalies. They are support structures—but not in any traditional sense. These are Resonant Pillars.

The Resonant Pillars

These massive vertical constructs—referred to in ancient Templar texts as *Anointed Pillars*—function as frequency stabilizers. Composed of a crystalline-limestone composite, their inner lattice is responsive to Earth-based and cosmic frequency patterns. When activated, they serve three primary purposes:

1. **Resonant Amplification** – Enhancing planetary energy flow through Earth's crystalline grid.
2. **Dimensional Anchoring** – Locking the pyramid's energetic field into interdimensional coordinates.
3. **Portal Stabilization** – Maintaining gateway integrity to subterranean cities, the Moon, and distant star systems.

Templar maps record twelve such pillars, forming a downward spiraling helix beneath the pyramid, converging into a subterranean node known as *The Labyrinthum*. These twelve resonate with the 12-number frequency system documented in Dossiers 1 and 2, forming the structural analog to the sacred mathematical pattern underlying all nodal resonance.

The Labyrinthum: City of Custodians

Located at the deepest point beneath the Giza node, *The Labyrinthum* has long been veiled in legend as "the city beneath the Sphinx." It is real—and it is active.

This subterranean metropolis is maintained by a cooperative alliance of Greys, Pleiadian emissaries, and select human initiates. It contains:

• Massive crystalline data vaults encoded with holographic knowledge
• Healing chambers calibrated to the 12-number resonance model
• Antechambers for interspecies diplomacy and multidimensional attunement
• Teleportation platforms with confirmed destinations on the Moon and in the Arcturus system

These are not mechanical technologies alone—they are *consciousness-responsive environments*. Access is not granted through excavation or force, but by achieving *resonance alignment* with the frequency matrix of the node itself. Entry is a rite, not a right.

Key Entry Points

While the central shaft remains sealed by a multi-frequency energy lock accessible only during planetary resonance alignments, additional access points exist across the Giza Plateau:

- The Tomb of the Birds (*Saqqara*)
- A frequency chamber beneath the ruins of Abu Rawash
- A chamber mislabeled as a "cistern" near the Sphinx's right paw

Each location served as a staging ground for ancient initiatory rites and vibrational assessments. Passage required harmonic coherence with the grid—a process overseen by sentient architecture and guardian beings still active within the system.

Templar Involvement

During the early 14th century, ancient Templars uncovered Crusader-era vaults containing pre-Flood maps of Giza's underworld. Despite the suppression that followed—most notably the issuing of the Papal bull ordering their extermination—the knowledge survived. These maps and instructions were preserved in what modern OTSI members refer to as *The Tectum Arcanum Scrolls*.

Today, the Order of the Temple of Secret Initiates has reestablished contact with the Labyrinthum's custodians. Select initiates are chosen to descend—but only during planetary alignments initiated by global node activation events. Joe Monroe's awakening of the Giza Star Lock, documented in Chapter 12, served as the energetic catalyst that reopened resonance access to the inner sanctum after centuries of dormancy.

Conclusion

The Giza node is not simply an ancient monument. It is the capstone of Earth's multidimensional operating system. The *Anointed Pillars* beneath it serve not only as technological spinal cords for Earth's crystalline body but also as harmonic bridges linking our planet to cosmic allies, memory archives, and healing technologies far beyond current human comprehension.

The alien cities below are not fiction. They are sanctuaries. They are libraries. And they are waiting.

The Templars were never guarding treasure.

They were guarding a door.

And now—after the resonance pulse of Chapter 12—the door has begun to open.

DOSSIER 6: MUGANDA'S MAP OF THE INVISIBLE

PSYCHIC CARTOGRAPHY FROM THE UFO WHISPERER

In the hidden corners of our reality—far beyond the reach of satellite imaging or GPS tracking—there exists a network of cities not built of stone or steel, but of **energy, resonance, and intention**.

Muganda, known in awakened circles as *The UFO Whisperer*, is a psychonaut and seer whose consciousness-traveling abilities have charted what conventional instruments cannot: the **Invisible Cities**.

Muganda's journeys are not navigated by compass or coordinates, but by attunement to **vibrational signatures** aligned with planetary chakras, cosmic leyline intersections, and the resonance of awakened DNA. Each city he uncovers reveals a unique **purpose, frequency, and species of inhabitants**—some terrestrial, some extraterrestrial, and others suspended between timelines.

Below are five such cities, recorded in Muganda's dream journals, resonance diagrams, and telepathic transmissions.

1. Elorak

- **Location**: Deep within the Amazon rainforest, dimensionally veiled
- **Inhabitants**: Tall crystalline beings called the *Kairoth*, who speak in ultraviolet harmonics
- **Purpose**: Earth's detoxification and harmonic calibration center. Elorak pulses vibrational signals that cleanse environmental and psychic toxicity from the planetary grid.

2. Tal'Mara

- **Location**: Under the Pacific Ocean, near a trench off the coast of Micronesia
- **Inhabitants**: Amphibious Greys and blue-skinned Lemurians
- **Purpose**: Aquatic knowledge archive housing ancient data from pre-Atlantean civilizations. Also serves as a sanctuary for lost souls seeking **soul-fragment integration** through emotional resonance fields.

3. Thron-Drake

- **Location**: Beneath the Ural Mountains, Russia
- **Inhabitants**: A philosophical sect of Reptilians and peaceful human hybrids
- **Purpose**: Dimensional diplomacy enclave. Thron-Drake functions as a neutral council ground where interspecies and ideological adversaries resolve conflicts before they materialize in physical realms.

> *Note: This portrayal of Reptilians refers to a breakaway minority aligned with non-interventionist principles, distinct from the controlling factions mentioned in other records.*

4. Savirah

- **Location**: Inside Mount Erebus, Antarctica
- **Inhabitants**: Arcturian time engineers—interdimensional beings who regulate temporal flow
- **Purpose**: **Time-stream maintenance** and paradox prevention. Savirah serves as a correctional node for fractured timelines, ensuring

the continuity of stable realities and shielding Earth from catastrophic temporal collapse.

5. Halos'varn

- **Location**: Sub-lunar orbit, phase-locked with Earth's energetic tides
- **Inhabitants**: Light-beings often misinterpreted as angelic—actually **trans-dimensional observers**
- **Purpose**: Emotional resonance translator. Halos'varn converts Earth's collective emotional waveform into harmonic codes uploaded to the **Universal Heart Grid**, influencing galactic empathy bandwidths.

Muganda's Mapping Techniques

Muganda does not draw maps in any traditional cartographic sense. His maps are **resonance diagrams**—comprised of spirals, standing waves, interlocked geometries, and symbolic overlays—encoded in dream journals and sketched during trance states.

- Some pages *self-animate under moonlight*.
- Others emit *subtle frequencies* when touched by those with expanded perception.
- A few are encoded with glyphs that align with **planetary memory nodes**, much like those described in Joe Monroe's resonance files.

According to Muganda, **"The map cannot be followed—it must be remembered."**

Each reader may find personal attunement to one of these cities, using it as a gateway to consciousness work, ancestral contact, or timeline anchoring.

Templar Acknowledgment

The Templars, particularly those within the **modern Resonance Council**, regard Muganda's work as **critical to locating the energetic threads** that bind humanity to alien civilizations—and, more importantly, to its own multidimensional soul structure. His diagrams are now archived in resonance sanctuaries across Peru, Turkey, and the Moon's Hollow Archive.

As **Joe Monroe** once scribbled in the margin of Muganda's field notes:

> *"You don't need to see the city to know it exists. You just have to feel the pull of home."*

Closing Reflection

The Invisible Cities are not figments. They are soul cartographies— psychic waypoints left by interdimensional architects and remembered by those who dare to look inward.

Not all maps are made for the eyes.
Some are made for the soul.

DOSSIER 7: THE PATH OF MODERN TEMPLAR INITIATION

FROM PAGE TO GUARDIAN — THE ESOTERIC ASCENSION OF A KNIGHT IN THE RESONANCE ERA

Throughout history, the Knights Templar have been revered not merely as warrior monks or protectors of sacred relics, but as initiates of deeper, multidimensional truths. In the post-Remembrance era, the modern incarnation of the Templar tradition has begun to resurface— offering a path for awakened individuals who feel the call of chivalry, mystery, and cosmic guardianship.

This dossier outlines the spiritual progression known within the inner circles of the *Templar Collegia* as the **Path of Resonant Knighthood**. While the process draws inspiration from historical rites, it has evolved to meet the needs of the current planetary frequency. It is no longer just about defending pilgrims in the Holy Land. It is about safeguarding the soul's journey through dimensions and anchoring cosmic memory back into Earth.

◈ Phase I: The Calling of the Page

Identity: The Seeker
Symbol: The Uncarved Pillar

To become a Page is to formally declare one's intention to remember. Candidates enter a sacred probationary period known as *Collegia Orientation*, which includes the study of esoteric wisdom from multiple traditions—Hermetic, Christian, Pythagorean, Vedic, and extraterrestrial in origin. Each initiate is assigned a unique resonance sigil, functioning like a vibrational fingerprint encoded to their soul's frequency.

Tools Received:
- *Codex Secretum*, Volume I (the foundational teaching scroll)
- Access to inner Collegia forums or gatherings (if geographically available)
- A symbolic cloak or ring (based on local chapter traditions)

Ritual Insight:
Pages must submit a vow of secrecy, light a candle while reciting the *Templar Oath of Listening*, and begin dream journaling for 33 nights.

◈ Phase II: The Rising of the Squire

Identity: The Apprentice Guardian
Symbol: The Sword and Chalice

Once the Page has demonstrated humility, intellectual curiosity, and commitment to service, they are ritually knighted as a Squire. This level introduces astral disciplines and the beginnings of *resonant shielding*—the conscious modulation of one's energy field to withstand lower frequencies. Squires are required to participate in at least one planetary energy working, such as a ley line alignment, lunar gateway meditation, or node harmonization.

Teachings Introduced:
- *The Squire's Primer on Interdimensional Ethics*
- *The Martian Chronicles* (a scroll documenting the fall of the Red Planet)
- *Codex Secretum*, Volume II

Challenges Faced:
- *The Trial of Stillness* (72 hours without speaking)
- *Mirror Gate Dreamwork* (invoking past lives as ancient Knights or Seers)

Phase III: Martinist Initiation (OMOT)

Identity: The Initiate of the Inner Flame
Symbol: The Rose Cross in Starlight

The *Ordre Martiniste of the Temple (OMOT)* represents a deeper mystical current within the Collegia—focused on inner alchemy, divine union, and the resurrection of the Christ Light within. Initiates at this level are taught the ancient meditations of the *Cosmic Templar*, including how to access akashic scrolls stored beneath Rosslyn Chapel and how to bilocate during resonance events connected to planetary grid fluctuations.

Practices Introduced:
- *Planetary Guardian Protocols*
- Vibratory Mantra: *Lux in Tenebris Lucet* ("The light shines in darkness")
- *The Lunar Crosswalk*: A guided visualization that reactivates the **Twelve Templar Memory Codes**

Phase IV: The Invitation to OTSI

Identity: The Keeper of the Gate
Symbol: The Anointed Star within the Shield

The *Order of the Temple of Secret Initiates (OTSI)* is the most private and protected circle within the Templar Collegia. Membership is by invitation only and extended only after deep observation of the candidate's vibration, devotion, and integrity. These Initiates serve as stewards of classified resonance technology, time-locked relics, and ancient scrolls buried beneath **Montségur, Sinai, and Giza**—sites activated during the planetary alignments referenced in *We Are the Aliens*, Chapter 12.

Responsibilities May Include:

- Overseeing planetary node reactivations (in coordination with the *Resonance Council*)
- Training Pages and Squires in dream-travel and memory glyph activation
- Holding the vigil for new incarnates who carry the Templar flame

Artifacts Guarded:

- *Atlantean Mind Crystals*
- One of the surviving *Twelve Number Tablets*
- *The Codex of the Hollow Moon Treaty*

◆ Notes on Entry and Application

While the process outlined above carries deep symbolic weight, the earthly form of this journey begins simply—with a seeker's heartfelt desire to serve. Today, the *Templar Collegia* maintains communication portals through digital means (email, study groups, and encrypted channels), but the initiatory current remains ancient and unbroken.

Applicants must:

- Complete an honest spiritual autobiography
- Submit to an energetic background scan (and mundane one)
- Acquire the *Codex Secretum* within 14 days of acceptance
- Uphold the *Vow of the Flame*: To protect esoteric teachings in all forms and serve the awakening of humanity

Final Words to the Initiate

There is no deadline for the soul's awakening. The path of the Templar Knight is not about speed—but resonance. Not power—but remembrance. You will be tested. You will be humbled. But if the flame within you is real, and the compass of your heart is true, the gates of initiation will open.

And when they do, you will not stand alone.
>   You will stand as a brother or sister among the Hidden Guard—
>   In alignment with Earth, the stars, and all that lies beyond.

Welcome to the path.
Lux Templum.

DOSSIER 8: SECRET ORDERS WITHIN THE TEMPLARS

HIDDEN BRANCHES, FORBIDDEN SCROLLS, AND THE ESOTERIC STRUCTURE OF THE ORDER

Beneath the public legends and surface history of the Knights Templar lies a labyrinthine network of inner circles, invisible colleges, and secretive councils—each entrusted with specific roles in humanity's awakening and the guardianship of extraterrestrial knowledge. These secret orders have operated continuously for centuries, often without name, crest, or historical record. But within the Resonance Era, their roles are emerging from the shadows—encoded in cathedrals, scrolls, sacred geometry, and memory glyphs.

This dossier outlines the five known secret branches of the Templars, their functions within the greater mission, and the esoteric systems they have preserved—sometimes at great cost. Their influence stretches from medieval strongholds to Martian ruins, from the vaults beneath Rosslyn Chapel to crystalline libraries on the Hollow Moon. The Orders described here are not speculative. They are whispered through dreams, recovered in regression, and confirmed by Templar memory-keepers like **Benjamin Arthur Templar** and **Timothy A. Hooligan**.

◈ **The Order of the Crimson Star**

Function: Guardians of Resonance Artifacts and Dimensional Seals

Among the most ancient of the inner orders, the Crimson Star safeguards tools that could alter planetary timelines if misused—resonance crystals, fragmented memory glyphs, and portable Stargate rings. Their sigil, recovered in the Martian glyph transmission described in Dossier 1, is a six-pointed crimson star surrounded by twelve nodal points—each representing a forgotten cosmic law.

Known Sites:
- Beneath the Sanctuary of Glozel, France
- The vaults beneath the Shrine of the Book, Jerusalem
- A resonance-locked corridor behind the west altar of Rosslyn Chapel

Seal Phrase: *Nulli perire memoria.* ("Nothing truly remembered is ever lost.")

◈ The Order of the Veiled Flame

Function: Stewards of the 12-Number System and the Flame of Inner Sight

Formed after the destruction of the two forgotten number tablets—*High* (^{h}) and *Low* (L), detailed in Dossiers 1 and 2—this order ensures the twelve-digit resonance code is never lost again. Its initiates are encoded with memory glyphs and trained to detect distortions in base-10 calculations that suppress dimensional access.

Sacred Tools & Symbols:
- Twelve-faceted crystal abacuses
- Hidden tattoos of mirrored ^{h} and L digits on the forearms
- The mnemonic: *"Twelve the path. Ten the cage."*

Key Artifact: The *Codex Luminara*, a living scroll said to contain transdimensional math for gravitational wave riding, LM-115 synthesis, and harmonic teleportation.

Templar Whisper: Some believe the Veiled Flame protects one of the original twelve tablets left by Jesus of Nazareth before the crucifixion.

◆ The Order of the Black Labyrinth
Function: Navigators of Inner Earth Portals and Dimensional Drift Corridors

Tasked with safeguarding (and, when necessary, sealing) the interdimensional gateways referenced in Dossier 3, this Order trains its members in resonance navigation and reality-fold mapping. Initiates are selected only after demonstrating dream-state bi-location or rein-carnational memory from Lemuria, Agartha, or ancient Mars.

Guarded Nodes:
- The North Pole Vortex to Agartha
- The subglacial crystalline temple above the South Pole Stargate
- The spiral stairwell beneath the Atlantean Triangle

Initiation Trial: The Silent Walk through the Invisible Labyrinth—a rite said to awaken the soul's inner cartography. Most return changed. Some never return.

◆ The Order of the Silent Archive
Function: Custodians of Forbidden Scrolls and Multiplanetary Records

While others protect objects, this Order protects memory. Its members are scribes, resonance recorders, and dream-channelers tasked with preserving ancient texts—many of which were transmitted by Pleiadi-ans, Greys, and Arcturians during the Lemurian era.

Known Archives (Rumored):
- Beneath Montségur, France
- Inside the Vatican's resonance-sealed sublevel
- Digitally encoded into the crystalline lattice of the Hollow Moon (see Dossier 3)

Primary Script: *Primordial Glyph Syntax*—understood only through resonance-based retrieval. These scrolls document the rise and fall of civilizations across Sirius, Orion, and the moons of Jupiter.

◆ The Order of the Celestial Choir

Function: Sonic Activation of Stargates and DNA-Harmonic Missions

This mystical Order works with sound—the first language of creation. Members use harmonic chants, triadic tones, and crystalline instruments to re-tune sacred sites and catalyze memory activations within human DNA.

Their sonic rituals were essential to the activation of the Giza Starlock and the opening of the Remembrance Grid, as recorded in Dossiers 4 and 5. When three or more members sing the correct tri-tone in harmony at a resonance node, the grid responds—sometimes with light, sometimes with memory.

Instruments & Tools:
- Meteorite-forged harmonic bells
- Voiceprint frequency tuners
- DNA-lattice crystal flutes

Choir Sites:
- Chartres Cathedral, France
- The Temple of the Wind, Mexico
- The subterranean amphitheater beneath Cairo's oldest foundations

◆ A Final Note from the Order of the Temple of Secret Initiates (OTSI)

The five Orders do not represent hierarchy—but harmonic differentiation. Each vibrates at a frequency aligned to a specific mission within the greater remembrance. Some serve as guardians.

Others as messengers, healers, or archivists. But all answer the same call: to awaken Earth to her place in the cosmic symphony.

To know your Order is not to receive a title. It is to feel a resonance that hums through your bones when you hear the call.

If you feel it, you already belong.

Lux Templum.

DOSSIER 9: THE TEMPLAR CODE OF CONDUCT FOR COSMIC CONTACT

PROTOCOLS FOR INTERSTELLAR INTEGRITY AND MULTIDIMENSIONAL RESPECT

Throughout history, encounters with non-human intelligences—whether angelic, extraterrestrial, or interdimensional—have been filtered through fear, power structures, or opportunism. But for the modern Templar, contact is not a conquest. It is communion.

This dossier outlines the Templar Code of Conduct for ethical, honorable, and heart-centered contact with extraterrestrial civilizations and multidimensional beings. It blends ancient chivalric principles with modern resonance protocols and remote communion techniques used by advanced consciousness operatives. The goal is not to summon aliens for spectacle—but to align with the frequency of remembrance that makes contact a sacred act.

◈ I. Core Tenets of the Code

1. Contact Must Be Consent-Based

Never attempt to initiate contact with the intention of control, spectacle, or manipulation. Only seek communion with beings who consent, resonate, and respond freely. This protects both the human seeker and the visiting intelligence.

2. Remember: You Are Not Inferior

Do not bow. Do not grovel. The myth of alien superiority is a false construct designed to disempower humanity. Approach with reverence, not subservience. You are not less—you are simply remembering later.

3. Purity of Intention Unlocks the Channel

Consciousness is the antenna. If you seek to "see a ship," you may not see anything. If you seek to serve the greater good with humility, the veil may part. Presence, peace, and purpose unlock contact.

4. Contact Is First Inner, Then Outer

Before lights appear in the sky, the signal arrives in the soul. True contact begins within—through dreams, downloads, meditative impressions, heart coherence, and telepathic resonance. External manifestations are secondary confirmations, not the point of origin.

5. No Contact Is Better Than Dishonorable Contact

If the field is not coherent—if there is fear, ego, or chaos—do not proceed. The Templar path insists on integrity before curiosity. It is better to wait than to invite dishonorable energy.

◈ II. The Modern Templar Contact Protocol

Based on harmonic principles, CE-5 methods, and ancient resonance scrolls

Step 1: Sacred Preparation

- Bathe beforehand and wear white or natural fibers.
- Fast from animal products, alcohol, or synthetic chemicals for at least 24 hours.
- Begin with invocation of protection (such as a Templar light shield or inner prayer).

Step 2: Establish the Field

- Create a circle, facing outward. Use crystals or resonance tools if desired.
- Use a tone generator or sing specific harmonic frequencies. (Examples: 528 Hz, 111 Hz, 963 Hz.)
- If you have the 12-number system mnemonic chant, recite it internally.

Step 3: Open Communication Channels

- Enter heart coherence: breathe slowly, rhythmically, and center your awareness in your chest.
- Project peaceful intention outward—imagine your frequency rising as a beam of coherent light.
- Invite contact only with beings in service to the Source and aligned with the highest benevolence.

Step 4: Wait in Stillness and Receive

- Do not chase signs. Allow impressions to come.
- Look for flickers of light, high-pitched tones, synchronicities, internal visions, or time distortion.
- Remain seated for at least 20–30 minutes after the protocol. Journal any impressions.

◈ III. Advanced Techniques

- **The Resonance Triad Method**
  In groups of three, one serves as the anchor (meditating), one as the

observer (eyes open, skyward), and one as the communicator (tele-pathically transmitting peaceful contact invitations). The roles rotate every 15 minutes.

• **Frequency Modulation Beacons**

Some Templars experiment with modulated ultrasonic frequencies —like modified dog whistles—to replicate contact initiation tones reported in crop circles or abduction reversal protocols. These must be used ethically and cautiously.

• **Glyph Projection**

Projecting glyphs from Joe Monroe's chest glyph (see Dossier 4) has been shown to stimulate recognition from certain Greys and Pleiadian groups. These can be visualized or drawn physically in chalk, crystals, or digital light patterns.

◈ IV. The Nine Virtues of Cosmic Conduct

Every Templar who seeks contact must embody the following:

1. **Clarity** – Purity of purpose and inner alignment
2. **Honor** – Keep all contact sacred; never disclose irresponsibly
3. **Non-Interference** – Do not try to change the being or extract secrets
4. **Reciprocity** – If gifted information, offer service in return
5. **Vigilance** – Be discerning of deception or false light phenomena
6. **Steadfastness** – Contact may not come immediately; remain steady
7. **Joy** – Let the process be rooted in lightness, not seriousness
8. **Humility** – You are not here to "prove" anything to the world
9. **Love** – The universal signal understood by all civilizations

◈ V. Known Contact Zones

These are locations where Templars and other contact practitioners have reported high-frequency encounters:

- **Mount Shasta (California)** – Lemurian and Pleiadian contact zone
- **Lake Titicaca (Peru/Bolivia)** – Interdimensional dolphin grid convergence
- **Göbekli Tepe (Turkey)** – Portal harmonized during Chapter **10**'s activation
- **Tuscany Sanctuary (Italy)** – The gardens where Joe's memory glyph resonated
- **Subsurface Hollow Moon Dome (Lunar Zone Delta-4)** – Templar-verified command hall *(see Dossier 3)*
- **Dream state transmissions** – Not location-bound; accessed via soul frequency

◈ Final Message from the Order of the Temple of Secret Initiates (O.T.S.I.)

In this age of Remembrance, contact is no longer science fiction—it is the sacred unfolding of human potential. But like all rites of passage, it demands more than curiosity. It demands coherence. It demands love. It demands your frequency.

The universe is listening. Are you singing the right song?

"Before the stars appear in the sky, they appear in the soul."

— *Ancient Templar Codex*

Lux Templum.
Let contact begin with the Light in You.

ACKNOWLEDGMENTS

I WANT TO express my deepest gratitude to **God**, for giving me the wisdom, clarity, and unwavering sense of identity that led to the creation of this book.

To my daughters, Brianna Angelina Templar, Hazel Autumn Templar, and MacKenzie Arwen Templar, you are the star systems I orbit. You inspire me to be bold in who I am, and to live my truth unapologetically. *Through playing with you as the innocent voice I once was—Benji, before the soul split—you're helping merge me back with who I truly am. In doing so, you're not only restoring my soul... you're quietly, mischievously, and completely healing my heart.*

To my wife, **Gelsey Aidan Templar**—your love, belief, and unwavering support gave this mission its anchor. You stood beside me as I traveled through timelines and galaxies, holding space with grace. Thank you for being both my home and my horizon.

To my spiritual parents, **Jim Norman** and **Marcie Rotenberg Adery**—your love and guidance have meant the world to me.

To the **Galactic Federation**, whose silent guidance and multidimensional stewardship have protected Earth through millennia of forgetting—thank you. You've held the resonance line while we struggled to find our own frequency. This book is offered in remembrance of the pact made long ago: that when humanity was ready to awaken, you would meet us not as saviors, but as **equals in conscious-**

ness, **partners in peace**, and elders of the stars. Your unseen support echoes in these pages—and in the hearts of those who now remember.

To the real-life truth seekers, experiencers, whistleblowers, and memory-keepers—your courage lit the path I followed while writing. Though your names aren't written here, your presence is felt in every word. I remember you.

To those who don't believe yet—thank you for existing. Your doubt gave this book direction, and your eventual remembering is part of the plan.

To my many teachers, guides, and inspirations—both human and non-human—who have expanded my understanding of consciousness, cosmic heritage, and what it truly means to be human, including but not limited to: **Joseph McMoneagle, Danny Sheehan, Dolores Cannon, Jennifer Carmody (JK Ultra), Sarah Breskman Cosme, Dr. Steven M. Greer, Dr. Brian Weiss, Matias De Stefano, Darius J. Wright, Graham Hancock, Bob Lazar, Jeremy Corbell, George Knapp, Lue Elizondo, Ross Coulthart, David Grusch, Jake Barber, Regina Meredith, Timothy Hogan, Scott F. Wolter, Muganda (the 'UFO Whisperer'), Chris Ramsay, Nick Pope, Sir Robert Edward Grant, Richard Dolan, Dr. Garry Nolan, Dr. Russell Targ,** and many more.

And most importantly, **to YOU—the reader**. Whether you're a lifelong experiencer, a curious skeptic, or someone just beginning to question the story we've been told about who we are and where we come from —thank you. Your open mind, your courage to remember, and your willingness to explore the unknown are what make this journey possible.

And finally, to the cosmic allies beyond human form—the **Pleiadians**, the **Greys**, the **Arcturians**, and even the **Reptilians** who've chosen peace—you've been patient. We're learning. And yes, we're finally listening.

May this book help awaken not just minds, but memories.

With resonance and remembrance,
Benjamin A. Templar

ABOUT THE AUTHOR

Benjamin A. Templar is a distinguished storyteller, award-winning actor, filmmaker, and author whose work spans multiple artistic and intellectual disciplines. Born on October 9, 1978, he cultivated his passion for the arts through dedicated training at the esteemed William Esper Studio in New York City. Under the tutelage of master instructors, he refined his craft, laying the groundwork for a remarkable career in film and literature.

An Acclaimed Actor and Filmmaker

Templar's presence on screen has been defined by his compelling performances and deep commitment to storytelling. His portrayal of Manny DiStefano in the cult-favorite post-apocalyptic series *Plaga Zombie* solidified his status as a dynamic actor, while his versatility has been showcased in over 30 independent films. His talent has earned him two prestigious Best Actor awards—one from *The Actors Awards Film Festival* and another from *Festigious International Film Festival*—for his performance in *The Street Photographer*.

As a filmmaker, Templar's vision extends beyond acting. In 2021, he founded *SunBow Media LLC* and directed the award-winning sci-fi film *The Street Photographer*, which received the *Buenos Aires Indie Film Award* for *Best Sci-Fi Film*. His work behind the camera reflects a keen artistic sensibility and an unwavering dedication to cinematic excellence.

A Visionary Author and Thought Leader

Templar's literary endeavors span a breadth of subjects, each infused with his signature depth and insight. His works include *How to Buy a Car at the Dealership*, a practical guide to navigating automobile purchases, *Princely Chess: A Chess Variant Manual*, which challenges the intellect with innovative gameplay, and *Masterplan Your Success: Deadline Your Dreams*, a book that empowers readers to transform ambition into achievement.

His latest work, *Divine Incomparable You (D.I.Y.)*, is a profound exploration of self-discovery, spiritual healing, and personal transformation. In this deeply introspective book, Templar shares invaluable wisdom, blending his experiences with philosophical and spiritual insights to guide readers toward wholeness and self-realization.

Master Life Coaching Professional and Mentor

Beyond his work in film and literature, Templar is a certified *Master Life Coaching Professional*, accredited by *The International Association of Professions Career College (IAP Career College)*. His passion for personal development and human potential drives his commitment to guiding others on their journey toward fulfillment and excellence.

A Legacy of Creativity, Knowledge, and Family

In addition to his artistic and literary accomplishments, Templar has a strong foundation in Information Technology, holding a *Magna Cum Laude* degree in *Computer Systems Management* from the *Community College of Vermont* and membership in the *Phi Theta Kappa honor society*. His career in IT has spanned critical roles in customer support across healthcare and digital mapping industries, underscoring his analytical and problem-solving expertise.

At the heart of his life's work is a profound devotion to family. As a loving husband and father to three daughters, he views his greatest mission as fostering an enduring legacy of love, wisdom, and inspiration. His unwavering commitment to the values of loyalty, honor, and personal transformation—deeply influenced by the spirit of the *Knights*

Templar—resonates throughout all his creative and intellectual pursuits.

With a career that seamlessly blends artistry, intellect, and mentorship, *Benjamin A. Templar* continues to make a lasting impact as an award-winning actor, filmmaker, author, and life coach. His journey stands as a testament to the boundless potential of human creativity and resilience.

facebook.com/BenjaminTemplar
x.com/BenjaminTemplar
instagram.com/benjamintemplar

ALSO BY BENJAMIN A. TEMPLAR

We Are The Aliens: Saving Earth from Alien AI Conquest

TransNationals: Reclaiming Your National Identity Beyond Birth

Divine Incomparable You (D.I.Y.)

Masterplan Your Success: Deadline Your Dreams

Princely Chess

How to Buy a Car at the Dealership

———